This month's prize:
A FABULOUS SHARP VIEWCAM!

This month, as a special surprise, we're giving away a Sharp ViewCam**, the big-screen camcorder that has revolutionized home videos!

This is the camcorder everyone's talking about! Sharp's new ViewCam has a big 3" full-color viewing screen with 180° swivel action that lets you control everything you record—and watch it at the same time! Features include a remote control (so you can get into the picture yourself), 8 power zoom, full-range auto focus, battery pack, recharger and more!

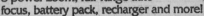

The next page contains two Entry Coupons (as does every book you received this shipment). Complete and return *all* the entry coupons; **the more times you enter, the better your chances of winning!**

Then keep your fingers crossed, because you'll find out by November 15, 1995 if you're the winner!

Remember: The more times you enter, the better your chances of winning!*

PRIZE SURPRISE
SWEEPSTAKES
OFFICIAL ENTRY COUPON

This entry must be received by: OCTOBER 30, 1995
This month's winner will be notified by: NOVEMBER 15, 1995

YES, I want to win the Sharp ViewCam! Please enter me in the drawing and let me know if I've won!

Name_____

Address _____ Apt. _____

City   State/Prov.   Zip/Postal Code

Account #_____

Return entry with invoice in reply envelope.

© 1995 HARLEQUIN ENTERPRISES LTD.   CVC KAL

Carly closed her eyes and tried to calm her suddenly racing heart.

For Tracy's sake, she had to find out if Mitch Scanlon recognized her. No matter what, Tracy had to be protected.

The resemblance between father and daughter was subtle, but it was there nevertheless. Anyone with any suspicion at all could see a more innocent, trusting replica of Scanlon's cynical golden eyes, the same tumble of thick hair framing the same square face.

No, she wouldn't let Tracy be hurt. For Tracy's sake she would be strong, just as she'd been strong during those terrible first months of her pregnancy. For Tracy's sake she would be polite and cool and every inch an Alderson.

For Tracy's sake...

Dear Reader,

This is another spectacular month here at Silhouette Intimate Moments. You'll realize that the moment you pick up our Intimate Moments Extra title. *Her Secret, His Child,* by Paula Detmer Riggs, is exactly the sort of tour de force you've come to expect from this award-winning writer. It's far more than the story of a child whose father has never known of her existence. It's the story of a night long ago that changed the courses of three lives, leading to hard lessons about responsibility and blame, and—ultimately— to the sort of love that knows no bounds, no limitations, and will last a lifetime.

Three miniseries are on tap this month, as well. Alicia Scott's *Hiding Jessica* is the latest entrant in "The Guiness Gang," as well as a Romantic Traditions title featuring the popular story line in which the hero and heroine have to go into hiding together—where of course they find love! Merline Lovelace continues "Code Name: Danger" with *Undercover Man,* a sizzling tale proving that appearances can indeed be deceiving. Beverly Barton begins "The Protectors" with *Defending His Own,* in which the deeds of the past come back to haunt the present in unpredictable—and irresistibly romantic—ways.

In addition, Sally Tyler Hayes returns with *Our Child?* Next year look for this book's exciting sequel. Finally, welcome our Premiere author, Suzanne Sanders, with *One Forgotten Night.*

Sincerely,

Leslie Wainger
Senior Editor and Editorial Coordinator

Please address questions and book requests to:
Silhouette Reader Service
U.S.: 3010 Walden Ave., P.O. Box 1325, Buffalo, NY 14269
Canadian: P.O. Box 609, Fort Erie, Ont. L2A 5X3

PAULA DETMER RIGGS

HER SECRET, HIS CHILD

Silhouette®

INTIMATE ™ MOMENTS®

Published by Silhouette Books

America's Publisher of Contemporary Romance

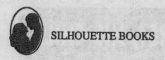

SILHOUETTE BOOKS

ISBN 0-373-07667-3

HER SECRET, HIS CHILD

PAULA DETMER RIGGS

discovers material for her writing in her varied life experiences. During her first five years of marriage to a naval officer, she lived in nineteen different locations on the West Coast, gaining familiarity with places as diverse as San Diego and Seattle. While working at a historical site in San Diego she wrote, directed and narrated fashion shows and became fascinated with the early history of California.

She writes romances because "I think we all need an escape from the high-tech pressures that face us every day, and I believe in happy endings. Isn't that why we keep trying, in spite of all the roadblocks and disappointments along the way?"

To Nancy Roberts
with thanks

Prologue

He was running, his feet pounding the turf beneath his cleats. Eighty thousand fans were on their feet, screaming, and the frenzied sound roared in his head. Yes, he thought. Yes! He had broken free....

Mitch Scanlon woke to find his heart pounding and his naked body drenched in sweat. For the third night in a row he'd been dreaming, and yet, for an instant before he'd opened his eyes, he'd been so sure he'd actually felt the ground under his feet.

Eagerly, he lifted his head and stared down at the body that had once been as perfect and reliable as a well-tuned machine. He was still lean, still hard, his stomach muscles clearly visible, his hips still fluid. At thirty-three, he was a man in his prime. A conditioned athlete. A superstar.

Lying back, he ran his hand over his flanks until sensation faded into numbness. What he couldn't feel, he couldn't control. Little by little, the once powerful muscles of his thighs and calves had atrophied until they were as wasted and thin as a kid's. He hated the way his legs looked. He hated the way they refused to move, no matter how hard he tried to make them.

But this time the dream had been so real. He'd felt his muscles respond, he was sure of it. Maybe, if he tried harder...

Digging desperate fingers into the mattress, he poured all his strength into straining every tendon, torturing every sinew, willing his muscles to obey. He felt... something. Didn't he? *Didn't he?*

But the legs that had once taken him fast and far remained motionless. Withered. Dead.

Exhausted and spent, he buried his face in the pillow. He was as helpless as a baby. Useless.

It had been a year since he'd felt like a man instead of a collection of mangled nerves and flaccid muscles, a year of pain and struggle and discouragement so deep it was like a cancer eating at him from the inside. Still, he hadn't given up, not even once. When they'd asked him for a hundred sit-ups, he'd given them two hundred. When they'd asked him to endure an agonizing hour of stretching contorted muscles, he'd pushed himself and the therapists for two. Yet all he'd done was become more skilled as a cripple.

Inching closer to the side of the narrow hospital bed, he reached between the mattress and springs and took out the cellophane bag filled with small pink capsules. His hand was steady as he shook them onto the sheet covering his belly. Without counting, he knew there were thirty sweet, beautiful little pills, his ticket to oblivion, one for every night he'd spent tossing and turning in agony from the spasms that tortured his hips and thighs while the nurses thought him nicely sedated.

The cramps had gotten worse after he'd been fitted with full leg braces. Just balancing himself between parallel bars for five minutes at a time had him sweating and swearing and close to passing out by the time they made him sit down. According to his therapist, he had months of struggle and brutally hard work ahead of him before he achieved even minimal mobility. Lord, but he hated that word. Not since the first few weeks after he'd gotten out of traction had anyone used the word *walk* to him. Instead, they promised to teach him to drag his legs and ten pounds of metal and leather between two crutches everywhere he went.

It's the best we can offer, Mitch. Even so, you're very fortunate to have come back as much as you have. At least you have some feeling in your thighs. Some possibility of movement. Perhaps, if he got lucky, the ability to make love again someday.

Damn them, why couldn't they understand?

He was an athlete, a guy who threw a football for a living. It was all he'd ever done. All he knew. Without it, he had no identity. No worth. Football had given him more than fame and money. It had given him back his self-esteem. His very life.

California's Golden Boy, the media had dubbed him. Nothing could be further from the truth. A bastard who'd never known his father's identity and didn't care to, he'd been on a fast road to trouble when Tyrone Williams, an ex-football player turned social worker, had found him sleeping under an oleander bush in the garbage-littered park near the apartment he shared with his mother and her latest "boyfriend." Bettina Scanlon and the man Mitch had been ordered to call Uncle Duane had been coked-up for two days, ready to take out their manic mood swings on him the minute he'd showed his face. Tired of getting hit and spat upon and pushed into walls, he'd taken to the streets, waiting until the john's money ran out.

A few days shy of eight years old at the time, he'd been dirty and hungry and ready to fight even the gentlest kind of restraint. Streetwise himself, Tyrone had taken him by the scruff of his dirty collar, hosed him down at the youth shelter and taken him off to a UCLA-USC football game. That had been the first of many Saturdays they'd spent together.

When the court had finally freed him from his mother's control, he'd gone to live with Tyrone and his wife, Arletta. Tyrone had bought him shoes that actually fit and his first toothbrush, taught him hygiene and manners and the best way to throw a perfect spiral. Arletta, a Baptist minister, had taught him self-control, respect for his elders and her mother's recipe for the best barbecue sauce in Los Angeles County.

Both had encouraged his love of football, knowing that he needed the discipline belonging to a team would force on him. Scrawny and short for his age, he'd learned to play sandlot ball first, taking his lumps from the bigger boys over and over until he'd finally mastered the intricacies of the game.

Pressing his hand over the pills so none would be lost in the rumpled sheets, he dug his head deeper into the pillow and tried to ignore the scalding pain in his knotted thigh muscles. He rarely allowed himself to think about the night that had changed his life forever, but when he did, he felt an icy, killing rage.

There had been two of them, one to hot-wire Mitch's Porsche, one to watch for the cops. Instead of the police, however, Mitch had been the one to surprise them in the act. He'd had a split second of premonition, felt a jolt, a scalding numbness, and then . . . nothing. According to the doctors, the hopped-up kid swinging the crowbar had pretty much turned his lower spine to mush with the first blow.

God in heaven, why me? he cried silently. What did I ever do to deserve this kind of punishment? He'd asked that question before, sometimes in a delirium of pain, sometimes in fury, and, ultimately, with no expectation of an answer. In a few hours it would no longer matter, he thought as he collected the pills and returned them to the plastic bag for safekeeping.

Glancing around, he saw that his roommate, Franco, was still sleeping. Poor kid had just turned fourteen when he'd broken his neck in a surfing accident that had turned him into an instant quadriplegic. As though sensing his gaze, Franco slowly opened his eyes and smiled. He'd already made it plain that he thought Mitch was some kind of god, just because he'd made it to the pros.

"Morning, Mitch," he murmured, shifting his gaze, all that remained under his control, toward the window. "Looks like it's going to be a great day. Maybe you and I can get outside during lunch, soak up some rays."

Mitch felt his stomach twist. Wouldn't that be a sight? Two gimps in bathing suits. He glanced down at his legs. The surgeon might as well have sliced them off, for all the good they would do him.

"Not today, kid," he said, wondering how long it would take for the pills to put him out of his misery.

"That's what you said yesterday," Franco reminded him with a grin. "Besides, I sorta promised Lupe we'd be out on the patio this afternoon when she came to work."

"Lupe?" Mitch asked, curious in spite of himself.

"C'mon, Mitch. She's that cute candy striper who's got the hots for me. Remember, I introduced you two day before yesterday?"

Mitch cast his mind backward, finally coming up with a vague picture of a short, plump cheerleader type with black curls down to her fanny and big brown eyes.

"Yeah, I remember. Cute kid." And young enough to be his daughter, if he'd been lucky enough—or man enough—to father a child.

"What do you mean, 'kid'?" Franco protested, his tone indignant. "Lupe's sixteen and one prime example of womanhood. As soon as I get myself sprung from this place, me and her are gonna have us a picnic on the beach."

Mitch pushed himself higher on the pillow. "I hate to be the one to give you the bad news, kid, but your surfing days are over."

"Surfing maybe, but sex, never!"

"Yeah? How are you going to manage that?"

Franco lifted his black eyebrows and clucked his tongue. "That's between me and Lupe."

The nurse bustled in with the morning medication and her usual cheery patter. Mitch ignored her. Franco gave as good as he got, asking rude questions about her love life and laughing at the insults she shot back in return.

From the first, Franco had never given in, never stopped grinning, never stopped talking about the future. Dumb kid, didn't he know he didn't have one?

Reluctantly, yet compelled by a gut-knotting feeling he didn't want to define, Mitch glanced down at his fist. Yeah, he had the means to end his life, all right, a handful of them. And he had the courage to swallow them.

So what if a few sorry do-gooders claimed suicide was a coward's way out? Everyone knew Mitch Scanlon had never backed down from a fight in his life. Mitch Scanlon was a man. A winner!

Or was he?

Is that what Franco would say about him when they zipped him into a body bag? Or would he shake his head and decide he'd picked the wrong guy for his hero?

Hell, it was no better than he deserved. Franco was the real winner. The real hero. And big, tough, kick-ass Mitchell Scanlon, best quarterback in the NFL since Unitas, was the real loser. Admit it, Scanlon, the kid has more courage than you had on your best day.

He shut his eyes tight, trying to escape the shame tearing at him. Slowly, relentlessly, a determination to beat this thing filled him until it burned in his soul. He'd made himself into a football player and a role model for a lot of would-be quarterbacks. Maybe he could turn himself into the kind of man that a kid like Franco could respect. It wouldn't be easy; he wasn't even sure he would succeed. He just knew he had to try.

Franco was watching him when he opened his eyes again. "How about it, Mitch? Looks like a winner of a day outside."

It cost Mitch to smile. He knew it would cost him every day. "Sure kid," he said as he tossed the bag into the waste basket by the bed. "We'll get some sun today. You have my word on it."

Chapter 1

It was rush hour in Sacramento. Traffic was snarled from one end of the civic center to the other. Peter Gianfracco had been away from the fast-paced California sprawl for almost seven years, long enough now to admit that the doctors had been right when they'd ordered him to retire from his stress-filled job as a coach for the Los Angeles Raiders or risk another massive heart attack.

He lived in north central Oregon now, where he was athletic director for Bradenton College, and it was college business that had brought him south. The college was in desperate need of a head football coach, someone who could turn a bunch of talented but dispirited kids into instant winners. After forty years in football, thirty of those in the NFL, the man everyone still called Coach knew of only one person who had the combination of intelligence, knowledge and grit to get the job done.

"Say, ain't I seen you someplace before?" the cabby asked as he pulled over to double-park in front of the K Street Gym. Wincing at the sudden cacophony of blaring horns behind them, Gianfracco added a precise fifteen percent to the amount on the meter and handed it over as he asked, "You ever watch the Raiders on TV?"

"Every chance I get," the cabby boomed, nodding his thanks for the gratuity. "Are you with the team?"

"Used to be, yeah. Quarterback coach."

"Must be where I seen you then, on the sidelines." The cabby narrowed his gaze. "No offense, but the damn team ain't been the same since Mitch Scanlon retired a few years back."

"Can't argue with you there." Coach opened the door and stepped out. Setting his overnight bag on the pavement, he reached back for his briefcase.

"Guess you know Scanlon owns that there gym," the cabby said, nodding toward the two-story brick building opposite. "Heard he made a pile of money designing exercise equipment for cripples like himself."

Gianfracco scowled. "Thanks for the ride," he said, slamming the door. Head down like the charging bull he resembled, he headed for the entrance.

Not sure what he would find in a place devoted to physical fitness for the disabled, he decided he was impressed. The place was bright and nicely decorated, with splashes of color on the white walls and soothing New Age music playing in the background. To Gianfracco's eye, it seemed as large and well-equipped as any NFL training room. The only real difference appeared to be a half dozen shiny parallel bars set waist high in one section and a bank of thick raised mats along the sidewall, the kind that he'd seen in the rehab departments of sports medicine centers. A man without legs was doing push-ups on one, a woman in a neck brace doing leg lifts on another.

Averting his gaze and feeling guilty about it at the same time, he headed toward the small reception area to the left of the door. A young woman stood behind the counter, studying a large yellow card. He couldn't help noticing that she was dressed in skintight workout clothes, revealing a figure that had an old man's blood pressure shooting sky-high.

When she saw him approaching, her pixie face brightened into an infectious smile. "Hi, I'm Jeannie," she said, before returning the card to a file box. "Beautiful day, isn't it?"

"Sure is," Coach agreed, enjoying the rush of blood through his veins. Just because a man had been a widower for the past eight years and mostly celibate didn't mean he was over the hill.

"Is Scanlon around?" he asked, scanning the room once again.

She nodded. "His office is in the back, just past the aerobics studio and to the left."

"Thanks." Taking a tighter grip on his case, he made his way to the back, enjoying the familiar grunts and groans of those working out on the machines. In the glassed-in aerobics studio, a class was in progress, and the room was crowded with men and women in wheelchairs or straight-back chairs. Muffled music accompanied the equally muted shouts of the leader, who was also seated in a chair.

Slowing as he approached the corridor's end, Coach took a deep breath, then straightened his shoulders and prayed that his poker face was still in working order. The last thing a man as proud as Mitch needed to see in his former coach's eyes was pity.

The office door was ajar. He was about to knock when he heard voices. He paused to listen, then grinned. It sounded for all the world like his old buddy Mitch was working hard at getting a lady into bed. But then, Mitch Scanlon had always been wildly popular with the ladies in his playing days. No reason to think that had changed any just because he was a paraplegic. Still grinning, Coach was about to retreat when the sudden blare of music caught his ear, followed by a pitch for laundry detergent. What do you know, it's a damn soap opera, he thought, pushing open the door without knocking.

Scanlon was seated behind a large oak desk, a pair of brown forearm crutches propped against the wall behind him. Frowning slightly, he was running the nib of a black fountain pen down a column of figures on a thick computer printout. He was dressed in a white polo shirt bearing the gym's logo in blue across his still impressive chest, and his tanned arms seemed even more muscular than Gianfracco remembered. The photogenic face that had seemed custom-made for a camera lens had permanent lines etched into the wide brow and a look of hard-won control around the mouth. And even though Gianfracco couldn't see the long, muscular legs that had taken a troubled kid from East Los Angeles to national glory by the time he'd been old enough to drink legally, Coach knew they would never move at Mitch's command again.

"Yo, Mitchell. Long time no see."

Scanlon looked up, his lean face registering fleeting pain before lighting in pleasure. "Hell, Pete, I thought you'd be six feet under by now."

"Might as well be, the way the doctors want me to live," Coach admitted as he approached the desk.

Scanlon leaned forward, stretching out a hand, which Gianfracco took eagerly, discovering as he did that he'd missed Mitch more than he'd thought. "Damn, but it's good to see you, boy," he said, his voice gruff.

Scanlon reacted with that same mixture of cautious warmth and streetwise toughness that Coach had first noticed in a touchingly eager rookie.

"Last I heard you were the Athletic Director for a college up north some place." Scanlon waved him to a chair, which he accepted gratefully.

"Still am, in a place called Bradenton," he said, placing his cases next to the chair. "It's up in north central Oregon."

"How do you like baby-sitting a bunch of spoiled college kids instead of prowling the sidelines, cussing out everyone in sight?"

"Actually, it's a pretty sweet life, all things considered. Got me a nice little town house next to the prettiest little golf course you've ever seen, and three months off every summer to enjoy it."

"Still hooking your drive to the right?"

Coach laughed. "Might have known you'd remember that, considering how much money you won from me over the years." Taking a chance, Gianfracco directed a pointed look at the small TV on the corner of the desk. "You taken to watching the soaps these days, Mitch?"

Scanlon glanced at the screen while at the same time switching off the set. "Hate to admit it, Coach, but I got hooked on them in the hospital, and I can't seem to shake the habit."

"Sounded to me like daytime TV has become X-rated."

Mitch looked sheepish. "More like R. Everyone keeps their clothes on until the commercial, then they hop into bed." His grin faded. "What brings you to Sacramento?"

"Football, what else?"

Scanlon capped his pen and put it aside. He had a restless look to him that was new, and Gianfracco wondered if his inability to move freely was the cause.

"Scouting trip?"

"Yeah, for a head coach." Pete leaned forward. "Your name is on the top of a very short list."

Mitch ignored the thud in his belly. Trading his helmet and cleats for a coaching job after his playing days were over had always been a secret dream. It had died a long, lingering death, but it had died. He'd built a new life for himself now, and there was no room in it for football.

"Don't waste your time, Pete, I'm not your man."

Gianfracco waved that aside impatiently. "I think you are. In fact, of all the players I've coached, you were the one I always figured would end up bossing me around. You were that savvy."

Mitch shifted. These days, sitting for any length of time was almost as taxing as walking. "It's been too long, Coach. I don't have the belly for it anymore."

Gianfracco rattled off a string of profanity that had Mitch shaking his head. "I've heard some creative swearing in my time, Coach, but you're the best of the best."

"Hell, in my old neighborhood in Brooklyn that kind of talk wouldn't even have rated notice." Gianfracco chuckled. "Nothing compared to what I'll say if you don't agree to take a look-see at what we've got to offer."

"I'm not a coach."

"How do you know that when you've never tried? Besides, coaching isn't much different from quarterbacking. In both jobs you have to be a father figure, big bad brother and kick-ass psychologist all rolled into one. Seems to me you did a good job at all three of those things."

"That doesn't mean I can teach someone else to do what I did. Or teach anything, for that matter."

Coach snorted. "That's bull, and you know it. Every rookie that joined the club while you were running the offense ended up praising you up one side and down the other for the things you taught 'em." He narrowed his eyes. "Tell me something, Mitch. Do you still have that notebook of plays you used to carry around with you? The one you were always scribbling in when the rest of the guys were swapping lies and discussing women?''

Mitch resisted a glance at the bottom drawer of his desk. "It's around somewhere," he hedged.

"Give me a few days of your time, Mitch. Let me show you around my part of the country, introduce you to a few people, maybe talk some football. Seems to me you owe your old coach that much, at least."

Mitch stared at the desk without really seeing it. Coach was right. He did owe the man. But how much? Enough to rip open old wounds that had finally healed?

He drew a breath, absently running his hand over the hard ridge of leather encircling his thigh. When he'd first gotten out of rehab, the need to return to football had been like a hot barb in his belly. Swallowing his pride, which he could admit now had been considerable, he'd approached a half dozen clubs about coaching. The owners who'd once tried to coax him away from the Raiders suddenly didn't want to know him. Without the use of his legs, Mitch Scanlon had been just another has-been. Coach had been one of the few who had kept in touch over the years.

"Tell you what," he said, looking up. "I'll take a look at your program for you and see if I can come up with some ideas for improvements. But I'm not promising anything more than that. Fair enough?"

"Fair enough. In the meantime, I'll buy you dinner, and you can tell me all about this place you've put together here."

Central Oregon was awash in another late April storm when Gianfracco returned to campus the next morning. He had three days to prepare for Scanlon's visit, seventy-two hours to put together an irresistible dog and pony show for a man who'd never been easy to talk into something he didn't think was right for him, even when he'd been a green as they come backup QB.

Arranging VIP treatment was first on the list. Grinning to himself, Coach picked up the phone and dialed the number of Bradenton's official hostess. Felicity Alderson was the widow of Bradenton's former president and the mother of the present one. A real Southern belle, she was dripping with class. If anyone could make Mitch feel special, it was Felicity.

After punching out the number, Coach swiveled his chair and glared at the team photos on the wall behind his desk. The Timber Wolves had gone through coaches like disposable tissues, four in as many years—good men, all, but still, Bradenton hadn't won a game in three seasons.

"Alderson House, this is Tilly speaking."

Coach pictured the round Irish countenance and all-seeing blue eyes of the Alderson housekeeper and grinned. "How're you doing, Tilly, me darlin'? This is Pete Gianfracco, and I sure would love to speak with Felicity if she's around."

"Mrs. Alderson's in the rose garden," Tilly replied with the clipped accent of her Irish birth. "I'll fetch her."

"Thanks."

Closing his eyes, Coach sent a fast prayer toward the heavens that everything would fall into place. The fate of seven thousand students and five hundred staff members and faculty, not to mention a goodly number of small businesses supplying the needs of those students, depended on these next few days. As President Caroline "Carly" Alderson had told him in her usual succinct manner, Bradenton was standing on the gallows, trussed and hooded and ready for the trap door to be sprung.

The problem was money, as it was these days for many private colleges. In eighteen months, the bank that held the mortgages on several buildings was expecting a six-figure balloon payment. If Bradenton defaulted, the bank had declared an intention to foreclose.

Project Cinderella Team had been Dr. Alderson's idea, born out of desperation, she'd said when she'd outlined his role in her plan. Bradenton was known for two things—an innovative admissions program and the longest losing streak in the history of the Northwest Central Conference. Area sportscasters made jokes about the hapless Wolves on the air, and students and graduates alike were soon ashamed to be seen at the games. Worse, a significant number of alumni had stopped donating to the general fund. Not that Coach blamed them. No one, him most of all, wanted to be labeled a loser, even by association. Which was what had given President Alderson an ingenious idea—turn a bunch of ragtag losers into a scrapping, give-'em-

hell underdog. Get the students and alumni fired up, spur them
to support the team.

Dr. Alderson had used words like *collective consciousness*
and *crowd dynamics,* stuff a social anthropologist like her
would know about. Him, he knew football and football fans.
Give 'em a team of fighting, spitting underdogs determined to
win and a couple hours of hoopla and excitement, and they'd
flock through the stadium gates in droves, their hands already
reaching in their pockets for the money to buy beer and hot
dogs and souvenirs.

Dr. Alderson's friend, Professor Kenworthy, said the same
thing, only in that Madison Avenue lingo she'd brought with
her from New York. Words like *star quality* and *charisma* and
media blitz.

A single-minded guy, Coach focused on the one thing all
three could agree on—everything depended on finding the right
man for the coaching job. Someone with a "name," someone
who could generate excitement just by breathing, someone who
knew football strategy and football psychology.

For the past three months Gianfracco had done things by the
book—logging innumerable hours on airplanes flying all over
the country in an attempt to recruit some of the game's best
coaches. He'd been laughed out of more locker rooms that he
wanted to remember. It was then that he'd thought of Mitch.

Maybe Scanlon hadn't coached, but the man knew football.
For a decade his name had been written in stardust, his reputation as one of the greats growing year by year, a reputation
that Coach considered well-deserved. After all, Mitch's work
ethic had always been exemplary, his dedication to the team
unquestioned. And best of all, he had the kind of guts and
mental toughness it took to ignore the odds. Hadn't he proved
the doctors wrong when they'd told him he'd spend the rest of
his life in a wheelchair? Maybe he didn't walk like most folks,
but he managed to get around pretty darn good, and as long as
they kept the sob-sister stuff in check, Bradenton was bound to
get a lot of publicity from the fact that a paraplegic was
coaching at the college level.

Coach grinned to himself as he added up the pluses. Caroline Alderson had been in Chicago, attending a conference of

college presidents, when he'd had his brainstorm. Normally a team player, he was all alone in this. His idea, his initiative.

According to Dr. Alderson's assistant, Sandy Brudinsky, the boss was due home on the same day Scanlon arrived. Coach couldn't wait to see the look on her face when he told her what he'd done. Hot damn, but she'd be pleased. He was sure of it.

"Hello?"

Coach felt a fast little jolt at the sound of Felicity's soft drawl. "Haul out the good silver, Felicity," he ordered, sitting up straighter. "You and I have important work to do."

Alderson House had the same Gothic turrets and stark granite construction as the rest of the buildings Mitch had seen as he'd driven through the campus to Coach's office. All it needed was a moat and it could pass as a medieval castle suddenly transported to a swath of green rolling hills and towering trees.

Mitch leaned his aching back against the heavy stone porch railing and watched Coach jam an impatient thumb against the doorbell. Beyond the huge carved door, the sound of chimes could be heard, echoing the same series of notes he'd heard earlier from the fortresslike carillon in the main quad.

"This place may have a lousy football team, but it sure has atmosphere," he told Coach with a grin.

"Around here we call that class, and Bradenton's got more'n its share," Coach retorted with a grin of his own. "But you'll find that out for yourself when you meet the Alderson ladies."

Mitch wasn't all that eager to meet anyone. Never knowing how his disability would be received was one of the reasons. But even before his injury, he'd struggled with a shyness so profound he'd stuttered like Porky Pig as a kid. Letting his athletic skill speak for him had helped, but even in the glory days, he'd thrown up every time he'd had to appear on TV.

"Felicity said seven, damn it," Gianfracco muttered as he scowled at his watch. "It's seven sharp, so how come we're still cooling our heels out here?"

Mitch eyed Coach speculatively. Pete's wife had been dead eight—or was it nine?—years now, time enough to blunt Pete's grief. "Felicity?" he asked blandly.

Coach grunted. "Carleton Alderson's widow. He was the man who hired me for this job."

"How long has Mrs. Alderson been a widow?"

"Three years. Around here the Aldersons are like royalty, which sort of makes Felicity the Queen Mother. Since old Artemus Alderson founded this place in the 1880s, no one but an Alderson has ever sat in the president's chair."

"Apparently Carleton didn't produce a son, or was he one of those enlightened males Jeannie keeps trying to make me into?"

Coach's raisin brown eyes twinkled. "One thing Carleton wasn't, and that's enlightened."

"Sounds like you've gotten to know his widow pretty well."

Coach grinned. "Not as well as I'd like. We're still stuck someplace between the first kiss and her bedroom." He took another stab at the bell, while Mitch studied the vista spread out below.

The entire campus seemed visible from here, looking for all the world like an ageless English village plopped down among distinctively American firs and pines. Only the stadium seemed out of place. Like him, he thought, flexing his tired shoulders.

"Say, Pete, are you sure you've got the right night?" he asked when Coach leaned sideways to peer through the closest window.

"Hell, yes. Confirmed it yesterday when I got your call saying you'd be here by five. Felicity's—"

The door swung open suddenly to reveal a rotund woman wearing a spotless white apron and a cheery smile. Mitch figured her for midfifties, with more salt than pepper in her short curly hair. Her lively blue eyes made short work of assessing him, then shifted back to Coach.

"Good evening, gentlemen," she said, retreating a step so they might enter.

"Evening, Tilly," Coach said warmly. "Meet Mitchell Scanlon," he added as he stepped across the threshold. "He's going to be visiting the campus for a few days. Tilly keeps this place humming, or so she reminds me every time I bump into her."

"And don't you be forgettin' it," Tilly said, shaking her finger in Coach's face before turning to greet Mitch pleasantly. "Won't you please follow me? President Alderson's plane was delayed in Chicago by bad weather, but she should be arriving shortly. In the meantime, Mrs. Alderson is in the small parlor."

Coach glanced at his watch, then shrugged. "Lead on, Tilly me girl. I feel a yen for some of Felicity's favorite sherry."

Mitch caught the look Coach sent his way and grinned. "Sherry?" he asked, lifting his eyebrows.

"Don't knock it till you've tried it, old son. There's a lot to be said for class."

Mitch took a tighter grip on his crutches and wondered what he'd gotten himself into.

Carly Alderson dropped her bags just inside the back door and turned to pull it closed. "Remind me to refuse any invitation that requires flying," she said to Tilly as the housekeeper came bustling into the kitchen.

"Bad trip?" Tilly asked as they exchanged hugs.

"My plane didn't crash. That's the good news." Carly managed a grin, but it took some effort. She was exhausted, and her head was still aching from the recycled air in the 737.

"I assume our guests have already arrived, or is that your silver Jaguar parked in front?" she teased as she filched a cherry tomato from the colander where Tilly had set them to drain.

"It is not, and yes, the gentlemen are in the small parlor with your ma."

"Darn. I was hoping to sneak in a shower and a nap before I had to go into VIP welcoming mode."

"Go ahead. I'll put off dinner for another half hour."

"Thanks, but I'll survive. I always do." Carly slipped her purse from her shoulder and set it on the counter. She'd been thrilled when Sandy had called her at the hotel in Chicago with the news that Coach had found a promising prospect and invited him to the campus for a visit. Though Sandy hadn't known the candidate's name, Carly trusted Coach's judgment and had been looking forward to meeting the man she'd privately dubbed Bradenton's answer to Rocky Balboa. Unfortunately, she was also suffering from jet lag and six days of exhausting meetings.

Wearily she removed her small makeup bag from her purse and zipped it open. Bending slightly, she used the microwave door as a mirror, touching her lashes with a hint of mascara and applying gloss to her lips. She returned the makeup to her purse before extracting a brush.

"Is Tracy in her room?" she asked Tilly, smiling at the prospect of seeing her daughter again.

"No, she's having dinner at Karen's."

Carly sighed in disappointment. "How'd she do on her chemistry test?"

"An A, what else?" Tilly grinned. "She and Karen have been practicing their cartwheels in the upstairs hall for three nights straight—and driving your ma crazy."

Carly grinned. Her beautiful, bubbly daughter was captain of her high school cheerleading squad and determined to make the junior varsity next year as a Bradenton freshman. "Poor Mother," she murmured, picturing her mother's disapproval. Felicity meant well, but she was horrified by her granddaughter's rebellious need to embrace life, just as she'd once been horrified at Carly's.

"Mrs. A is afraid they'll loosen the chandelier in the foyer and it'll come crashing down on some poor soul's head some day," Tilly amplified.

"I sincerely hope not. The last thing Bradenton can afford right now is a law suit."

Tilly chuckled. "Not to worry. Just to make sure, I called McNabb from maintenance, and he checked it out. Said a herd of elephants could tap-dance on that ceiling and that big old fixture wouldn't so much as sway."

Carly grinned. "That's a relief."

Tilly nodded. "McNabb also mentioned that Bessie is out of order again. Said he'd called the elevator repair people, and they're sendin' someone out on Friday, but told me to tell you to wear your sneakers to the office till then."

Carly groaned. She loved the old elevator that had been installed in the administration building in the early part of the century, and she didn't want to see it replaced by something made of chrome and plastic. Preserving Bradenton's unique character was akin to a sacred trust with her, though at the moment she was more concerned with just keeping the doors open.

"First the water main breaks in the science hall, and then the fire marshal finds frayed wiring in the library, and now this." Just thinking about trudging up three flights of stairs to her tower office every day made her more exhausted than ever. "Remind me to buy a lottery ticket next time I'm in Bradenton Falls."

Tilly took the lid from a large pot and inhaled the rich aroma before stirring. It was lobster bisque, Carly's favorite, and her mouth watered. She hadn't eaten since the end-of-conference brunch.

"Needs more garlic," Tilly muttered before replacing the lid and opening the door to the spice cabinet.

"Is Tracy planning to spend the night at Karen's?"

"No, she'll be home later."

Carly ran her brush through her chin-length Dutch bob and felt the electricity crackle. Her hair was a medium brown, as thick and glossy as a mink's winter coat, and poker straight. After several disastrous perms, she'd resigned herself to the simplest of styles.

"I just hope I can stay awake long enough to see her." Carly dropped her brush into her purse and adjusted the collar of her silk dress. It was her favorite, a deep rich purple that made her feel calm and competent.

"So what's your read on Coach's latest prospect?" she asked, straightening her shoulders and lifting her chin.

"He has a strong face and sad eyes and a nice, steady way about him, like he's wrestled the Devil himself and won." Tilly added a nod of approval for good measure, and Carly let out a low whistle.

"That's praise indeed," she said before filching another tomato. "And I fervently hope that you are one hundred percent right, because spring practice starts in six weeks and two days."

"I still say football is a barbaric sport," Tilly muttered, giving the bisque an extra-vigorous stir. "I've never been able to understand why you love it so."

"Because watching football games with my father was the only time I ever had him totally to myself."

Tilly sniffed. "He could have done with a good lesson in priorities," she muttered, and Carly chuckled.

"Tilly, my Tilly, what would I have done without you?"

"Probably the same as you did with me," the housekeeper retorted brusquely.

"Just the same, I'm glad you're part of our family." Carly gave Tilly a hug and then left the kitchen.

The parlor where Felicity preferred to serve drinks when the occasion was an intimate one was on the other side of the mansion, and as she headed that way, Carly's heels tapped a muted tattoo on the priceless rugs covering the polished hardwood.

Sunset was just starting, giving the light flooding through the front windows a pink tinge. The house seemed still, as though brooding about the crisis threatening its existence.

Bankruptcy. The very word made Carly recoil. As president, she should have known. But she hadn't. None of the senior administrators, including Bradenton's long-time controller, had had more than a vague inkling. The auditor had blamed the downturn in the economy for a drastic shortfall in alumni donations. The trustees had blamed her.

She was the one with the ambitious plans, the one who'd pushed through the "Youth at Risk" scholarship program for ex-gang members that had made a new dormitory necessary. And she was the one who had bullied the trustees into approving an expensive revamping of the curriculum. But all those things had been necessary, darn it, she reminded herself firmly. And every one had been done with the trustees' approval. Only when serious trouble started rumbling their way did the trustees suddenly come up with second thoughts.

Carly refused to waste time on the blame game. What was done was done. The important thing now was to replenish the sadly depleted treasury, and fast. Most of the elements of her plan were already in place. Marca Kenworthy had the publicity campaign ready to go, and Carly had freed enough money to finance it by personally taking on part of next year's teaching load, left open by two retiring professors. All they needed now was the right coach, someone photogenic and irresistible to the media, "a taller Robert Redford with tree-trunk shoulders," Marca had quipped. Carly would be satisfied with someone with a passion for winning, no matter how long the odds. And while you're at it, Carly, why don't you make the guy rich enough to contribute a chunk of the money himself? she thought, pushing her shoulders back an extra inch.

As she approached the parlor, Carly heard her mother's finishing-school diction countered by Coach Gianfracco's harsh Brooklyn consonants. Those two, she thought, shaking her head. Neither one had anticipated an attraction for the other, but to anyone seeing them together, it was more than obvious. And really quite endearing, Carly thought as she paused outside the door to gather her wits.

Felicity was in her usual attire of tailored chic and pearls and her usual spot, holding court from the wing chair by the fireplace, the picture of a gracious hostess in every carefully attended detail, including the small glass of excellent sherry in her hand.

Coach was sitting bolt upright on the small damask and rosewood settee facing her, looking as though he would kill for a cigar. But it was the large man sitting in Carly's father's chair on the other side of the fireplace who drew her eager gaze.

Casually but impeccably dressed in a camel-colored sport coat and a pale blue Oxford cloth shirt open at the throat, he was a big man, with enough breadth of chest and width of shoulder to please Marca twice over. At first glance he appeared to be in his early forties, with the brooding look of a man given to solemn moods and bouts of deep introspection.

Carly's heart began racing, and her throat went dry. A long habit of enforced composure kept her from gasping aloud, but one hand went to her stomach nevertheless.

The deep-set eyes she had fought to forget were the same intense shade of gold, the lashes still thick, the eyebrows quirked at a sexy angle. But the lazy glint of supreme self-confidence was gone, replaced by a world-weary watchfulness.

There were other changes, too. His thick, sun-burnished hair was now heavily salted with steel, and the lion's mane that had tumbled almost to his shoulders had been shorn to collar length. The firm lips that had smiled so easily seemed cast in a somber line now, and his face had been honed to a new leanness. Under perfectly tailored slacks he was wearing braces on those long legs, once thick with muscle and rippling with en-

ergy, and now so utterly still. The brown forearm crutches by
the chair spoke very clearly of the extent of his disability.

A younger man's face rose in her mind, equally tanned, with
the same fiercely proud jut to the strong square chin, the same
resolute mouth. It was a face she'd seen on the covers of sports
magazines when he'd won the Heismann Trophy, the same face
that had smiled with such cocky pride when the Raiders took
him in the first round of the NFL draft his senior year.

Sometimes she wondered if she hadn't been half in love with
Mitch Scanlon before she'd actually laid eyes on him. He hadn't
been a pro then, merely UCLA's latest golden boy, but everyone knew he was headed for superstardom. To top it off, he had
been gorgeous at twenty-two.

Six feet four, hard as rawhide and deeply tanned, he'd had
sandy hair burnt nearly blond by the sun and nut brown eyes
that seemed to be smiling even when he wasn't.

They'd met her freshman year, when she and Marca had
driven down to Palm Springs for spring break. Everyone had
been talking about him that week. Of course, Marca, with her
passion for new experiences, had been the one to spot him
leaning against the bar. Carly had just tagged along as Marca
had approached him, scarcely believing her luck at being near
her idol.

She had been close to speechless when he'd smiled her way.
His lazy gaze promised an excitement she'd only dreamed
about, and yet his smile was oddly shy, touching an as-yet-
undiscovered chord deep inside her.

Afraid he would lose interest once he found out how inexperienced she was, she made up an alter ego on the spot—a girl
named Sarah from the big city of Seattle. Sarah was twenty-one
and adventurous. Sarah was fun; Sarah drank.

He'd bought her a beer and then another, laughing when
she'd licked the foam from her upper lip. The room had begun
to spin, and she'd felt as though she were floating above the
peanut-strewn floor. While other girls glared jealously her way,
he'd slowly wooed her in that rough cat's purr of a voice that
stirred feelings of excitement she couldn't seem to control, no
matter how hard she tried. And when he asked her to go with
him to his motel room, she hadn't stopped to think twice. Six

weeks later she'd found out she was carrying his child, a little girl she'd named Tracy and raised alone.

Drawing a long breath into her burning lungs, she closed her eyes and tried to calm her suddenly racing heart. For Tracy's sake, she had to find out if Scanlon recognized her. No matter what, Tracy had to be protected.

The resemblance between father and daughter was subtle, but it was there nevertheless. Anyone with any suspicion at all could see a more innocent, trusting replica of Scanlon's cynical golden eyes in Tracy's, the same tumble of thick hair framing the same square face.

No, she wouldn't let Tracy be hurt. For Tracy's sake she would be strong, just as she'd made herself be strong during those terrible first months of her pregnancy.

For Tracy's sake, she would be polite and cool and every inch an Alderson. This was her turf, her home field advantage. She was a professional now, a woman at the top of her career, the president of a well-respected college. Taking another deep breath, she stood tall and curved her lips into a polite smile of welcome. President Alderson had guests waiting.

Chapter 2

While Coach regaled their hostess with another of his football stories, Mitch sipped enough sherry to be polite and wondered how things were going in Sacramento without him. He trusted Jeannie, but she was new to management and still a little shaky when it came to making decisions.

A quick glance at the ornate clock on the spindly table near the French doors off the terrace told him it was still early, not quite seven-thirty. Later, when he was settled in his motel, he would give her a quick call. If she had a problem, she would likely let him know then.

Not that he was worried, he reminded himself as he took another sip of the too sweet wine and watched Coach punctuate the story he was recounting with his usual expansive gestures. Okay, so maybe he was edging toward worry, but the spa was his baby, the only one he was ever going to have. Putting it together little by little had given him a reason to get out of bed every morning. And watching it prosper had bumped his self-esteem up a few badly needed notches.

"I understand you're from California?"

It took Mitch a moment to realize his hostess had swung her gaze his way. Unlike most women he'd known, she had a knack of concentrating completely on a man when she spoke to him.

"I live in Sacramento now, but I grew up in East Los Angeles." In a neighborhood boasting a shooting gallery on every other block and the thickest concentration of hookers in the entire city.

"My late husband and I attended a conference of college presidents in Los Angeles in—now let me see—1981?" Mrs. Alderson's patrician forehead puckered daintily as she reflected. "Yes, that is correct," she declared with a genteel nod of her perfectly coiffed head. "I remember because it was the same June Caroline graduated from Bradenton. She was the third Alderson to matriculate here, you know, although, sadly, she missed being the valedictorian by two percentage points. Her father was terribly disappointed."

"Yes, ma'am," Mitch repeated while mentally adding bottle-thick horn-rim glasses to the picture forming of Coach's lady boss.

"Did you attend college in California?" she asked brightly.

Mitch shifted, heading off the hamstring cramp he felt clutching at his left thigh. "Yes, UCLA."

"Best quarterback the Bruins ever had," Gianfracco inserted. "Mitch still holds the record for passing yardage. Played his last collegiate game in the Rose Bowl. Beat Ohio State by thirteen points."

"My daughter's hoping for a bowl bid this season. Not the Rose Bowl, of course, but perhaps one of the smaller, regional bowls."

"She's not the only one hoping," Coach declared before swallowing the remainder of his drink. "I'd like to end my career with a winning team myself."

Felicity nodded. "More sherry, Peter?"

"Don't mind if I do, thanks."

Felicity's gaze came to Mitch, and she smiled. "Mitchell?"

Mitch indicated his nearly full glass and shook his head. As he did, a whisper of silk and skin drew his gaze to the door. He stopped breathing and for a split second felt as though he'd just been body slammed into a wall. If this was President Alderson, he and every other man within a ten-mile radius were in big trouble.

Simply put, Coach's dragon lady was a knockout, all the way from the sheen of her sleek brown hair to the tips of her classically simple high-heeled shoes.

From where he sat, she looked to be half a head shorter than six feet, every inch designed to steal a man's breath and, unless he had completely lost his male compass, enticingly packaged in smooth white skin.

She was wearing purple, an appropriate color given her family history and the regal angle at which she held her slightly cleft chin. Her eyes were a muted green, somewhere between emerald and a morning sea, and fringed with curly brown lashes just short of lush. Her nose was standard female issue, shaded toward small, and her mouth was wide, with enough fullness to keep a man's blood pressure in the red zone.

Though younger than he'd expected—early to midthirties was his first guess—she gave off pulses of power that didn't surprise him, along with waves of hidden vulnerability that did. Steel and velvet, an unusual combination and definitely classy, he thought, watching her gaze sweep the room with perfect poise before coming to rest for an instant on his face.

Unbidden, a smile tugged at his mouth. Maybe his stay in Oregon wasn't going to be all work and no play. As though privy to his thoughts, she firmed her lips, and the smoked green of her eyes iced over.

Whoa, what'd I do to deserve that? he wondered, and then he remembered the last woman he'd taken to bed, and the pity in her eyes when she'd seen his withered legs. She hadn't even stayed around long enough to button her blouse. Probably gave some half-sloshed conventioneer a real thrill when she left his Tahoe hotel room. He'd spent the rest of the evening getting drunk, alone.

"There you are, Caroline," Felicity murmured with the barest trace of annoyance hardening her vowels. "I heard your car pulling in quite a long time ago, and I was beginning to worry."

Carly offered her mother the same tolerant smile she'd been using for most of her life. "I stopped to chat with Tilly."

"I see." Felicity smiled then. "Sherry, dear?"

"A small one," Carly said before gliding forward to greet Coach Gianfracco.

"How was the conference?" Coach asked, after lumbering hastily to his feet.

"Challenging."

"Bet you wowed all those other presidents with your speech," he said before introducing her to Scanlon. "Mitch, meet the best boss a man ever had, Carly Alderson."

"Ms. Alderson."

Carly had forgotten the gritty, bone-shivering quality of his deep voice—or, more accurately, erased it from her mind, just as she'd tried to erase everything else about him.

"Mr. Scanlon," Carly said briskly, her hand extended as she approached his chair. "How nice of you to accept Coach Gianfracco's offer to visit."

Scanlon didn't rise, nor did she expect him to. Leaning forward slightly, he took her hand in his. His touch was impersonal, his grip strong but not designed to impress. Even as her mind processed the feel of hard calluses against her palm, her body was recoiling inside. Her emotions churned toward violent, but she made herself concentrate on her breathing. One slow, even breath. Another. The need to strike out leveled, and she felt some of the tension lift. He hadn't recognized her, and that was all that mattered.

Needing distance, she retreated to the settee, conscious that he was watching her with a glint of lazy amusement in his tawny eyes. Did he ever think about that plump, too eager virgin he'd charmed into his bed one hot spring night seventeen years ago? she wondered, tasting a bitterness she'd thought she'd mastered long ago.

"Have you ever visited Oregon before, Mr. Scanlon?" she asked politely, crossing her legs.

Scanlon's gaze lingered a beat too long on her ankles before skimming up to meet her eyes. Schooling her features to remain calm, she met his gaze squarely.

"Once. The Raiders played an exhibition game in the stadium in Portland right after it was built. It was a nice place, and best of all, it had natural grass."

Carly nodded. "The sportscasters are always saying that players hate artificial grass. Sounds as though you did, too."

She saw that there was a coiled tenseness about him, even as he acknowledged her question with a slight smile. "No matter what those suits in the front office claim, playing on artificial grass is like playing on a blanket spread over concrete.''

Coach grunted his agreement. "Too many good men had their careers cut short on account of it."

"But, gentlemen, isn't football always played on natural grass?'' Finished pouring Carly's drink, Felicity directed her question to Coach, managing to look both mystified and remarkably pretty, something that Carly was fairly certain Coach had already noticed.

"Only in older stadiums," Coach told her in an almost courtly way. "In others, it's played on an artificial surface."

Felicity beamed her thanks, and Carly visualized a long line of Southern belles stretching back a hundred years, hiding their intelligence behind lace hankies and questions carefully crafted to inflate a man's ego.

She didn't blame her mother for choosing a subservient role. Felicity was only being the woman she'd been raised to be. Carly hadn't set out to break the pattern, but having a child out of wedlock had forced her to.

"Speaking of Portland, what did you think of this last Super Bowl?'' She shaded her voice to convey polite interest in a guest of the college, nothing more.

"I heard it was pretty boring.'' Scanlon's smile was slow, with just enough of a twist to let her know he didn't much like talking about the past.

"Heard? You didn't watch?'' Her surprise was genuine.

"I had other things to do.'' He shifted restlessly in the chair, one big hand resting on the arm, the other flattened on his thigh. He'd worn shorts in Palm Springs, and his thighs had bulged with muscles. Even a casual glance told her that those huge thighs had shrunk. She refused to feel sorry for him.

"I have to admit I watched until the bitter end. It was a good game, even if the press thought lousy officiating cost Portland the win.''

"Yeah, well, the press gets paid for offering stupid opinions.''

Mitch knew he was supposed to be impressing Bradenton's cool and collected lady president, but the pity he'd seen in her eyes at first meeting had gotten his back up before she'd even opened that very unschoolmarmish mouth of hers. For some reason he couldn't pinpoint, he wanted to ruffle her feathers but good. He also, he discovered with some annoyance, wanted to find out if that pouty mouth was really as soft as it looked.

"Isn't that a rather prejudiced viewpoint?" she asked, shifting slightly to face him more squarely.

Mitch allowed his expression to reveal just how prejudiced he was. "You might as well know up front, Ms. Alderson. I have zero respect for all but a few members of the media."

She accepted that serenely, with only a slight lifting of one eyebrow. He wondered what it would take to rile up the sea green calm in those eyes.

"I guess that's putting it plainly enough. And it's Dr. Alderson."

The sudden edge to her voice had him grinning to himself. So she liked to call the shots, did she? He'd always liked that in a woman. It made her surrender that much sweeter.

"Sorry," he drawled, though they both knew that he wasn't. "I'd forgotten how important those extra letters after a person's name can be."

"Some of us have had to work very hard for those letters, Mr. Scanlon. Harder, I suspect, than you had to work at earning your bachelor's degree—in physical education, I believe it was."

Mitch never minded taking a shot from a worthy opponent and saluted her with his glass to show that there were no hard feelings. "Best training for an NFL career that UCLA had to offer."

Frowning to let him know that she wasn't amused, she reached forward to lift her glass of sherry from her grandmother's prized Chippendale table. As she sipped slowly, she was conscious that Scanlon was watching her. For seventeen years she'd worked hard not to see reminders of him in her daughter's face. Now she realized that she would never be able to look at Tracy again in quite the same way. Anger poured through her. Just another reason to hate this man.

"Naturally it would have been better for our purposes if you'd gotten an advanced degree, but most colleges do make an exception in their hiring practices for—how shall I put this?"

"Washed-up ex-jocks with bum legs?" he prompted blandly.

Her soft, pink mouth relaxed momentarily and then tightened even more. It wasn't just run-of-the-mill pity he was getting from her. Something else was all mixed up with the usual
reaction of a stranger to an up close and personal view of his
handicap.

"I was about to say instructors with specialized talent. Like
yours, Mr. Scanlon." She reached forward to return her glass
to the table. "Your record as a quarterback speaks for itself."

"I can tell you he was a darn good strategist, too," Coach
put in. "Almost as good as me."

"That *is* high praise," Carly said with a spontaneous smile
for Gianfracco that he returned with interest.

"Mitch and I spent a couple hours after he arrived going over
play books, kicking around a few ideas. Like I told him then,
the talent's there, all right. Just needs the right man at the top
to bring it out."

Carly's heart thudded hard. So Scanlon was actually considering taking the job. As though the fact that it would be offered to him was a given.

"Talent, yes," she admitted, folding her hands in her lap.
"But there are some major weaknesses, too, especially in the
backfield."

Scanlon's tawny eyes narrowed, and she sensed that she'd
surprised him. Good, she thought.

"I won't argue with any of that, but I can tell you right now,
Dr. Alderson, it will take a lot more than raw talent to turn
around a forty-eight-game losing streak."

"Forty-seven. We tied one game."

"A major distinction, I agree." His strong fingers loosely
gripped the stem of his wineglass, which, in contrast, seemed
impossibly small. It was also nearly full. But then, he had fa-
vored beer the last time they'd met, hadn't he? A pitcher, at
least. Perhaps more. She'd lost track.

"I see you have a knack for sarcasm as well as football, Mr.
Scanlon."

She was annoyed and working hard not to show it. Most men
would be too busy checking out the body under the expensive
tailoring to notice much else. But he'd made a good living for
a lot of years because he'd trained himself to watch the eyes
first. Hers were alive with intelligence and what he suspected

was a carefully hidden passion. At the moment they seemed intent on putting him in his place, which, undoubtedly, wasn't anywhere he cared to be.

"Just following your lead, Dr. Alderson."

Carly shifted, her shoulders tight with tension and her skin clammy. What had made her think she could sit face-to-face with him for more than a few seconds without remembering the hot demand of that hard mouth? Or the crush of that big body on hers?

For an instant she had trouble breathing, then she regained control. "If I've given you the idea that I or the rest of the faculty take Bradenton's dismal football performance lightly, you are mistaken," she said firmly. "No one faults the player who gives his all and comes up short, but to a man, our players seem to have given up, which is not—I repeat *not*—in keeping with Bradenton's philosophy."

"Can't argue with that, either."

Carly reached for her drink and took a careful sip, conscious as she lifted the glass to her lips that Scanlon was watching her with those lazy cat's eyes. It made her sick inside to know that she remembered their hot, frantic coupling in a lumpy motel bed and he didn't. She took a deep breath to settle herself. It didn't work.

"I have to admit, I've never cared that much for football," Felicity commented when the silence stretched toward awkward. "It always seemed like such an uncouth game to me. On the other hand, Carly has always adored it. Haven't you, dear?"

Carly offered her mother an agreeable smile. "I wouldn't put it quite that strongly, Mother, although, of course, I do follow the Wolves."

"Does that mean you attend the games, Dr. Alderson?"

She let her smile fade as she met Scanlon's steady gaze. "The ones at home, yes."

"Coach here has given me the bare bones of the team's past troubles. Suppose you give me your read on the problems a new coach would face."

"Apathy, for one thing," she said briskly. "Among the players as well as the fans."

He eyed her steadily, his eyes shadowed. "Which came first, I wonder?"

The question gave her pause. It was one she'd never asked herself, but, she realized now, one she should have. "It's hard to say for certain," she said slowly, working backward in her memory from the last game in the losing streak to the first. "This is just a guess, but I'd say the fans gave up first."

His mouth took on an intriguing slant. "Usually happens that way."

"Sure does," Coach declared. "Remember your rookie year, Mitch? The Raiders had just come off the worst year in franchise history. A guy coulda aimed a cannon behind the goalposts at the stands any place but the fifty-yard line and not hit a paying customer." He waved a hand, then let his gaze rest on Carly's. "One year later—just one, mind you—and this guy here had 'em packed in those same seats like sardines."

Reluctantly, Carly shifted her gaze to Scanlon. "That *is* remarkable." It was also something she'd already known before Coach brought it up.

"But not much of a recommendation for a guy who wants to coach instead of play?"

"No," she said bluntly. "It isn't."

Carly slanted her mother a look, then slid her gaze toward the door. Leaning forward, Felicity returned her glass to the coffee table before rising.

"Shall we go in to dinner?" she murmured with a polite smile.

"Thought you'd never ask," Coach said, getting up quickly to offer Felicity his arm.

Carly took a deep breath and got to her feet while Scanlon bent to retrieve his crutches, then pushed himself up and slipped his arms through the cuffs.

"I'd offer you my arm, but I need it," he said with a faintly mocking smile. If he pitied himself, it didn't show.

"That's okay," she murmured, moved in spite of herself. "I can take care of myself."

Carly toyed with her crème brûlée, far too tired to appreciate Tilly's exceptional cuisine. For most of the dinner party, she'd kept herself going on her reserve of nervous energy, but even that had been depleted, and now she was wondering how soon she could excuse herself without appearing rude.

Fortunately, no one else seemed to notice her distress. Coach had eaten like a starving lumberjack. He'd also done most of the talking, punctuating his stories with quick stabs of the fork he seldom put down.

Scanlon had said little. He'd smiled even less, and there was a tautness around his mouth that hadn't been there earlier. Now and then he moved restlessly, as though the chair where he sat was too confining. Listening to Coach wind down yet another football anecdote, she risked another peek at her watch.

"Are we keeping you from something important, Dr. Alderson?"

"Not at all, Mr. Scanlon," she said, reluctantly meshing her gaze with his over the centerpiece. "I'm still on Chicago time, that's all."

"Long day?"

"Yes, with a little bit of jet lag thrown in."

His smile slanted a shallow dimple in one cheek, his right, awakening painful memories she'd worked hard to erase. "Try tomato juice and lemon, with a whiskey chaser," he said with perfect seriousness.

She winced. "Good heavens, where did you come up with that?"

"A guy I used to play with. Swore it worked on hangovers and jet lag. I've used it for both. Works like a champ. Of course, maybe that's because you're so busy gagging you forget whatever else ails you."

Her soft mouth curved, erasing much of the strain from her face. Even as Mitch found himself noticing the sensuous fullness of her lips, he was wondering what there was about her that aroused protective instincts he'd thought he'd lost years before. In spite of the perfect manners and impressive poise, she seemed oddly tense to him, as though she had pulled her emotions deep inside. Or perhaps it was only a trick of the candlelight that had him seeing shadows in those fascinating green eyes.

"Now that's what I call a great dinner!" Coach sighed like a man who had just made love.

Felicity beamed. "How about another helping of dessert?"

"Better not. Got to watch my waistline."

Right on cue, she turned her attention to their other guest, her smile warm and coaxing. "How about you, Mitchell? Another helping? We have plenty, especially since my granddaughter was unable to join us as I'd hoped."

Mitch shook his head. Another ten minutes, tops, and he would politely excuse himself and head for the nearest motel. He was tired from the long drive, and his braces were giving him fits. His entire plan for the rest of his first night in Oregon consisted of a long soak in a hot tub and as much sleep as he could manage. Only his respect for Coach had kept him around for dessert and coffee.

"How old is your granddaughter, Mrs. Alderson?" he asked because the question was expected. And because he liked her enough to haul out his party manners.

Felicity brightened, and he was glad he'd asked. "Tracy will be seventeen in November."

"Pretty as a picture, too," Coach threw in. "Like her mom and grandmom."

"She'll be a freshman here next year," her grandmother added with visible satisfaction. "Her grandfather would have been so proud." She shifted her gaze to her daughter. "Wouldn't he, dear?"

Carly took a sip of water, then dabbed politely at her pale lips. Watching without seeming to, Mitch felt a sexual stir. Remembering other times, other women, had him backing down hard. It wasn't as easy as it should have been.

"We're all proud, Mother, and I'm sure Mr. Scanlon isn't interested in a recitation of Tracy's talents."

Mitch was interested in a lot of things—the woman opposite, at the moment.

"Is your husband a graduate of Bradenton, too?" he asked her directly, rubbing his thumb over the fragile bone china cup.

Her gaze flickered only slightly. "I'm not married."

Mitch wasn't surprised. Most people he knew had at least one failed marriage behind them. It was almost a badge of honor among some. "Divorced?" he asked, figuring he already knew the answer.

She took a second sip of water, then carefully returned the heavy goblet to the table. "In politically correct terms, I'm what is known these days as a single parent, which is a polite way of saying I'm an unwed mother." Her gaze met his calmly.

"Caroline!" Felicity murmured disapprovingly.

President Alderson flicked her gaze toward the head of the table, a quick, defiant smile curving her lips. "Don't fret, Mother. Given Mr. Scanlon's colorful past, I'm sure he isn't the kind to pass judgment on the morality of others."

Mitch lifted his cup to his mouth and drank the last of his coffee. At the same time he studied the face of the woman across from him. Something about her seemed vaguely familiar, and he wondered if they'd crossed paths before. It was possible. He'd met a lot of ladies in his hell-raising years. Took more than his share to bed, too, and bruised a lot of tender feelings fending off the advances of the ones he hadn't, before he got sick and tired of the jerk he'd become. Since he was positive he'd never romanced the aloof Dr. Alderson, he couldn't help wondering what he had done to set her off.

"I may not be the best educated guy around, but I have learned a few things here and there," he said with a deliberately lazy smile. "Not to judge someone by what I've read or heard is one of them."

He watched her mouth snap shut and her eyes grow frosty. Good, he thought. Anything was better than the careful way she had kept her eyes trained above his waist since he'd unlocked his braces to sit down.

"Point taken, Mr. Scanlon," Carly said quietly, fighting for control. "Like life, people are not always what they seem at first glance."

Scanlon studied her face for a long moment, then shrugged his big shoulders easily. "Apology accepted."

In spite of her good intentions, Carly bristled. "I wasn't apologizing."

His mouth slanted. "It's hell being in the wrong and hating to admit it, isn't it?"

"I wouldn't know," she shot back without thinking.

Scanlon's shout of laughter took her by surprise. When Coach and her mother joined in, Carly felt heat surge into her cheeks. "Touché," she said with as much grace as she could muster.

His gaze touched hers briefly, soberly, and she could have sworn he was silently reaching out to apologize for scoring at her expense before he reached down to retrieve his crutches. After propping them against the table, he levered himself to his feet. Carly was moved by his quiet poise in spite of the old resentments.

"Thank you for dinner, Mrs. Alderson. It's been a while since I had a home-cooked meal."

Felicity preened. "You're most welcome." Without missing a beat, she turned to Carly and smiled. "Dear, I wonder if you would do the honors and show Mr. Scanlon the guest suite?"

"That's not necessary. I figured I'd check into a motel in town." Mitch shot Coach a look that had the old man shooting to his feet so fast his chair nearly toppled over.

"Thought I told you, we've got you all set up in deluxe accommodations right here in the President's Mansion."

"Thanks, but I'll bunk in town. Besides, you'll need a ride back to your place, remember?"

"Not to worry," Coach said. "The campus taxi service operates until eleven. I'll just give them a quick call."

"Peter's right, Mr. Scanlon," Felicity said, rising to offer Mitch a dazzling smile. "I would be terribly insulted if you refused."

Mitch recognized the look she gave him. It was the same one Arletta used when she wanted something. He was already working on turning her down when Caroline Alderson rose from the table.

"Please don't feel obligated, Mr. Scanlon. If you would prefer to stay elsewhere, we will of course respect your wishes."

"Nonsense, Caroline," her mother put in quickly, clearly annoyed. "There isn't a decent motel between here and Medford, and you know it."

Mitch was trapped. If he refused the invitation now he would look like the uneducated jerk Dr. Alderson clearly thought him to be. He would also embarrass Coach, which was something he didn't much care to do.

"In that case, Mrs. Alderson, I accept," he said, his gut knotting at the thought of dealing with an unfamiliar setup.

"I'll say good-night, then," Felicity said, smiling. "Breakfast is served at seven, but feel free to roam the kitchen if you're up earlier. If there's anything you need, please don't hesitate to ask."

He took his hand from the handle of his crutch to shake hers. "Thanks, but I'm sure your daughter will take good care of me." And then, because he'd never been one to walk away from a scrap, he looked Caroline Alderson squarely in the eyes and grinned. Her own eyes flashed, but she merely clamped her soft lips together and returned his gaze with a cool confidence he envied.

"Guess it's time for me to hit the road," Coach said before thanking Felicity for her hospitality.

"Hey, Pete, before you go, how about grabbing my gear from the Jag's trunk?" Mitch pulled his keys from the pocket of his jacket and flipped them Coach's way. Caught off guard, Coach managed to snag the keys before they hit his chest.

"Sure thing, Mitch. Be right back."

Felicity offered to see the athletic director to the door, and they walked out together, leaving Carly alone with Scanlon. Like a poison dart, her mind zoomed unerringly to the last time they'd been alone. It had been a steamy night, and the motel had smelled of disinfectant. Ever since that night, she'd hated the scent of pine.

"If you'll come with me, Mr. Scanlon," she said a bit too abruptly, "I'll show you the guest suite."

Carly led the way. When they reached the foyer, he eyed the elaborate flight of stairs with silent resignation. The thought of dragging his legs up those stairs one by one while Caroline Alderson watched had him going cold inside.

"Is something wrong, Mr. Scanlon?" Glancing his way, she arched a shapely eyebrow inquiringly.

Mitch nodded toward the staircase. "I'm not great with stairs these days."

She followed his gaze for a moment, then understood. "Don't worry. The guest wing is on this floor."

"Score one for the good guys," he muttered, moving forward.

Carly allowed herself a small frown as she challenged, "Is that how you see yourself, Mr. Scanlon? As a good guy?"

"Depends on the game, Dr. Alderson." His grin was just shy of devilish. Carly felt a flutter in her belly and told herself it was a reaction to the memory instead of the man.

"It's been my experience that life can be a lot more serious than a game," she told him to the accompaniment of her sharply clicking heels. Realizing that she was walking faster than he could manage, she slowed her pace, her jaw set and her nerves raw. By the time they reached the door to the guest suite, she was so tense she had trouble regulating her breathing.

"It's not large, but I think you'll find it comfortable," she said, pushing open the door and entering first in order to switch on the light.

Mitch had an impression of pale walls and dark furniture offset by splashes of purple and blue in the bedspread and drapes. A quick look told him that the bed was oversize and easily accessible for a man with limited mobility.

"This door opens onto the terrace. Father had it enclosed after his first stroke, and a lap pool and Jacuzzi installed."

She opened it wide enough for him to see a tile-lined pool and an adjoining spa before swinging it closed again. "Feel free to use either one or both," she said, turning to face him. He was closer than she'd expected. It made her uneasy.

"The bath is through there," she said, glancing toward the door, which was open far enough to offer a glimpse of peach tile and chrome fixtures. "I'm sure Tilly's left plenty of towels. She's very efficient."

"Must be nice having a housekeeper," he offered.

"With a house this size, it's a necessity. Besides, Tilly has been with us since I was a child. She's more family than employee. I suspect we'd be lost without her, and she without us."

"Anybody home?" Coach came through the door toting a well-traveled leather suitcase in one hand and an armload of notebooks in the other. He dropped both to the floor and handed over Mitch's keys.

"All set?" he asked, glancing around curiously.

"Looks like." Mitch tossed the keys on the nearest table.

"See you tomorrow, then. Come to the stadium about nine and I'll show you around."

"You're on."

After saying good night to Carly, Gianfracco left the room and closed the door to the hall behind him. Carly glanced around, satisfied that she hadn't neglected anything. It was becoming difficult to concentrate. She was so tired that her head was buzzing.

"If there's nothing more—"

"But there is." He came toward her, the muted click of those cruel braces already familiar enough to seem a part of him. "Have we met? All evening, I've been working on this hunch we've met before."

Carly felt a cold hand seize her heart. "Not to my knowledge," she bluffed with a skill that she'd worked long and hard to master.

"You like football, so I figured maybe you'd come to one of the Raiders' games."

"Actually, I've never been to a professional game at all."

"UCLA, then?"

"Sorry. I'm an Oregon native. The only other place I've lived is Providence, Rhode Island."

"Never been there." He'd been a great scrambler because he'd read body language better than most quarterbacks, but hers wasn't easy to read, especially when he kept getting distracted by the nagging feeling he'd seen those eyes before.

"Caroline Alderson. Pretty name. Not easy to forget," he said slowly, narrowing his gaze while he ran the face and name through his admittedly flawed memory. He came up blank, but the feeling of having known her before just dug in harder. Oh well, he thought. If it was important, it would come to him sooner or later.

"Will I see you tomorrow, Caroline?"

Mitch watched wariness take over her eyes and tried to put a name to the shade of her irises. Part green, part gray. If there was a name for that particular color, he didn't know what it was.

"Of course. This is my house, remember?" Forcing a smile, she murmured a polite "Good night" and left the room.

Chapter 3

It was close to eleven when Carly removed her earrings and tossed them into the velvet-lined jewelry box on her dresser in the walk-in closet adjoining her bedroom.

"Of course I'm annoyed, Mother," she said, returning to the bedroom to face Felicity, who was seated sedately on Carly's bed. "You should have consulted me before you invited Coach's guest to stay here."

Felicity didn't look the least bit chastened, but then, her mother had always possessed a supreme confidence in everything she did. It was one of the traits Carly had always admired in her. The other was her ability to ignore anything she didn't want to deal with.

"But, darling, I did it for you. Peter explained how important it is that Mr. Scanlon be impressed by all that Bradenton has to offer. And you have to admit, this house is the nicest one in the area."

"Since when have you taken orders from Pete Gianfracco instead of me?"

Felicity's gaze sharpened. "I don't take orders from either of you, Caroline. I was simply trying to do my part in this plan you've concocted, even though I've told you repeatedly I don't think it will work."

Carly sighed. "I'm sorry, Mother, I didn't mean to snap. I know you meant well."

Felicity glanced down at her hands. "I don't know if I've ever told you how grateful your father was when you agreed to return to Bradenton. I think he knew he didn't have too many years left, and he so desperately wanted you to succeed him."

Carly stared at her mother, astounded by her confession. "I feel as though I've let him down," Caroline said softly. "He was always so cautious about instituting changes. I'm beginning to think I was too impulsive."

Felicity drew a breath. "Perhaps, though these troubled times seem somehow to beg for changes."

Carly let her gaze trail around the room that had been hers from the age of two. Pale peach and gray now, it had once been bright yellow, with dotted Swiss curtains and an imported dollhouse in one corner. And then, in her high school years, she'd talked her mother into letting her paint the walls a psychedelic blue.

Other, far more fundamental, changes had taken place in this room, as well. A rowdy tomboy had grown into a young woman so eager to please she'd suppressed her natural zest for living. And, most significant of all, that same insecure young woman had prepared to become a mother, knowing that the rest of her life would be centered around the child she'd first felt move inside her womb while lying in this same bed.

The weight of those decisions had never felt heavier, she thought as she walked to the window and looked out. The security lights bathed the mansion grounds in blue-white light. The daffodils that had just popped their heads from the still-barren soil shone an eerie gray-green next to the brick walk.

"I'll never forgive myself if Tracy isn't able to graduate from here because of my determination to remake Bradenton into my personal ideal," she said softly.

"You did your best, which is all your father or I ever asked of you," her mother said, surprising Carly into glancing back at her.

"You expected perfection," Carly murmured with a resigned smile. "And I did try."

Sadness flitted over Felicity's face. "I know you did, dear. At the time we didn't realize just how excessive the demands we

made on you were. Or how they might eventually push you into
the very kind of behavior we were trying to prevent.''

"You were afraid I would tarnish the Alderson name, and I
did exactly that. I'll always regret that.''

"Just as I'll always regret not supporting wholeheartedly the
decisions you made then,'' Felicity said softly before drawing
a long breath. "I offered you blame when you needed acceptance and understanding, and for that I am very sorry.''

Too astounded to speak, Carly simply stared at her mother's pale face. "Don't look at me like I've suddenly stripped
naked and climbed on the table,'' Felicity chided in a half
amused, half teary voice. "I have been known to apologize to
you before, you know.''

Carly started to answer, then found that her voice still eluded
her. After clearing her throat, she tried again. "Forgive me,
Mother, but I can't seem to recall your ever having apologized
to anyone for anything before.''

Felicity frowned, then rose and joined Carly at the window.
"Then perhaps it's time I started,'' she said, touching her
daughter's hand. "And while I'm trying new things, I might as
well add that I'm very proud of you.''

Carly blinked, feeling totally at a loss. "Mother, have you...I
mean, are you ill?''

Felicity seemed taken aback for a long moment before she
broke into soft laughter. "No, dear, though it must seem that
way to you.'' Her laughter faded, replaced by an air of sadness. "I've been doing a great deal of thinking since your father passed away, and perhaps I've grown up a bit, as well.''

"I don't understand,'' Carly admitted.

"It occurred to me that I've been very fortunate in my life.
My parents raised me with every indulgence, and your father
did his best to grant my every wish. He was always ready to
protect me from disappointment or hurt. When you became
pregnant, it was I he comforted, not you. And yet, when he
needed help, it was you he turned to, just as I turned to you for
comfort when he died.'' Tears sparkled in Felicity's gray eyes,
and her subtly glossed lips trembled before she found the
strength to firm them. "It was then that I realized you've had
no one to support you all these years, no one to comfort you in
times of pain or disappointment.''

"Oh, Mother," Carly murmured, deeply touched, yet not quite able to fully trust her mother's abrupt change of heart.

"I know how desperately hard you're working to keep Bradenton going, which was why I was so hoping that this little dinner party tonight might have been of some help to you." Felicity glanced at the vista beyond the window and sighed. "Try not to be too discouraged, darling, though I know it's difficult not to feel terribly disappointed that Mr. Scanlon isn't the right man."

Carly allowed her confusion to show. "He isn't?"

"Because of his unfortunate circumstances," Felicity amplified, then smiled. "I saw your face freeze when you shook his hand, and I realized then that you had come to the same conclusion as I. That a man as severely handicapped as he couldn't possibly manage the job."

"No, I suppose not." Carly realized that it hadn't occurred to her that he couldn't handle the job, just that she didn't want him to have the opportunity.

Felicity's expression turned pensive. "He really is an impressive-looking man in many ways, especially when he smiles. And an enormously proud man, I would guess, from the determined way he has of putting everyone at ease around him. Still and all, it must be very difficult for him to accept the kinds of restrictions and frustrations his handicap must impose on him."

Felicity drew herself taller and, patting her hair in a way Carly recognized, offered Carly a serene smile. "But then, that is what we were talking about, wasn't it? Changes?"

Carly laughed softly. "Yes, Mother, we were. And I appreciate your sharing your feelings with me. I love you, you know? Even if it is taboo for an Alderson to actually say those words."

A slow flush rose to Felicity's cheeks, and the tears that she'd somehow kept from falling reappeared in her eyes. "I love you, too," she murmured. "I always have."

Carly leaned forward to kiss her mother's cheek, and Felicity held her daughter close for a long moment before they separated. Looking somewhat embarrassed, yet relieved, Felicity cleared her throat, then murmured, "It's been a long day. I'll say good-night now."

"Good night, Mother," Carly said in a husky voice. "Sleep well."

"You, too, dear. And try not to worry. Maybe Mr. Scanlon will surprise us both and turn out to be the perfect man for the job."

Carly smiled, but remained silent as Felicity glided from the room. Then, letting out the air she'd been holding, she left her bedroom and headed down the hall. Tracy's door was ajar. Carly rapped once and entered on her daughter's muttered response.

Tracy glanced up from the sentence she had just typed into her word processor. Model tall, with a willowy figure and an athletic grace, Tracy was blossoming into an exceptionally lovely young woman, with masses of thick honey-toned hair and a ready smile that lit her eyes from within. Even though it was barely fifty degrees outside, she was dressed in shorts and a Bradenton T-shirt.

"Hi, Mom. You look tired."

"It's been a long day," Carly murmured as they hugged. "Sorry I missed seeing you before dinner, but I tried. Blame the weather gods for keeping my plane on the ground in Chicago."

Tracy giggled, then caught herself. At sixteen, she had become enormously conscious of her dignity. "Did you have a good time with all those other bigwigs?"

"Yes, but I missed you."

Carly passed a hand over the golden hair fluffing around Tracy's face. It seemed like yesterday when she'd held her daughter for the first time and saw Scanlon's imprint on the tiny face. For an instant she'd been overcome with fear that she would never be able to love his child, and then Tracy had screwed up her face and let out a hungry bellow.

Carly had laughed and cried at the same time, and from that moment on, Tracy had been the fulcrum upon which her life had balanced. Not once since that moment had she ever regretted her decision to have her baby.

"Looks like you're putting in a long day of your own," she commented with a nod toward the glowing computer screen.

Tracy exhaled loudly. "I'll say, but it'll be worth it if I get the A I need for a 4.0."

"Even if you don't, I want you to know I'm proud of you."

Tracy looked pleased. "You're my mother. You have to say that."

"No way, toots," Carly protested around the lump in her throat. "I'm as objective as they come. Ask anyone who knows me, and they'll tell you I never brag about you without an absolutely authentic reason."

Tracy slanted her an impish grin, and Carly's heart did a slow tumble. Her little girl was still there, hiding behind a newborn maturity.

"So how was the dinner party for the visiting VIP?"

Carly felt her stomach tighten. The thought of Scanlon sleeping one floor below had all of her protective instincts humming, even though, years ago, she'd consulted an attorney about custody issues. According to the law, Scanlon had zero claim on his daughter. None.

"It was like any other business dinner, boring."

Tracy grimaced. "I figured it would be, which is why I begged off. Grandmother was not happy with me."

"Grandmother means well, honey, honestly she does. But I agree that sometimes she seems a bit out of touch with modern times."

Tracy snorted. "I'll say. Last week she about took my head off because I asked her if she and Grandfather used condoms when they had sex."

Carly nearly choked. "Oh, my," she muttered. "I can just imagine Grandmother's reaction to that little gem."

"She freaked but good. Turned about six shades of red, and then proceeded to lecture me about what were proper topics of discussion for young ladies and what were not."

"Aha. That would be Lecture Number One, usually followed a day or two later by Lecture Number Two."

Curiosity deepened the amber cast of Tracy's eyes. "Which is?"

"Which is the proper behavior for young ladies in a social setting."

"Oh, I got that one years ago when Grandmother found me wrestling with Randy Small in the backyard one summer when I was visiting."

"Yes, I heard about that. Grandmother was afraid you were going to grow up wild, like your mother."

"You? Wild? Come on! You're about the most conservative person I know."

Carly angled one hip on the desk and folded her arms. "You might as well know, Trace. I was a big disappointment to your grandmother—mostly, I think, because she had to cancel my coming out party."

"Because you were pregnant with me?"

Carly laughed softly. "Can't you just see it, me in my very expensive white dress with a belly out to here, marching into the Debutantes' Ball on my father's arm?" She shook her head. "Poor Mother. And after she'd invited the governor, too."

Tracy's eyes were suddenly pensive. "Mom, if you had it do over, would you keep me?"

Carly had already anticipated the question. According to the books she'd read on adopted and out-of-wedlock children, it was a common one for them to ask. Also according to the experts, the best way to handle it was calmly and with total honesty.

"Of course! You're the best thing that ever happened to me. I'm a much better person because of you."

Relief flickered in her daughter's eyes for a moment, only to be replaced once more by questions. "Grandmother is worried that you'll be lonely when I move out."

Carly drew a careful breath. She'd done her share of grieving at the thought of Tracy all grown up and on her own. Chances were good she would have to leave Bradenton Falls in order to build her own career, whatever that might be.

"I'll miss you, sure, but it's time you tried your wings. And it's not as though I'll never see you."

Tracy's smile was shaky. "Just don't rent out my room, okay?"

Carly heard a note of anxiety in Tracy's voice and made herself smile. "Are you sure Bradenton is what you want?" she asked, flavoring her tone with a heartfelt urgency. "It's not too late to apply someplace else, you know, especially with your grade point average."

Tracy made a face, the same face Carly used to make at her mother in her teenage years. "Are you kidding? I love this place almost as much as you do." Her eyes suddenly glinted with mischief. "Besides, I already know a lot of guys on this campus, and there's this one, Ian Cummings III, who is the sexiest, most gorgeous male on the planet."

Carly hid the sudden sharp jab to the heart behind a mother's look of warning. "Don't even think about accepting a date with him or any of those other 'guys' until you officially start classes in September."

Tracy drew her eyebrows together and pouted, but they both knew it was just for show. Other than the normal mother-daughter scuffling, they were extremely close, closer than Carly and her own mother had ever been.

"Okay, but I can still look, right?"

Carly laughed. "You can still look." Carly bent to hug the almost grown-up young lady who would always be her baby. "And now, kiddo, I think you should call it a night. You need your sleep."

"As soon as I finish this biology report." Tracy hesitated, then added, "It's on genetics. We're supposed to trace our eye color and hair color and special traits that run in our families, like diabetes or left-handedness. Things like that. Grandmother helped me with your side of the family, but I don't know what to put down for my father. Grandmother said to ask you, but it's no big deal if you don't want to tell me about him. I mean, I can just explain to Mrs. Zacharias about…well, you know, him not being a part of my life." Tracy shrugged one shoulder, giving her an uncharacteristically uncertain look that nearly broke Carly's heart. "Some of the other kids are adopted, so they got excused."

As a child, Tracy had asked a lot of questions about her father, questions Carly had answered with generalities. Now she realized that she herself knew very little about the details of Scanlon's family.

According to the last story she'd seen written about him, he'd never married. It was possible he'd fathered another child, perhaps more than one, but there had been no public mention of a paternity suit. And now, disabled as he was, he might not even be able to sire a child.

It would be a fitting punishment if he had someday hoped to have children and then, when it was too late, found himself sterile. Or, better yet, impotent. Carly felt an instant moment of shame that she should be wishing that kind of sorrow on anyone. And then she reminded herself that he deserved that and more. Seeing the curiosity in Tracy's eyes, she forced herself to smile, but her heart was racing.

"Well, let's see," Carly said briskly, striving for a clinical detachment. "Your father had blond hair and brown eyes." Even as she said the words, she had to acknowledge privately that what sounded so ordinary was anything but.

"Like mine."

Carly nodded. "He was a California native, an only child, and liked to laugh. I know he'd had chicken pox as a boy, because he had a few scars." On his right shoulder and low on his flat, corded belly. She drew a breath. "I don't know about other childhood illnesses or family traits."

"Did he have a temper, like me?"

Carly recalled the articles she'd read about Scanlon's fury when a fellow player had made a boneheaded mistake. "Yes, but he didn't hold a grudge." Or so those same articles had stressed.

Tracy picked up a pen to scribble some notes on one of the papers at her elbow. Carly sensed that she was still troubled. "Trace? You didn't miss having a dad too badly, did you?"

Tracy suddenly busied herself with a stack of textbooks. "Sometimes, but it's no big deal, Mom. I can handle it."

"I know you can, sweetheart, but there's nothing wrong with wishing your life had been more conventional. Sometimes I wished that, too, but you wouldn't have wanted me to marry someone I didn't love just to give you a father, would you?"

Tracy shook her head, her gaze fixed on her notes. "I'm not blaming you, only I still don't understand why you won't at least tell me his name."

"We've had this discussion before, Trace. When I die, my attorney will give you his name—if you're still interested in knowing—but not before."

Tracy had always been an easy child, but there had been moments when she'd exhibited a streak of stubborn determination. Carly saw the sudden tension in her face and knew that this was one of those moments. "I'm not a child anymore. I'm not going to do something stupid, like showing up at his house someday. I just think I have the right to know his name.''

''I disagree.'' Carly had to lock her knees to keep them steady. ''I love you dearly, Tracy. I've done all that I know how to make sure that you grew up knowing how precious you are to me. You'll just have to trust me to know what's best for you in this one thing at least.'' She hesitated, then rested her hands on Tracy's shoulders. Beneath her fingers, her daughter's body trembled slightly. Guilt twisted a hot blade beneath her heart.

When Tracy remained silent, Carly rested her cheek against her daughter's cloud of honey-colored hair before saying goodnight. She made it all the way back to her room before she started shaking.

Marcella Kenworthy lived on the outskirts of Bradenton Falls in a house that had once been a stable. Weather-beaten and forlorn, it had sat unwanted and unloved for nearly twenty years before Marca had bought it six years earlier. Claiming she was tired of living in rentals, she had moved in the day the roof had been repaired, and bit by bit she'd turned the battered derelict into a cozy home, doing much of the work with her own hands. Only the smaller of the two bedrooms upstairs remained to be done, and the last time Carly had stopped by, she'd found Marca happily stripping four layers of ancient wallpaper from the walls.

Acting on an impulse that she herself hadn't fully understood, Carly had borrowed a pair of jeans and an old sweatshirt from Marca, kicked off her shoes and waded in with putty knife in hand. They'd had a ball, and Carly had come away envying Marca her privacy—and the freedom to be utterly herself.

It was close to midnight when Carly pulled into the carport behind Marca's bright red Bronco. Marca had the floodlights on and the front door open almost before Carly switched off the ignition. Unlike the chic Professor Kenworthy who wore classic suits and Italian pumps, Marca at home was generally seen in an old paint-spattered sweatshirt and leggings. Tonight, as usual, her feet were bare.

Gypsy dark, Marca was barely five feet tall, with masses of curly hair and snapping black eyes. In what had to be one of life's greatest mysteries, her waif-thin body managed to radiate energy and health and more than her share of sex appeal.

Men from twenty to eighty found her irresistible, especially when she laughed. But Marca was still recovering from a marriage gone wrong, and had sworn to keep her relationships with attentive males strictly platonic. As far as Carly knew, she had kept that vow.

"It's about time you got here," she called out as Carly exited the old MG roadster that was her pride and joy. "I've just about worn a groove in the floor waiting for you."

"It's only been fifteen minutes since I called," Carly reminded her as she entered.

"A long fifteen."

Carly tossed her jacket and purse on the nearest chair before sinking gratefully into the sinfully cushy sofa in front of the lava rock fireplace.

"Wine?" Marca asked, holding out a brimming glass.

"Lord, yes," Carly muttered, accepting with a guilty grimace. One was usually her limit, and she'd already permitted herself a glass of sherry. A very small glass.

"Are you all right?" Marca asked, seating herself opposite.

"I don't know yet. Mostly I'm numb." Carly tasted the wine, grimacing at its tart bite as it slid down her throat. "I thought dinner would never end. If Coach had told one more story, I swear, I would have gone for his throat."

Marca grinned, but her eyes remained shadowed. "How did you feel when you saw Scanlon again?"

Leave it to Marca to ask the one question she'd deliberately avoided asking herself, Carly thought. It took her a moment to sort out her thoughts.

"I'm not sure I can describe my initial reaction." She set the wine on the refinished chicken crate serving as a coffee table and allowed herself to slump against the pillow behind her. "Consumed by rage that he was intruding into my life comes closest," she offered slowly, feeling her way. "Followed by this overwhelming determination to keep him absolutely and totally out of Tracy's."

"If he takes the job, that might be more difficult than you think, especially if Tracy makes the cheerleading squad. In case you've forgotten, they practice on the same field and, quite often, at the same times.''

Carly drew a slow breath. ''Maybe she won't make the squad.''

''Which would break her heart,'' Marca said softly.

''Oh, Marca, I know that,'' Carly murmured, brushing lint from her skirt. ''And I want her to make the squad because she wants it so badly. I've always wanted her to be happy, you know that.''

Marca nodded. ''Of course I do. And I wasn't criticizing, just playing devil's advocate.'' She frowned, as though she'd just had a sudden thought. ''He didn't recognize you, I hope?''

Carly drew a breath. *Have we met?* he'd asked in that too-familiar way, and for an instant her heart had stopped. ''I think he did, in a fuzzy sort of way, but I'm positive he doesn't know why. And no, I don't think that's wishful thinking on my part,'' she hastened to add when Marca opened her mouth to speak. ''Believe me, if I thought there was any chance of that, I would have broken my own rule about never interfering with my department heads and ordered Coach to send Scanlon packing.''

''It's too bad you can't just tell Gianfracco the truth.'' Marca took a sip, then waved an impatient hand. ''In fact, it's too bad you can't tell the whole world what he did to you.''

''You know I can't do that! No matter what, I won't have Tracy hurt by my mistake.''

Frowning, Marca lapsed into thoughtful silence, while Carly listened to the crickets chirping outside.

''Hey, I just had a thought,'' Marca said, her tone hopeful. ''Scanlon's a southern California boy, remember? Used to three hundred days of sunshine every year. I'll lay odds he'll hate our gray skies so much he won't even stay a week, let alone an entire school year.''

''Maybe, but that's not something I'd care to count on.'' Carly drew a long breath. Her heart was still beating much too rapidly, though not pounding, as it had done through much of dinner. ''The solution is actually pretty simple. All we have to do is convince Pete Gianfracco that Scanlon's not our man.''

Marca shifted and drew her raven-dark eyebrows together. ''I'll buy that. The question that comes to mind first, however, is how?''

"Well, for one thing, he's never coached before, which should be the cornerstone of our argument. The last thing Bradenton needs right now is a beginner trying to learn on the job." She sighed. "Lord knows, we've had miserable enough results from experienced men these past few years, which is what got us in this mess in the first place."

"Do you know he's a beginner for sure, or are you guessing?"

"I know." Carly saw surprise spark in Marca's eyes and sighed. "I do read the sports pages, you know." Carly didn't want any more wine, but she took a sip anyway, hoping it would wash away the sick feeling in her stomach. "After he was forced to retire as a player, there was all kinds of speculation about his becoming the Raiders' new quarterback coach. It didn't happen."

"True, but that was five years ago. He could have done a lot of things since, including coaching."

Carly sat forward and waved a hand. "I doubt that very much."

"Why? Because of his handicap?"

"No, because of his notoriety. If Mitch Scanlon had gotten back into football, it would have been splashed all over the evening news, just like everything else he did. You know how the press loves that kind of human interest story, and—" She stopped, appalled at her own words. "Oh my God, what am I saying?"

Marca glanced away, a look of pain on her face. When she made eye contact again, Carly winced. "Don't say it, please."

"All right, I won't." Sitting back, Marca sipped her wine and regarded Carly with an impassive face. Carly reached for her glass, then changed her mind. Instead, she slipped off her shoes, drew up her legs and rearranged herself until she was curled snugly into the corner of the sofa.

"I would kill for a cigarette," she muttered, fervently wishing she hadn't promised Tracy to quit after her last bout of bronchitis.

"Sorry, I gave up the habit years ago," Marca gloated mercilessly.

"Fifteen months ago, you mean," Carly groused, shifting. "Feels like more than that to me."

Carly managed a wan smile, which quickly faded. "Don't look at me like that."

Marca arched her eyebrows, the very picture of innocence. "Like how?"

"Like you're humoring me."

"But I am humoring you," Marca declared patiently. "You don't want to talk about the man you've hated for seventeen years, and I understand why. I'm willing to talk about anything else you like. Your choice."

Carly snorted. "Isn't that like trying to ignore a prowling tiger who's targeted you for lunch?"

Marca bit her lip, then laughed. "An apt analogy, or a random thought?" she wondered aloud.

An image of Scanlon's deep-set amber eyes rose in Carly's mind. "There was this . . . moment in the sitting room when he first looked at me, when I was sure I felt . . ." She paused to clarify her jumbled thoughts. "When I sensed a terrible, well, aloneness, I guess, is the best way to describe it, in the man he is now." She moistened her lips and tried to banish his image from her mind. And she failed.

"I suppose it does tend to set a man apart when he goes from being a world-class athlete to a paraplegic in the span of one night."

The sympathy in Marca's voice had Carly's head jerking up. "That's not the worse thing that can happen to a person," she declared on a flare of anger. "I wish everyone would stop talking about his handicap. He might have crippled legs, but he's the same man inside."

"Sorry," Marca muttered. "And you're right, of course. A disability doesn't necessarily come with instant sainthood."

Carly shivered, cold on the inside in spite of the room's cozy temperature. "I will not feel sorry for that man," she declared, her jaw suddenly tense. "If he's suffered, it's none of my doing or my concern."

"No, it isn't," Marca said very quietly. "But I can't help thinking that on some cosmic level, what happened to Scanlon has a certain element of justice to it." She shifted, frowned to herself, then sought Carly's gaze. "It's been a long time since I was in Sunday School, but I remember one of my teachers telling me once that no sin goes unpunished, no matter how privately it was committed.''

"In the best of all possible worlds, maybe, which we already know this one is not.''

"I'm serious, Carly. Think about it for a minute. Seventeen years ago Scanlon took something very precious from you without a second thought. And now he's lost the one thing that was precious to him, his athletic ability. Sounds like some higher power at work to me.''

Carly managed a wan smile. Her slight headache had gradually turned into a hard pounding in both temples. "It does have a certain logic, doesn't it?"

Even when he was seated and his crutches were out of sight, there was a stillness in his lower body that sooner or later became evident. While others shifted and moved easily, he had to work at it. And when others stretched out their legs to relax, his remained motionless. So why wasn't she gloating? Or at least feeling a certain satisfaction?

"I think I'd better call it a night,'' she muttered, sitting up. "I hate jet lag. It makes me feel like I'm underwater, and I have a full calendar to deal with tomorrow.''

Marca finished her wine and stood up. "Including a five o'clock appointment with yours truly to go over the media campaign for Project Cinderella—unless you'd rather reschedule?''

"No, but thanks for offering.'' Carly slipped into her jacket and retrieved her purse, then turned slowly to pin her best friend with a look.

"From a public relations standpoint, hiring Mitch Scanlon would be a terrific idea, wouldn't it?''

Marca nodded, a rueful smile curving her lips. "It would be pure magic. The press would eat it up. The headlines practically write themselves.'' She traced the words in the air. "'Injured hero returns to football after five years of self-imposed exile.' 'Legendary quarterback turns to coaching.' With Scanlon on the sidelines, the Wolves wouldn't even have to win a game and the stands would be jammed.'' She dropped her gaze. "If I didn't know what I know, I'd be urging all of us to grovel at the man's feet if that's what it would take to get him on board.''

Carly's laugh was strained. "Leave it to you to bring things back into perspective."

Marca's head came up, her blue eyes solemn, her gaze brutally direct. "Oh, hell, kid, you know I'm on your side, and I always will be. But I think you'd better be very clear on your priorities before we go much farther with this."

"Tracy comes first. She always has, and she always will."

"And she should," Marca agreed. "But you love Bradenton almost as much as you love your daughter. And, with your exaggerated sense of responsibility, I know that you would feel personally at fault if Bradenton closed its doors."

Carly felt a shiver of raw fear at the thought. "Not necessarily," she hedged, glancing past Marca toward the distant lights of the campus, framed by the large picture window. "It's just a college, after all. A bunch of old buildings on a few hundred acres of land, and a random number of trees that just happen to predate Oregon's entry into the Union. Nothing really earth-shattering would happen if it closed its doors." She shifted her gaze to Marca's face. "Right?"

"I could live with that. The question is, could you?"

"I don't know, Marce. I wish I did." Carly drew a shaky breath. "I wish I'd never come up with this idea in the first place."

"Yeah, but you did, and now that the train is on the track, you can't stop it without causing a major wreck."

"What is this, Madison Avenue lingo?"

Marca grinned. "Sorry, I'm still going through withdrawal."

Carly managed a laugh. "Thanks. I can always count on you for something profound."

"Hey, what are friends for?"

Marca walked her to the door. They exchanged hugs, and then, with a wave, Carly headed into the night.

Mitch tucked his hands under his head and stared at the ceiling. In his playing days he'd slept in his shorts, a remnant from his years in one training camp or another. Since his legs had become paralyzed, he slept naked. Pulling on a pair of skivvies took more effort than he wanted to expend when he was already dead tired from a day of dragging around full leg braces.

He heard a distant creak, like a footfall overhead, and he glanced toward the door to the hall. Coach had been right about one thing—the accommodations were four star. A decent bed, a soft pillow, even a bathroom with a bathtub he'd actually been able to get in and out of without too much trouble.

It had been a while since he'd gotten the VIP treatment. He should be happy as a clam. Instead he was lying there brooding about a pair of distant green eyes and a ripe little mouth that smiled at everyone but him.

He dug his head deeper into the pillow, trying without a lot of success to ignore the burning ache in his legs. He'd worn the braces longer than he should have, and now he was paying for it.

His chair was still in the trunk of his car. No sweat to haul it out and use it part of the day, the way the therapists had drummed into him. Half the clients at the gym used wheels, some part-time, some all the time. It got so he was more used to seeing someone in a chair than out.

It wouldn't be that way if he got back into football. He would be the one everyone looked at then. The way Caroline Alderson had looked at him—with pity.

Damn Gianfracco and his wild hare of an idea, he thought, shifting his gaze to the travel clock by the bed—2:00 a.m.

Who are you trying to kid here? he thought as he maneuvered to his side and closed his eyes. He wanted to get back into football almost as much as he wanted to be able to make love freely again.

How long had it been since he'd been with a woman? he wondered. Six, seven months maybe. Longer since he'd had the kind of sex that made a man feel full inside instead of empty. Before his paralysis, he would have already been planning his campaign. Wine, roses, candlelit dinners. Dancing. A turn in one direction, a slight swaying in the other. Gradually, he would pull her closer until her thighs were melded with his, and then together they would move more and more slowly until they were simply standing, so close he could feel her heart beating. So close that her scent was a part of him.

He would kiss her then, his mouth hot for hers. Her lips would be soft and welcoming, her breathing as strained as his. Perhaps he would tease her with his tongue. Perhaps she would tease him with hers. When they were both trembling, their breathing frantic, he would lift her into his arms and carry her to her room.

He would undress her slowly, taking his time, building the fires hotter. Her skin would be creamy in the moonlight, her breasts full and quivering, her thighs parting eagerly.

Tension skittered through him, twisting and turning his flesh into hard painful ropes. Just thinking about the first few times he'd had sex after he'd gotten his braces had his hands balling on his thighs and his gut tightening. For the first time since he'd lost his virginity at the age of sixteen, he'd failed to satisfy his partner. Worse, he'd actually reduced her to tears of pity.

It had gotten better, but not much. Reduced mobility had a way of making a guy plan every move. Most women he knew wanted spontaneity in their lovemaking. And a man to take charge. Sometimes, he actually wished he'd ended up impotent. Maybe then he would be content with making love to Caroline Alderson in his mind without wanting more. Much, much more.

Carly woke suddenly to find herself sobbing silently into her pillow. Her cheeks were wet, the linen pillow slip wetter. Her heart was racing, her breathing erratic. She'd been dreaming of that night. Party time in the desert. Meet the guy of your dreams and fall in love.

Because he was so big, she hadn't expected gentleness, but he'd drawn off her clothes piece by piece with such sweet patience, each kiss more draining than the one before.

His mouth had toyed with hers while his long, supple fingers stroked her breasts. His skin was bronze perfection, slick with the sweat of anticipation. His long legs stretched between hers, the lean muscles hard, their strength prodigious.

Carly remembered how her heart had raced, how her lungs had gasped for air. At the same time she'd dug her hands into the taut line of his shoulders, her fingertips barely making a dent in the layered muscle and sinew.

"Relax, Sarah, honey," he'd murmured, his mouth skimming her cheekbone, her temple, her ear. "We have all night."

She could still feel the sheets slick and clinging beneath her back as she writhed uncontrollably. His hands had been skillful, skimming her newly tanned skin, leaving her flesh tingling and alive.

He'd known just where to kiss her, just how to stroke her to make her forget eighteen years of dutiful compliance with her mother's teachings. Wildly she'd arched upward, tangling her legs with his, legs she had admired from a distance, legs sheathed in skintight football pants, shifting with power and dexterity as he uncorked another touchdown bullet.

"Ah, baby, you're beautiful, so beautiful." He ran his palm over her skin. "You make me crazy...can't wait much longer."

His fingers slipped between her thighs to caress her, and she cried out in surprise and pleasure. His finger explored gently, and then more aggressively, until it was fully extended inside her.

She stopped breathing, a thousand sensations assailing her. His breathing was loud in her ear, and his skin was damp and hot, causing the white-blond hair on his chest to coil tightly.

"Tell me you're ready," he demanded hoarsely, his eyes nearly bronze in the dim light. Unable to speak, she stared up at him, her heart racing and her body screaming for his.

He shifted slightly until his engorged body was nestled between her thighs. She felt slick heat, an insistent pressure.

Panic burst someplace in her head, and then she was struggling, pushing hard at the arms that held him over her. "Wait," she tried to shout, but her cry was muffled by his mouth coming down hard on hers. What had been pleasure was now terror. Worse, she was helpless, trapped by the weight of heavy sinew and bone. Jerking her head sideways, she gulped air, her heart trying to pound through her skin.

She tried to cry out, but his mouth was hot on hers again. Helpless, she raked his biceps with her nails, drawing thin bloody lines against the deep tan. His eyes glittered, his expression intense, and then, with a low guttural cry, he thrust throbbing and hard into her.

The pain was beyond bearing, a knife slicing her in two. It seemed to go on and on, and then he collapsed on top of her, his face buried in the hollow of her shoulder. She tasted blood and realized she'd bitten through her lip. Through force of will, she swallowed her tears and waited for him to get up.

The only sound in the room came from the mingling of their breathing, his slowing now, hers still frantic. Beyond the motel walls, she could hear the splashes and shouts of her fellow college students playing in the pool.

"Please," she whispered. "Please let me up."

There was no answer. Mitchell Scanlon, the man she'd thought she'd loved from the moment she'd seen his picture on TV, was sound asleep, oblivious to her silent sobs of remorse and pain, and the blood on the sheets.

Chapter 4

Carly had slept poorly, when she'd slept at all. She was already awake when the alarm rang at five-thirty. Her head was still fuzzy as she slipped into her favorite swim suit and padded through the silent house to the pool.

Tilly was just putting out the coffee on the poolside table when Carly slipped into the glassed-in enclosure. Warm, chlorine-flavored air enveloped her instantly, chasing some, but not all, of the chill from her bones. Outside, the morning mist formed exotic patterns on the panes.

Stomach growling at the enticing aroma rising into the steamy air, Carly returned the housekeeper's cheery greeting with a smile. "Did I smell cinnamon when I passed the kitchen, I hope, I hope?" she asked, just as she'd asked countless times as a child.

"You hope right. I thought our guest might like some of my crumb cake for breakfast." Tilly cast a critical eye at the table she'd just arranged, then, frowning, wiped a smudge from the silver coffee service with the hem of her apron. When it was just the family in the house, they drank their coffee from sturdy mugs poured directly from the pot. But guests rated the heirloom silver and linen napkins, one of Felicity's ironclad rules.

"How come you never make crumb cake when it's just us?" Carly asked as she stepped out of her robe and tossed it over the back of the nearest chair.

After giving the silver one more swipe, Tilly shifted her attention to Carly's face. "Because your mama and your daughter are forever on a diet, that's why." Frowning, she allowed herself a thorough inspection of Carly's figure before clucking a maternal tongue. "You, on the other hand, could use another five or ten pounds. You're way too thin."

Carly drew a deep breath and stretched her arms overhead, trying to work out some of the kinks from her restless night. "I always lose weight when I travel, you know that," she murmured, bending from side to side. "Just give me a few days of your cooking, and I'll be as plump as a little butterball again."

Tilly sniffed. "Not if you don't stop working day and night seven days a week, you won't."

"Don't fuss, Tilly. I love my job." Bending from the waist, she let her hands drop toward her pink-tipped toes.

"So did your pa, but he also had a family."

"I have a family."

"Half a family. You need a man next to you when the nights turn cold."

"I have an excellent electric blanket." Carly grasped her ankles and visualized the tight muscles of her back and legs relaxing and warming. "And I'm perfectly content with my life just the way it is."

"Perfectly *stubborn* is what you are. A regular little mule. Always were, always will be, by my way of thinking."

Laughing, Carly straightened slowly. "Then why do you keep trying to change me, darling Tilly?"

"Because I have some of that mule in me, too," Tilly shot back. "And because I miss the loving young girl you were before you left a piece of your heart in Palm Springs."

Carly felt a chill. "I left my childish illusions in Palm Springs. There's a difference." Finished stretching, she walked to the shallow end and executed a racing dive. The water was warmer than the air, and almost as soothing as a bubble bath.

At the end of the pool, she flipped quickly and slipped into her rhythm without losing her concentration. Warm now and fluid, her muscles flexed and contracted easily.

Her mind drifted, lulled by the hypnotic stretch and pull of her movements. The water stroked her skin, lap by lap releasing the tension she'd brought with her to the pool.

Winded now, she forced herself to concentrate on the last turn. Her arms and legs felt heavy, and her lungs burned. One lap to go, and then she would have earned her first cup of coffee.

Sensing the narrow pool's midpoint, she gave her all for the last few strokes, pushing herself to the limit. Her hand hit the slick tile at the shallow end, and she relaxed, exhilarated and exhausted. Straightening, she let her feet hit bottom as she tossed back her head and wiped the water from her face with both hands.

"Looked like a sure first place to me."

She recognized the voice before her startled gaze found the man himself. He was standing a few feet from the lip of the pool, the robe she'd left on a nearby chair now tossed carelessly over one broad shoulder. Viewed from below, he seemed taller than ever, with half his height in his legs and a heavily muscled chest that gave him the look of an extremely powerful man.

True to his image, he was casually dressed in pleated twill slacks and a pale yellow polo shirt sporting the logo of his fitness center. The loafers attached to his braces were meticulously shined and obviously expensive.

"Good morning," she managed to get out when she realized his grin had turned quizzical. "You're up early. I hope the splashing didn't wake you."

"It didn't, but it did intrigue me enough to get me out of bed for a look-see."

"Sorry. I guess I forgot how close the guest suite is to the pool," she said as she climbed the steps toward him.

"Don't apologize. I was enjoying the view." Releasing one crutch, he handed her the robe.

Belted safely inside the warm terry cloth, she retrieved her towel and wound it securely around her dripping hair. Barefoot, she padded to the table and poured herself a brimming mug of steaming French roast. Sipping greedily, she gestured to the extra cups on the tray, along with sugar and cream.

"Do join me," she said as she slipped into her usual chair.

"Thought you'd never ask."

"Black?" she asked, leaning forward to pour.

He nodded. "And two sugars." At her surprised look, he shrugged. "A guy's got to have some vices."

"As long as they don't hurt anyone else." Settling back, she reached for her own mug. Cradling her cup under her chin, she let her eyes drift half closed as she breathed in the steam. She wouldn't permit herself to think about the past, only the future. The present was simply a means to an end.

Scanlon went about the chore of sitting down and stowing his crutches, conscious that she was surreptitiously watching his every move. He wanted to be flattered. He knew better. She was simply curious. Everyone was. He figured he would get used to it someday.

"What about you? What are your vices?" he asked, drawing the mug toward him.

"Sorry, that's privileged information." She hooked a spare chair with her foot and drew it close enough to use as a footstool. He had a quick glimpse of shapely calves and tanned skin before she flipped the robe closed again.

He felt his interest spike and then, like the persistent ache in muscles he could only half control, refuse to be leveled. "Nice place," he said, glancing around. "Yours or the college's?"

"The college's now."

"Now?" He lifted the mug to his mouth and drank. The coffee was stronger than he'd expected in a household of women.

"The house and seven acres of land around it had always belonged to my family until three years ago."

"What happened then?"

"My father died. When his will was read, we discovered he'd left the house to Bradenton, with residency rights for my mother until her death."

Not much for nuance, he nevertheless heard a sudden strain in her voice and wondered about her relationship with her father. "What about your rights?"

She shrugged. "Father knew I could take care of myself. Besides, I intend to be Bradenton's president for a long time, so, in a way, the house is still mine."

She tugged at the lapels of her robe until they were snug against her neck. Protecting herself? he wondered, shifting in the small wrought-iron chair.

"Good weather for spring practice," he said, glancing upward. There was a light haze hovering over the arching glass, the kind that would burn off as soon as the sun moved higher.

"Sunshine is always a pleasant surprise this time of year." Eyes narrowed against the glare, she lifted the cup to her lips for another sip, allowing herself a small sigh of pure enjoyment that had Mitch's lips twitching. So the cool and collected lady president was human after all.

"Sounds like the stories I've heard about Oregon's gray skies might be true."

"I'm afraid so." She glanced at the large, callused hand loosely curled around his cup. "If you're into a year-round tan, this isn't the place for you."

"Funny, that's exactly what I told Coach when he bullied me into coming up here for a look-see."

"Bullied?" She lifted one sleek eyebrow. "Surely not."

"True story. Pete has a way of staring a guy into doing what Pete wants him to. J. C. Cobb used to hide in the locker room after a game if he'd bobbled a ball, just so Pete wouldn't have a chance to stare him into agreeing to extra practice."

That won him the first smile of the day. It drew his attention to her lips, a serious mistake. No man working on nearly a year of celibacy should have to deal with such a lush mouth first thing in the morning. Averting his gaze, he brought the mug to his mouth and drank. The coffee slid down hard.

"I'm curious, Mr. Scanlon. What makes you think you can succeed with the team when so many other, shall we say *more experienced* coaches have failed?" she asked as she leaned forward to refill her cup and his, leaving him to add the sugar himself.

"Like I told Coach, I'm not sure I *can* succeed," Mitch admitted, giving his coffee a quick stir to settle the sweet. "I'm not even sure I want the job."

"Then why make the trip up here at all?"

He shrugged. "I owe Coach a few favors. I thought I might come up with a few suggestions that could help whoever does take the job."

She started to reply, then turned her head at the sound of raised voices. Mitch recognized Felicity's sugared tone, genteel even at an increased volume.

"Sounds like a difference of opinion," he commented wryly.

Carly gave a good imitation of calm as she nodded, but her hands were suddenly ice cold. Relax, she told herself urgently. Nothing's going to happen.

Tracy's musical laughter floated over the water as she and her grandmother entered the enclosure. "Oh, Grandmother, c'mon. You know these aren't rags. In fact, they're the latest style."

Felicity's sniff of disapproval was easily audible. "I know they're not one bit flattering, whatever you want to call them."

"Okay, we'll leave it up to Mom. She's got great taste."

As they both looked to the woman seated opposite him, Mitch noted a striking resemblance between Felicity and her granddaughter. Even more striking was the resemblance between the teenager with the dynamite grin and the woman across from him. Her name was...Tracy. Yeah, that was it. One of those unisex names, although the girl herself was already well on her way to becoming a knockout.

In spite of the oversize shirt flapping almost to her knees, she carried herself with the same poise as her mother, but the fair hair that seemed so carelessly tousled was more honeyed than Dr. Alderson's, framing a face that hadn't yet come into its full promise. Taller than her mother, she had enough curves on that long stretch of body to make some hapless adolescent forget his name, and yet her golden eyes radiated the guileless innocence of a child.

Mitch sipped coffee and thought about the man who had fathered her. Had he ever given a thought to the kind of rearing she would get? The environment that would form her? Or had he simply deposited his sperm and moved on?

God knows, he'd done his share of tomcatting. For an unsophisticated kid with a hunger for life and a lot of years of loneliness behind him, UCLA had offered ripe pickings. He'd dated—and bedded—his fair share of cheerleaders, sorority women and even several graduate assistants in his four whirlwind years. And then he'd taken the kiss-her-senseless-and-hustle-her-into-the-nearest-bed routine one step too far.

The details were hazy and distorted by a lousy drunk's selective memory. The girl had been older than Tracy by a good three or four years, and he could only remember her first name, Sarah, but he would never forget the shame that had scalded through him when he'd emerged from an alcoholic stupor to find her virginal blood on his sheets. For the rest of his stay at the Springs he'd searched for her night and day, but she'd simply vanished. He had prayed then, the way he'd never prayed as a child, that he hadn't made Sarah pregnant. To his dying day, he would always regret that one drunken, irresponsible night in the desert and fervently hope that Sarah had forgiven him for making her first sexual encounter a drunken disaster.

"Mom, you've got to settle this!" Flouncing over to the table, the girl gave her mother an intense look.

"Seems like I've heard that before." Laughing, Carly shook her head and pulled her daughter down for a hug. Mitch wasn't much for analyzing emotions, his own or anyone else's, but he recognized the real thing when he saw it, and Dr. Alderson was obviously crazy about her daughter. The kid seemed to feel the same about her mom. It was the kind of relationship he respected, even though he knew it wasn't for him. Caring meant sharing chunks of yourself with someone else, and that was something he no longer wanted to risk.

Catching sight of Scanlon, Felicity replaced her disapproving look with a warm smile. "Good *morning,* Mitchell. I hope you'll forgive the confusion, but it does appear that my granddaughter has suddenly lost her mind." Turning on her daughter, she bored in, her social mask still firmly in place. "She won't listen to me, darling. Perhaps you'll have better luck."

"Leave me out of this, you two," Carly protested, lowering her feet to free the chair her mother appeared ready to appropriate.

"Coward," Tracy said with a grin, but she was already looking at Scanlon. "Hi. You must be the new coach."

"More like an interested observer." Leaning forward, he reached out a hand. "I'm Mitch."

"Uh, I'm Tracy. Mom's daughter. I mean, Carly's . . . Dr. Alderson's daughter."

Carly had to take a moment to fight down the sudden nausea. The resemblance between father and daughter was subtle, but it was there, nevertheless.

"Honey, I hate to sound like a nagging mom, but you're going to be late for school if you don't get a move on."

"That *was* where I was going until Grandmother all but barred the door."

Felicity shook her head. "I merely asked if there was some kind of costume party going on at school today."

Tracy reached over her mother's shoulder to filch a sip of her coffee. "Needs sugar," she muttered, tossing her hair back.

"You shouldn't be drinking it anyway," Carly muttered, too aware that Scanlon was taking in the scene with a look of amusement in his eyes.

"Fine, then I'll leave."

"Caroline!" Felicity protested. "Surely you don't approve of your daughter going out in public dressed like a ragamuffin."

"Mother, I hate to tell you this, but teenage girls in this day and age do not have the same dress code you had at her age."

Felicity turned to Mitch and arched her eyebrows inquiringly. "What's your opinion of the way today's young people are behaving?"

Mitch had been shoved into no-win situations before. Before he'd learned a few basics of diplomacy, he'd invariably chosen the wrong side and come out bleeding. Now he knew better. "Let me put it this way. When I was playing, there were times when the only option was to eat the ball and pray."

Felicity looked crestfallen. Carly had to work hard to keep from laughing. Tracy gave him a thumbs-up and a grin before running for the door.

Felicity shook her head. "I give up," she said, a hint of a smile in her voice.

Carly poured her mother a cup of coffee and slid it toward her. "Don't give away Grandmother Carter's pearls just yet, Mother. Sooner or later Tracy will grow into them."

"They're supposed to be yours first, then Tracy's."

"I'd rather see you wearing them for a long time to come."

Felicity looked pleased. "Oh, I intend to."

Smiling, Carly rose and pushed in her chair. Higher now, the sun was streaming through the tall windows behind her, framing her figure. What the robe hid, Mitch remembered with a private moment of purely male appreciation. When her gaze came to his, he saw ice forming over the smile she'd given her mother.

"If you'll excuse me, I'll get myself organized while you have breakfast, and then we'll get started."

He didn't bother to hide his surprise. "Started?"

"On a tour of the campus." A hint of a smile curled one corner of her pale mouth. Mitch sensed more challenge than warmth. "I assume you're interested in Bradenton's history?"

"Absolutely." Though he would rather learn more about hers.

"Good. It's my custom to give the tour myself. That way I can get to know a prospective employee and gauge his reaction to the campus at the same time."

"In other words, I'd better be on my best behavior."

"Exactly."

Mitch saw the glint in her eyes and grinned. "There's just one problem. I'm supposed to meet Coach at one."

She took that in stride. "No problem. I'll end the tour by then. I'll even drop you off at the stadium." Turning to her mother, she asked a question about ordering flowers for some kind of faculty tea. It was as smooth a dismissal as he'd ever received. Both impressed and amused, he relaxed against the back of the chair and enjoyed the play of sunlight over her face.

Most women he'd met were bang on predictable. The pretty ones knew it and used the power it gave them over men like currency. A smile in exchange for dinner. A kiss in return for an evening of flattery. Sex in return for a long list of things, most of which boiled down to one thing—money or marriage.

But Caroline Alderson didn't fit into that tidy slot, no matter how hard he tried to put her there. In spite of a gorgeous face and a knock 'em dead figure, she didn't appear to trade on either one. No, it was more than that, he thought, rubbing his freshly shaved chin. It was as though she were as open and honest as her daughter. And innocent, he realized with a jolt, though he knew that was impossible.

"Fine, then I'll rely on you to take care of everything," he heard her say.

Felicity smiled sweetly at her daughter. "Yes, dear. I won't let you down."

Carly nodded. "Better not, or I'll tell Coach you have a crush on him."

With that she turned on her heels and headed for the house. leaving her mother with her mouth agape and Mitch chuckling to himself.

Damn, but he was looking forward to spending time alone with Bradenton's self-contained, self-assured and downright-sexy-in-spite-of-herself president.

The mansion's garage had space for three vehicles. One space contained a dark blue sedan, the next a four-wheel drive utility. In the third was an old green MG roadster with the top down. He had a feeling he knew which one was Caroline Alderson's before she led him straight to the classic.

"Sure you wouldn't rather take my car?" he asked, watching her dig into her purse for her keys.

"Don't worry, it's safe."

"That's not the problem. It's the size. British cars aren't made for someone my height."

She opened the driver's door and tossed her purse and briefcase into the well behind the seat. "You drive a Jag."

"A Jag sedan." Partial to sports cars himself, the Jag was the first car he'd ever owned with an automatic transmission, the only kind that would accommodate hand controls.

Mitch sized up the tiny bucket seats and the low-slung chassis, figured he had nothing to lose but his dignity and shrugged. "I think I can get in okay. Getting out might not be that easy."

"Can I help?"

He gave her a sideways glance. "Yeah. Promise you won't laugh if I fall on my can." Releasing a crutch, he managed to get the passenger door open without banging his shins. He stowed his crutches next to her case, then, unlocking the braces, lowered himself onto the seat and lifted his legs inside. He found the seat adjustment and managed to shove himself back a few inches.

"What is this baby, anyway? A TC?"

"No, a TD. His name is Nigel. I found him sunning himself in a junkyard by the Providence River when I was teaching at Brown, and he's been mad at me ever since."

He slammed the door and felt the little car shake. Considering its age, the damn thing had probably been made out of melted down World War II fighter planes. "I thought all cars were considered female."

"Not this one," she said, slipping behind the wheel. "He's too unreliable."

Carly flipped down the visor and moved her seat forward an inch. There wasn't much room to spare when both seats were occupied. Only a few inches separated his shoulder from hers. Grateful for the shift lever between them, she put on her sunglasses and stuck the key in the ignition.

"Don't forget your seat belt," she said, fastening her own. It was a lap belt, added on long after the little car had left England.

He cocked one eyebrow. "Is that an order or a warning?"

"Oregon law."

"Sorry to hear it." He snugged the belt around his flat middle, looking very much like a man going to the gallows.

She worked the throttle, pressed the starter, and the old engine roared to life. Glancing in the mirror, she reached for the gear shift. Her hand brushed his thigh, and she felt him jerk.

"Don't worry. I'm a very good driver."

Mitch kept his opinion to himself. It wasn't so much a question of tact as it was a moment of distraction. It was just his bad luck her hand brushed the one spot on his thigh that had almost normal feeling. More bad luck that he hadn't been touched by a woman who smelled this good in a long string of lonely months.

"So? Where to first?"

"East quad," she said, revving the motor. "Almost all the buildings there are original, drafty floors, leaking pipes and all."

She concentrated on backing out of the garage, then shifted into first and wheeled around, all in one smooth motion. By the time she'd worked her way through the gears and was cruising in high, Mitch had decided he liked her style. Fast in the straightaways, controlled in the curves. A woman who took chances, but not foolish ones. And she knew her own limits.

When she downshifted through a particularly wicked curve with the skill of a pro, he allowed himself to relax. She, on the other hand, seemed preoccupied. It showed in the tension in her fingers where they gripped the leather-wrapped wheel and in the stiff line of her slim shoulders.

Leaning back, he stretched an arm along the back of her seat and told himself to enjoy the scenery. Without California smog tainting his senses, everything seemed brighter and fresher, especially the air. Oregon was also mostly green, he decided as they approached a small pond populated with very fat, very noisy ducks. A goodly number of mallards were mixed with the white ones. He saw a few geese in the crowd, too.

"Looks like a popular place," he said, watching a fat Canada goose suddenly take to the air with an ease he envied.

"We're on their route," she said, glancing right. "In the fall the water's covered with them. Bradenton is an official wildlife preserve."

"Shouldn't they all be back north by now?"

"They should, but we always seem to end up with a few breeding pairs year 'round."

"Must like it here."

"What can I say? Bradenton's a great place."

"Not that you're prejudiced."

She shook her head. "Nope. Not a bit." She checked her mirror, then zoomed past a campus maintenance truck, tapping the horn as she passed. Rounding a curve, they came upon a group of cyclists taking a break on the grassy shoulder. Slowing, she waved, and the students waved back, some shouting greetings.

"Around here, it's not really spring until the bikes come out," she said, shifting up.

"I almost signed with the Bills because I wanted to know what it was like to live in a place with more than one season. Who knows? Maybe I'll finally find out."

There were a lot of things Carly didn't want him to find out about. The changing of the seasons wasn't included.

"That's Grayson Hall ahead," she said as they rounded a gentle curve. "Bradenton's founder, Artemus Alderson, named it after his wife's family."

"Your grandfather?"

"Great-grandfather. He was a self-educated logger who dreamed of educating others. Bradenton is the result of that dream."

"Sounds like an interesting man."

"He was."

Dutifully, Mitch swung his gaze right and saw another building with turrets. On the walkway out front, he spotted a handful of students, most of them on the far side of thirty, which interested him. "A lot of older students, I see."

She shrugged an elegant shoulder. "The mind never grows too old for more knowledge."

Smiling slightly, he lifted his gaze to the rooflines of the buildings. "Looks like you have a problem with moss up here."

"Consider it our version of California smog."

Leaving the shade of the overarching canopy of branches, the little car shot into the sunshine. Squinting, he took aviator sunglasses from his shirt pocket and put them on.

"What's the enrollment at Bradenton, anyway?"

"Just under seven thousand. Nothing to compare with UCLA."

The number he'd heard was 6,810. Up considerably in the last few years. "Not in numbers, maybe, but the people I talked to had great things to say about the graduates."

She shot him a quick glance, and he decided he liked the way the wind ruffled her hair. "You checked us out?"

"I made a few calls, yeah. I've been blindsided too many times by offers that sounded great but weren't."

"I hope that isn't meant as a criticism of Coach."

Pleased that she was clearly ready to defend the old man, he found himself wanting to probe deeper for the emotion he sensed cooking beneath the calm.

"I have a great deal of respect for Coach. I just wanted to make sure someone else wasn't using him to get to me."

Downshifting, she narrowed her gaze. "Who might that someone be, exactly?"

"Last time it was a reporter for one of the tabloids. When he couldn't get my doctors to tell him if I could still have sex, he paid a lady I'd taken out a few times in the past to try to renew old acquaintances. Seems she was supposed to seduce me for pay."

"That's sick."

"Yeah, but it's also part of the game the way it's played today."

"Not at Bradenton." She kept her gaze straight ahead, watching the road, while he watched her. Sunlight was in her hair where the wind feathered the silky strands away from her face. Though she'd been lovely in the lamplight last night, the sun's rays seemed to bring out a hidden sparkle, along with a subtle fragility that surprised him.

"That smaller building is Bandon Hall," she explained with a quick wave of her left hand "Next to it is the Science Building, and behind that is Language Arts. We've recently added a master's program in Mandarin Chinese. By this time next year we should have five candidates ready to take their orals."

"I don't suppose any of those five candidates can kick a fifty-yard field goal?"

"Possibly, although I doubt it." She hesitated, then surprised him with a grin that stole a good portion of his breath. "All five are female."

"Hey, a field goal's three points, no matter who kicks it."

"That's true enough." For an instant her soft lips had actually curved a little before they'd firmed. He wondered what it would be like to feel that softness pressed against his skin. It was a thought he didn't dare pursue.

For the next half hour she drove them from quad to quad, until all the buildings began to look alike. "And this is the stadium, newly spiffed up and ready for the crowds," she said, slowing to a snail's pace when it came into sight. "The painters still have the seats to finish and a little work to do in the visitors' locker room, but they tell me they'll be done in plenty of time for football season."

Braking, she pulled to the side and turned off the engine. He glanced around him, taking in the neat appearance of the grounds and the well-tended look to the buildings. The place had a lot of class.

"Well, what do you think of Bradenton so far?" Carly asked briskly, turning toward him. The ride had stirred her hair into a tousled cap that softened the sophisticated image, and her cheeks were brushed with color. But it was the sultry sweetness of her lips that held his gaze lingering a beat too long for his own good.

"I think my foster mother would love this place," he said dryly, glancing toward the turreted bell tower.

That threw her, but she recovered quickly. "Your foster mother?"

"Yeah. Arletta Williams. She pastors a church in Watts. When she's not reading her Bible or writing sermons, she's got her nose stuck in one of those gothic romances." He grinned, and she had to work hard not to let herself be charmed. "Even talked me into reading one or two while I was in the hospital."

"Did you enjoy them?"

"Enough that I didn't mind the ribbing I took from the nurses when they caught me reading after lights out." His grin was just shy of embarrassed, and Carly wondered how many times he'd used that same grin to charm and seduce. Her stomach rebelled.

"I'm sure you didn't mind the extra attention."

He shrugged. "Actually, there were a lot of times when I would have killed to have five minutes alone, with absolutely no one around. In the hospital, there's no such thing as privacy."

"Sounds a great deal like Alderson House."

Watching her, he saw a gentle smile play over her mouth for a moment before her lips set into the same firm line. He felt a stirring, stronger now, and found himself wondering about the current man in her life.

The campanile in the main quad struck the quarter hour, and within seconds the doors to nearby buildings opened, spilling students onto the sidewalks. Several called out greetings as they passed. One, a well-built kid of about nineteen or twenty with the look of a weight trainer, stopped by the driver's side.

"Dr. Alderson, long time no see." He shifted his stack of books from his right hip to his left and stuck out his right hand.

Smiling, she took the hand he offered and gave it a firm shake. "How's it going, Ian?"

"No sweat. Got me straight Cs so far this semester." No more than mildly curious, he flicked a gaze Mitch's way. "How's it going?" he asked halfheartedly.

"Can't complain." Mitch sized him up as running back material, or possibly a quarterback. Good legs, chest wide enough to develop decent wind, the loose-hipped walk of a runner.

The boy's gaze shifted away, then snapped back. Frowning, he narrowed his eyes for a long moment, then trained them on Carly. "Tell me that's not Mitch Scanlon," he said in an awe-struck tone that had her laughing out loud.

"Okay, if that's what you want, but I'm afraid that wouldn't be the truth."

Swallowing hard, Ian reached past her to offer Mitch his hand. "It's a real honor to meet you, sir. Really."

"Thanks." The kid had a good firm grip, and he looked a man in the eye when he shook his hand.

"Coach Gianfracco has films of just about every game you ever played. That play-off game against the Chiefs, the one in the snowstorm? Man, that was some Hail Mary pass you made. Every time I see it, it gets better."

Mitch grinned. He still got high thinking of the euphoria he'd felt when that sucker connected. "J. C. Cobb was a great receiver. Most of the credit for that play goes to him, as he never fails to remind me whenever we bump into each other."

"Coach said you used to practice throwing five, six hours a day. He said guys used to call out a seat number and you could hit it on the first try."

"Once, maybe. I got lucky."

The sidewalks were rapidly emptying, but Ian seemed in no particular hurry. Instead, he put his books on the hood and leaned a hard hip against the MG's frame. Settling in, Carly decided, glancing Scanlon's way. Sensing her gaze, he shifted his to meet it questioningly.

"Ian is the starting quarterback for the Wolves.'"

One eyebrow lifting lazily, Scanlon studied the boy thoughtfully. "What are you, six-one, one ninety?"

"One ninety-five. Ten pounds lighter than your playing weight, right?"

Mitch nodded. The kid knew how to make points, but then, so did he. "Tell me, son, what's your read on the team's problems?"

Ian's delight at being asked was readily apparent. "We have a lousy team," he declared heatedly. "Half the guys can't cut it, and the ones who can don't give a sh—pardon me, Dr. Alderson—don't care if we win or not."

"Including the quarterback?" Mitch kept his tone friendly.

Ian reddened. "Yeah, well, what's the use of busting your butt for nothing?"

"A little thing called pride, maybe?"

Carly drew a quick breath as Ian dropped his gaze. "Maybe in the beginning, yeah. But I got tired of spending all day Sunday in a whirlpool working out the soreness while the rest of the guys were off partying with the chicks."

"Guess I can't blame you for that."

Ian worried a stone with the toe of his expensive sneakers. Carly was about to suggest that he might be late for class when the boy suddenly lifted his head and looked at her. "How's Tracy doing with her genetics paper?"

Carly's hand tightened on the wheel. "Last I heard, she was planning to dump her word processor into the pool and run away from home."

Ian grinned. "Tell her I said hi, okay?"

"Yes, of course," she said with deliberate coolness. At the same time she made a point of looking at her watch. "One minute to the bell."

"Yeah, right." Straightening, Ian said a quick goodbye and headed down the street at a long-legged trot.

"At least he's honest," Mitch said, watching the boy's feet pound the pavement.

"Ian's father was the quarterback of the only Wolves team to win a conference championship. Ian had his heart set on attending the University of Washington, but Ian Senior insisted on Bradenton. I tried to talk him out of it, but he's pretty bullheaded."

"What about the kid's mother?" He shifted, his gaze finding hers again.

"She's—how shall I put it?—extremely impressed with Ian Senior's ability to sign checks."

Mitch watched frustration fill her eyes and wondered if she got as deeply involved with all of Bradenton's students. Or had Ian Senior's generosity with the old checkbook included the college endowment fund?

"Sounds like he's interested in your daughter."

"I hope not," she replied sharply, feeling her stomach knot at the thought of Ian and Tracy together.

"You don't like him?"

She took a slow breath. "As a matter of fact, I do, but I know his reputation. He's as slick as they come when it comes to the coeds."

"Maybe that reputation has been exaggerated. Happens that way sometimes."

"Perhaps, but I don't care to risk my daughter's happiness just to find out."

He lifted his hand and flipped down the silky shirt collar that had blown against her neck. Carly drew a slow breath but didn't retreat.

"Must be tough, being both mom and dad."

"I manage." Carly kept her chin high and her expression controlled. It hurt to discuss Tracy with him.

"You must have been very young when you had her."

"I was old enough." She reached for the key, only to find her hand trapped in his. She tried to pull free, but his grip tightened.

"For what it's worth, I'm sorry."

"Sorry for what?"

His thumb moved gently against her wrist. "For making you so uncomfortable whenever I'm around, for one thing." Her frown had his eyes crinkling behind the glasses, but his mouth stayed somber. "But mostly for asking questions I had no business asking. God knows I've dodged enough of them myself to know how deep idle curiosity can cut."

"Yes, I imagine you do." Carly drew a slow breath. His hand was warm against hers. She tried to draw away, only to find her back pressed hard against the door.

He grinned at her. "Going somewhere?"

"To my office—as soon as you let go of my hand."

"Only if you let me make amends by taking you to dinner tonight."

Her pulse leapt, then took on a faster rhythm. "I'm sure you can find something more exciting to do with your evening."

"Can't think of a thing."

He was crowding her. She didn't like it, but she found she could handle it.

"All right," she murmured, "but I get to name the restaurant. And the college will pay."

"No way. This is personal."

Carly set her jaw. "No, Mr. Scanlon, it isn't."

"You don't like me?" He folded her hand between his. His palms were muscular and rough with calluses. Strong hands, strong heart, Tilly always said.

"It's not a question of liking or disliking, Mr. Scanlon. Only of professional ethics. You are here as a prospective employee, and therefore you are Bradenton's guest. Not mine."

"I'm staying in your house—"

"Not mine, remember. The college's."

"—and sleeping in the room below yours."

She couldn't quite master her surprise. "How did you know that?"

"I heard you drive away about midnight, heard you come back a couple hours later. And then I heard you pacing the floor over my head. Must have something on your mind."

She shrugged, but her gaze slid away from his. "I had too much coffee at dinner."

"You drank decaf." He hid a smile. She was nervous and trying hard not to let on. He liked her better that way. When a guy was more vulnerable than most, he preferred to think the woman who fired his blood had a few insecurities of her own to deal with.

"Mr. Scanlon—"

"Don't you think it's time you started calling me Mitch?"

Carly glanced around. The quad was empty. No one would see if she bashed the man over the head with one of his own crutches. His low chuckle had her gaze jerking back to his.

"You know, Carly, guys like me are very sensitive to slights. Might even say we have a real problem with self-esteem."

"In a pig's eye," she scoffed.

He moved closer. With his free hand he removed her sunglasses, hooking them over the mirror attached to the dash.

Without them she felt exposed. Vulnerable. Because she had a feeling it was exactly what he'd intended, she refused to snatch them back.

"Now take my friend Dante. Keeps telling me I should get out more. Guess that makes sense, don't you think?"

She blinked. His tone was teasing. He seemed relaxed, certainly more relaxed than she was. So why did she have this strong feeling he was telling her things he usually kept to himself?

"Tell me something, Scanlon? Does this 'pity me' act usually work with women, or is this the first time you've tried it?"

His grin started as a twitch of those hard lips. By the time he let her go and sat back against the worn leather upholstery, he was laughing. "Why did I think this was going to be easy?" he said, angling to look at her.

"Exactly what do you mean by 'this'?" she said, lifting her eyebrows in the intimidating arch that was every teacher's last resort. It didn't faze him.

"Let's just say I'm a lot closer to signing on the dotted line than I was before we climbed into this spine-crippling crate of yours."

Carly tasted raw panic but somehow managed to keep her expression from changing. Her feelings were secondary. Bradenton was what mattered.

"On behalf of the college, I'm pleased to hear it," she murmured with only a slight rasp of emotion in her tone. "But I do feel a certain need to remind you that you have yet to be *asked* to sign."

"Obviously an oversight." His grin flashed. "We can talk about that tonight over dinner."

For an unsettling moment she thought he was going to kiss her. Instead he reached behind her for his crutches and went about the careful business of getting himself out of the car.

"See you tonight, Caroline," he said when she reached for the key.

"Carly," she said before thinking. "Only my mother calls me Caroline."

"And you don't like it?"

"I neither like it nor dislike it. I simply prefer Carly."

"So do I. Makes you a lot more approachable."

Carly frowned. "Seven o'clock in the parlor," she ordered, giving the key a hard twist. The engine roared to life, and she shoved the shift lever into first.

"It's a date," he said, unable to resist a grin.

"It's business," she corrected a split second before she roared off.

Definitely a challenging lady, he thought as he watched the roadster zip around the corner and disappear behind a building. And definitely a woman with secrets trapped in those bright eyes.

Coach was tied up when Mitch rapped on his door and suggested that Mitch wait for him in the stadium proper. As Carly had warned, the stands had a half-finished look, and the smell of fresh paint hung heavy in the air. Standing alone on the fifty, Mitch drew a long breath and gazed toward the east goalpost. Stretching in front of him like a newly laid carpet, the playing field was a brilliant green, pampered into a thick, cleat-resistant turf by the two groundskeepers he'd just met.

Unwanted emotion churned as he trailed his gaze along the tidy row of empty seats, half now painted a gleaming orange, the other half dull and faded. Blue on orange were Bradenton's colors.

A different team, a different uniform.

Just thinking about the first time he'd pulled on the intimidating black-and-silver Raiders jersey gave him a hit of adrenalin almost as good as sex. It had gotten as good as it gets after that—money, headline after headline, women.

A fast lane kind of guy, the reporters had labeled him his rookie year, everybody's idea of a winner. Oh yeah, he'd bought it all, every damn line of the hype. And then he'd spent half a lifetime trying to live up to an image he'd been dumb enough to let his good buddies in the media create for him. Arletta had called it right when she'd ripped into him for becoming a self-centered jerk.

Lifting his gaze, he sighted along the top of the stands, checking out the bank of lights, the flag poles, the press box. The people's right to know, he thought. What a farce! How many times in how many smoky bars had he listened to some pencil jockey or other pontificating drunkenly on the media's lofty dedication to the truth?

The truth was, guys he'd thought would stick in the bad times as well as the good had disappeared as soon as he'd stopped being salable copy. He'd spent a few lonely months nursing his bitterness until he choked on it. And then he'd started the long comeback climb, creating his own image this time. Most of the bitterness was gone now, or maybe he'd finally grown up.

Squaring his shoulders, he made his slow, careful way along the gleaming chalk line to the sidelines. By the time he crossed the sideline marker, Coach was waiting for him by the bench, an unlit cigar clamped in the corner of his mouth.

"Don't you ever light that thing?" Mitch asked, needing to rest a minute.

"Doctor says they'll kill me, so I'm trying to cut down." Coach tongued the cigar to the other corner of his mouth. "What do you think of the place?"

"Nice. Bigger than I expected."

"Football's always been big in these parts, too. Or it used to be, before the Wolves tanked." Eyes narrowed, Coach glanced around, then jerked his head in the direction of the President's residence. "So, what did you think of the Alderson ladies?"

"Intimidating."

Coach chuckled. "Which one?"

"All three." Releasing a crutch grip, Mitch lifted a hand to wipe some of the sweat from his forehead. He was used to the energy it cost to get from place to place, but he wasn't sure he would ever get used to changing his clothes a couple of times a day. "What's the story on President Alderson, anyway?"

Coach nodded. "She grew up in the President's mansion, used to sit in on classes from the time she was in grade school. Way I heard it, she was a shy little thing, never said more than a few words to anyone until she'd known them for a long time, which is probably the reason she goes out of her way to make every student feel welcome. Don't tell her I told you so, but I know for a fact she's paying tuition out of her own pocket for one or two that ran into some hard luck along the way."

Coach chewed on the end of the cigar. "'Course, there's some who say she got the job 'cause of who she is, too."

Mitch knew all about gossip and the jealousy that prodded it. "What do you say?"

"I'd say she's worked for everything she's gotten. Under all that silk and sophistication, she's as tough as they come. Had to be, considering all the cow dung she had thrown at her when she wasn't much older than Tracy."

"Had a rough time, did she?"

Coach glowered. "Nobody talks much about it, but a few things have slipped out over the years, bits and pieces mostly, enough so's I know it had to have been rough being pregnant in this town, without a man in sight to claim the kid as his own."

Mitch watched one of the painters swabbing orange paint over the last seat in one of the upper sections. "Any of those bits and pieces tell you anything about the guy?"

Instead of answering, Coach snorted a laugh. "Got it bad, haven't you?"

Mitch shifted his gaze. The old man might have slowed up a few steps over the years, but his mind was still sharp, maybe too damn sharp.

"Let's say she's got me wanting to turn some corners I've been avoiding for a while."

Pete's eyes crinkled, but his smile had an edge of warning. "She's a special lady, that's a fact. Smart, real smart, but not so's she flaunts it, you know? And sweet as they come, even if she tries to hide a damn soft heart under those plain suits she wears."

"There's plain, and then there's plain," Mitch said, enjoying a fast private fantasy.

Coach removed his cigar and carefully tucked it into his shirt pocket. When he was finished, he deliberately let Mitch see the rough-and-tumble of the Brooklyn streets in his eyes.

"I wouldn't want to see her hurt, Mitch. Not by you. Not by anyone."

Mitch acknowledged that with a nod. "Not my style."

Coach lifted both shaggy eyebrows. "Since when?"

Since he'd found himself with a lot of time for thinking about things that mattered, and things that didn't. "Since I got almost as smart as you," he said, jerking his head toward the locker room. "How about we finish this discussion sitting down?"

Coach's expression cleared, and his big hand clapped Mitch hard on the back. "I've got a couple of comfortable chairs in my office, and while we're there, there's a contract I want you to take a look at."

Chapter 5

Carly wore black linen, to match her mood. She chose long sleeves and a high neck because the severe lines made her seem taller and more dignified and in command.

She'd been tense and jumpy all day. Twice she'd picked up the phone, intending to cancel. Both times she'd talked herself out of it. It was important to remember that she was in control of her life and her feelings, no one else.

Consider it a business meeting, she told herself firmly as she zipped the dress up the back and cinched the matching belt. An appointment with a prospective employee. Nothing more.

She stepped to the mirror in the walk-in closet to put on her earrings. Just as she was fastening the last gold hoop, the phone rang. A quick glance at the clock radio had her frowning. It was nearly time for her to leave. "This is Dr. Alderson."

"You sound like you've been running." It was Marca.

"I don't run. It's not seemly for a person of my weighty responsibilities."

Marca's laugh always cheered her up, no matter how low she might be.

"Hey, I called to see if you wanted to grab something to eat with me tonight."

"I'd like to, but I'm tied up." She hesitated, then added, "Scanlon and I are having dinner together."

Marca's sudden intake of breath was clearly audible. "You're kidding!"

"Think about it a minute. He's a guest in this house. Tracy is in this house. Doesn't it make sense to keep them apart as much as possible?"

"I have to admit that does sound logical." There was a pause before Marca asked, "Is Gianfracco included in this business dinner?"

"No, although I had Sandy call to invite him. It seems he's addressing a Cub Scouts meeting tonight."

Already ajar, the door to her closet suddenly swung wider, admitting a sleepy-eyed gray tabby cat. Queen Tabitha was Tracy's cat, but most nights she preferred to sleep in Carly's bed, curled up next to her pillow. Tracy claimed her mother spoiled the hedonistic little creature. Carly preferred to think Tabby shared her taste in classical music rather than the atonal stuff Tracy adored.

Spying Carly in front of the mirror, Tabby trotted over and rubbed against her ankles, purring loudly. Grinning, Carly reached down to rub the sensitive triangle behind the cat's ears. The portable phone crackled with static as Marca spoke again. "What's your read on Scanlon so far? Does he want the job, do you think?"

"Yes. No. Oh, Marca, I don't know. I'm just trying to get through the next few days without falling apart."

"Don't worry, you won't."

"I did once."

"You were eighteen and scared."

"Now I'm thirty-five, and I'm still scared."

"Of what? Scanlon?"

"No, myself. A lot of stuff is coming up for me that I thought I'd addressed years ago."

"Like what?"

"Like my feelings for the father of my child. I should hate him for what he did. I *do* hate him, and yet..." Carly straightened, earning her a plaintive meow from Tabby.

"Yet what?"

"It's difficult to explain." She drew a thoughtful breath. "It's as though I have to keep reminding myself why I hate him. Does that make sense?"

Instead of an answer, Marca remained silent, causing Carly to frown at herself in the mirror. "Carly, you're not still attracted to the man, are you?"

"Of course I'm not!" Carly replied instantly, offended that Marca of all people would even ask such a question. "I'm just trying to make the best of a horrible situation."

"Now that I understand perfectly. You've had a lot of practice."

Carly laughed. "I have, haven't I?"

"Practice makes perfect."

"Perfect I'm not, but I am determined to get through this with a minimum of fuss." Carly cradled the phone against her shoulder and selected black pumps from the overhead shelf.

"How about if I just happen to show up while you're having dinner? You could invite me to join you."

Carly felt a surge of relief. It was a perfect lifeline, which was why she couldn't accept. "Thanks for the offer, but this is something I need to face alone."

"I understand, but the offer's still open. I'll be in my office for another ten minutes or so, and then I'll be heading home. You can always reach me there."

Sidestepping Tabby, who was now stretched out in the middle of the closet, Carly carried the shoes into her bedroom and dropped them on the bed.

"I'll keep that in mind, and—" She paused to listen and heard Tracy calling her name. "In here, sweetheart," she called out before adding into the receiver, "Marca, I've got to go—"

"Wait, don't hang up! There's one more thing I need to tell you."

She didn't like the sound of that. "Tell me."

"I got a call a few minutes ago from Chad Duncan at the *Times-News.* Seems Scanlon stopped for gas at a service station just off the interstate, and someone recognized him. That someone told someone else who told Chad."

"News moves fast in a small town."

"That's not all. Apparently Scanlon asked directions to the college from the pump jockey, and Chad smells a story." Marca breathed a heavy sigh. "Anyway, bottom line, our ferret-faced friend wanted to know if Scanlon is slated to become the new coach of the Wolves. I put him off, but good old Chad wants to ask the man himself. I figure he'll be showing up on your doorstep pretty soon, trying to score a scoop."

"Exactly what we don't need."

"You're telling me! We need surprise on our side to maximize the publicity value. Nobody's going to show up at a press conference to announce our new coach if every paper and TV station in the country has already leaked Scanlon's name."

"He doesn't have the job yet, Marca."

"Exactly. And in case he turns us down, we don't want a bunch of false rumors raising the hopes of the very alumni we're trying to woo."

"This is getting out of hand."

"Not yet, but it could. That's the problem with manipulating the media. One little unexpected hitch, and the whole house of cards comes tumbling down." Marca paused, then added more lightly, "Metaphorically speaking."

Carly closed her eyes and tried to find the quiet center inside her head where she went to draw strength. But all she could see was a pair of haunted brown eyes and a once cocky smile that was now touched with vulnerability.

"Remember that small girls' college in northern California that offered me the presidency a few years back?"

"The one in the redwoods?"

"That's the one. I'm thinking very seriously of calling them and seeing if the job is still open!"

"Good idea. Ask if they need someone to teach advertising and PR while you're at it."

"Right," Carly drawled before saying goodbye. She was returning the phone to the cradle when Tracy appeared in the doorway, looking almost formal in nearly new jeans and a sweater.

"Hey, you look great!" she exclaimed, looking her mother up and down with obvious approval. "Don't tell me you're actually going out on a date?"

"Nope. Just another dull business dinner."

"Who with?"

"Mr. Scanlon."

"Oh yeah?" Tracy glanced her way, her expression as guile-less as a baby's. "He's got a killer smile, don't you think?"

"I hadn't really formed an opinion one way or another." Carly took a last critical look in the gilt mirror over her dresser, fluffed her hair one more time and slipped into her shoes. The three-inch heels didn't quite bring her eye-to-eye with her al-ready gorgeous daughter.

"How was cheerleading practice?" she asked nonchalantly.

"So-so. Karen keeps saying we have to come up with some-thing unusual to wow the judges."

Carly wondered if she should take a wrap, decided on her purple velvet jacket, then changed her mind. Velvet was for festive occasions, not business meetings.

"What movie did you two decide to see tonight?"

"We couldn't agree, so we decided to go bowling instead." Tracy offered her mother a wheedling smile. "I was hoping I could borrow Nigel."

"Only if you promise to obey all speed laws." Carly punc-tuated her words with a maternal frown, which only made Tracy grin.

"Don't worry, I never break the rules, just bend 'em a lit-tle."

"Tracy Marie!"

"Just kidding!"

Mentally crossing her fingers, Carly returned to the closet for a black purse. Tracy wandered over to the dresser and, just as she'd done for years, opened the lid of Carly's antique jewelry box and began poking through the contents.

"Can I wear these sometime?" she asked, holding up small emerald studs.

"For a special occasion, yes."

"Tonight?"

"To go bowling?"

"Guess that's not really all that special, is it?" Tracy agreed as she returned the studs to the box and closed the lid.

"Not really, no." Carly glanced at her watch, saw that she still had five minutes before she was to meet Scanlon in the parlor and wondered if she'd left a pack of cigarettes in any of her old purses. If Tracy hadn't been there, she would have been tempted to sneak a few puffs, just to calm herself.

"Is this perfume new?" Tracy asked, removing the stopper from a small vial for a sniff.

Carly nodded. "I bought it in Chicago in a little shop near the Art Institute."

"Smells expensive," Tracy said with a grin. "And sexy."

"I was hoping for sophisticated." Carly said with a self-conscious shrug. "With just a hint of brilliant."

"Nope. Sexy." Before Carly could stop her, Tracy managed to get them both smelling like a bordello.

"That's enough." Carly ordered, laughing as she swatted Tracy's hand away.

"Hope so," Tracy muttered, grinning to herself as she stoppered the small crystal bottle and returned it to the dresser. "Are you going to hire Mr. Scanlon to be the new coach?" she asked as she scooped the sleepy cat into her arms.

"That's up to Coach Gianfracco."

Tracy nuzzled the cat's furry face. "You hired Coach, didn't you?"

"No, Grandfather hired him just about the time you and I moved back here from Providence." Carly selected a bag and carried it into the bedroom. "Get the light, please, Sweetie," she threw over her shoulder.

Tracy flipped the switch before following her mother into the bedroom. Tabby curled around Tracy's neck, her green cat's eyes half closed in pleasure.

Perching on the bed, Carly dug her car keys from her purse and tossed them Tracy's way before transferring the remaining contents to the black bag.

"Oh, I almost forgot. Nigel needs gas." She selected a credit card from her wallet and tossed it next to the keys. "I meant to fill up on the way home, but I was running late."

"I'll take care of it." Tracy transferred Tabby to the crook of her arm before slipping the keys and the card into the pocket of her jeans.

Carly held a fast debate with her conscience—and lost. "By the way, I ran into Ian Cummings today. He asked me how you were doing with your biology paper. He also said to tell you hi."

Tracy flushed, then glanced away, but not before Carly noticed the sudden glow in her eyes. "I saw him in the library when I was checking out those books on genetics. We got to talking, you know? About the difference between high school papers and college papers, stuff like that.''

"I'm sure Ian was most informative.''

"Oh, he was. And he was really interested in my paper, too. He's really easy to talk to, you know? Not at all like some of those other jerks on the team.''

Carly drew a breath. Careful, she told herself silently before saying aloud, "Tracy, he's still too old for you.''

Tracy angled her chin. "My father was older than you.''

"We aren't talking about me.''

Frowning, Tracy deposited Tabby on the bed, much to the cat's displeasure. Tabby leapt to the floor, then padded across the carpet with dainty steps, twitching the tip of her tail as she went.

"Mom, can I ask you something important?''

"Of course you can.''

"Did you really love my father?'' Tracy kept her gaze fixed on the cat as she spoke. "Or did you just say that so I wouldn't think you were a one-night stand?''

Carly hesitated. If she was ever going to tell Tracy the truth about her conception, now was the perfect time. And then what? Admit that she'd lied to her daughter for sixteen years? Raise doubts in Tracy's mind about her mother's integrity? Shatter her little girl's sense of security? Carly felt a chill invade the space around her heart, and she forced a smile.

"I thought I loved him, yes,'' she said, softly but firmly. "Otherwise, I never would have gone to bed with him.''

"Is that how you know when you're in love? Deciding to sleep with someone, I mean?''

Too restless to sit still, Carly got to her feet and walked to the window and looked down on the front lawn. The newly emerging daffodils in the front bed were a bright spot of color in the gathering darkness. The security lights had just come on, shining down on the familiar scene—and on the unfamiliar silver Jaguar parked to one side of the circular drive. A week ago the earth had still been touched with frost. A week ago Mitch Scanlon had been a distant memory.

"I think it's different for each person,'' she said slowly, thinking as she went along. "Nature gave us a strong sex drive for purely practical reasons, so finding yourself attracted to a man isn't unusual. But God gave us free will, so acting on that impulse is something else again.''

''So what was it that made you decide to do it with my father?''

Three glasses of beer, Carly thought immediately, and then realized that the truth was far more complicated than that.

''He listened,'' she said on a rush of unwanted sadness. ''I felt as though I could tell him anything and he would understand. And when he asked me questions, I had the feeling he really cared about the answers.'' She shook her head, her eyes suddenly stinging. ''That sounds silly now, I know,'' she added, turning to face her daughter.

''No it doesn't,'' Tracy said with an earnest frown. ''I think it sounds wonderful.''

''It was wonderful,'' Carly said softly, honestly. ''And when he smiled at me, he looked into my eyes, and I felt special. Cherished.'' She found that she was hugging herself and quickly dropped her arms to her sides. ''No other man has ever made me feel that way since.''

''You still love him, don't you?'' Tracy asked in a voice thickened by emotion.

Carly bit her lip, the ready denial stuck behind the sudden lump in her throat. ''No, Tracy, it doesn't work that way in the real world,'' she murmured, her eyes flooding with tears. ''Oh rats, now I've gone and ruined my makeup.''

Biting her lip, Carly went into the bathroom to repair the damage. Tracy hovered in the doorway, watching anxiously. ''Did you ever think about maybe contacting him again sometime?''

''Yes, when you were born.'' Carly opened the drawer containing her small store of cosmetics. ''You were so wonderful, and my hormones were going crazy. I was suddenly feeling guilty for not telling him about you. And in a way, I guess I still believe in fairy-tale endings.'' She shrugged. ''By the time I finally tracked down his telephone number, I realized that talking to him would be a mistake.''

''Why?''

Frowning, Carly swirled more mascara on her lashes before returning the wand to the drawer and closing it again. ''Because I was afraid he would want to be a part of your life, and

I knew that would only cause problems down the road." She'd also been terribly afraid that the notoriety Mitch had already garnered might end up hurting Tracy someday.

Tracy drew her eyebrows together and stared at the floor. At that moment she was so much like her father it hurt. "And now?" Tracy asked, glancing up, her eyes probing intently. "What if you ran into him someplace by accident? How would you feel?"

"Curious, I suppose, and maybe a little nostalgic," she hedged before turning on the tap to wash her hands.

"Would you want to go to bed with him?"

Carly felt a jab of fear, which was almost immediately replaced by an insidious, unwanted heat deep inside. "Absolutely not," she said, giving the faucet a hard turn before reaching for a towel. "And that's enough about good old Mom's past for tonight. Too much soul-searching gives me hives."

Tracy giggled, but her expression remained thoughtful, perhaps even a little sad, Carly noted with a pang. "I'm sorry you never found anyone else to love as much as you loved my father," she said softly. "Maybe then you wouldn't look so sad sometimes when you look at me."

Carly's throat tightened, and for an instant she couldn't breathe. "Sweetheart, I'm not sad, not at all. I have a terrifically charming, intelligent, beautiful daughter whom I adore, a satisfying career and neat friends like Aunt Marca. I'm making a difference here at Bradenton, and that makes me happy every single day."

Admittedly there were times when she longed to feel the same hot rush of emotion she'd felt that steamy night in the desert, but passion that strong, that incendiary, could destroy as easily as it could enthrall. Perhaps it was cowardly to choose safety instead of risk, and perhaps she sometimes felt an aching loneliness inside, but for the most part, she was content with the life she'd created for herself and her child.

No regrets, she reminded herself firmly as she turned to offer Tracy a reassuring smile. "Sweetie, I'm touched that you're worrying about me, but truly, your concern is misplaced. I made my choices years ago, and I'm satisfied they were the right ones for me—and for you."

Tracy's answering smile was endearingly off center and just a bit shaky. "It's just that you're still young, and like Ian said, as foxy as any student. And when I leave, you'll be alone."

"But that's the way it's supposed to be, Trace. You'll have your life and I'll have mine, just as Grandmother has hers." Carly smoothed her daughter's golden hair with a gentle, loving hand. "Darling, please believe me, I am not unhappy, and I am not afraid of being alone. So don't give that another thought, okay?"

Tracy nodded. "Okay, but that doesn't mean I don't wish a terrific, good-looking, sexy guy like Mitch Scanlon would fall madly in love with you and sweep you off your feet."

And then she was gone, leaving Carly with nothing to say and a lot to think about.

The parlor was empty when Mitch arrived a few minutes before seven. In deference to the still chilly nights, a fire was blazing in the fireplace, and the heavy drapes had been drawn over the windows facing the pool area.

He moved to the fireplace and warmed his hands for a long moment before moving to the glass-enclosed bookcase opposite the fireplace. The contract was still in his room, unsigned. Unlike his last contract with the Raiders, this one was actually pretty straightforward. Two years up front, with an option for a third, a decent salary with enough digits to give his tax accountant a few headaches, and a fairly substantial bonus for a winning season. Not a bad deal for a novice coach.

Coach had been disappointed when he hadn't signed on the spot. A few years back he would already have been out celebrating in some dark, smoky watering hole, buying rounds for the house, instead of squiring a woman he'd just met to a quiet dinner in what he figured would be the classiest place in town. Maybe he was getting mellow in his old age, he decided, turning toward the door.

He heard her heels clicking on the hardwood floor an instant before she stepped into the room. She was wearing a black dress that didn't so much cling as suggest, and silky black stockings that just begged to be stroked by a man's slow hand.

Mitch found himself swallowing hard. After a lot of years fending off sex kittens in low-cut spandex, Carly's tasteful attire had his imagination jumping through hoops.

"Good evening," she said, her lips curving slightly in that reluctant half smile he was rapidly coming to expect from her. She was wearing perfume tonight. Something feminine and alluring.

"You look terrific," he said, and then nearly laughed at the corny words. He started to loosen his tie, then realized he wasn't wearing one. Glancing down at the blue dress shirt and slacks, he frowned. "Maybe I should change."

Her impersonal gaze made a fast trip to the tips of his shoes, then back up. "Don't bother. Things are always more casual in a college town."

Mitch hitched a little more air into his lungs and jerked his chin toward the door. "All set?"

Her nod was brief, her expression cool. "I hope you don't mind taking your car. Tracy is using Nigel."

Mitch took a tighter grip on his crutches and slanted her a look. "If she drives like her mom, I hope she gives us a head start."

"Don't worry. She already left." Her smile lasted longer this time. Long enough for him to imagine her lips parting under his.

Outside, the daylight was nearly gone. In spite of the hint of winter still lingering on the air, the scents of spring had grown stronger over the past few days. Carly treated herself to a long, pleasurable sniff, then stiffened when she saw Scanlon's mouth twitch.

"Nice night," he said when she glared at him.

"Very."

She could have sworn he'd had his hair trimmed since they'd parted that morning. And the blue-and-white striped shirt looked surprisingly unwrinkled after a night in that scruffy duffel Coach had toted in last night. The Jaguar seemed to have lost the fine layer of road dust she'd noticed earlier, as well.

She paused by the passenger's side while he unlocked the door and opened it. "Wait," he said when as she started to slip into the bucket seat. "I have this problem."

"What kind of problem?" she asked, turning to face him.

"It's personal. I've tried to shake it, but so far, no luck."

"Maybe you need castor oil," she muttered.

"I'd rather try something else."

It was a testing kiss, all too brief, achingly gentle. But enough to send a flood of longing through her so fierce she shuddered.

"Aw, hell," he muttered as though he had just made a terrible mistake. But before she had time to recoil in hurt, he had somehow propped his crutches against the car and was pulling her against him. His body exuded heat, and his mouth, though that of an experienced man now, was just as eager and persuasive as she remembered.

No! she thought, stiffening. Instantly, he pulled away, his grip easing, as though he'd sensed her flash of fear.

"I've been wanting to do that since last night," he muttered, his voice rough. "Now maybe I can concentrate on something else."

His words seared her, arousing pleasure and triumph and hunger. Strong, unruly emotions that frightened her. Emotions she refused to feel again.

She took a deep breath and waited for the oxygen to calm her. "Don't do that again," she ordered, her voice cold and calm, even though her heart was pounding in her throat and her skin felt hot.

"He really hurt you, didn't he? Tracy's dad?"

"Yes," she said calmly. "He did."

Averting her gaze, she opened the car door and slipped inside. By the time he'd gotten himself around the car and into his seat with his crutches stowed in the back, she'd regained her composure.

"Are you all right?" he asked.

She took a long, cleansing breath. "Yes, of course. Why shouldn't I be?"

His mouth quirked. "Well, for one thing, you haven't buckled your seat belt. Oregon law, remember?" he said, reaching over his shoulder for his own belt.

Carly felt foolish and off center, two feelings she abhorred. "Thanks for the reminder."

"Always willing to assist a lady," he drawled as he started the Jag, then waited while she finished securing her belt before applying the gas.

He was a good driver, handling the manual controls deftly as though he'd never driven any other way. "Which way?" he asked when they reached the T at the end of her lane.

"Left to the center of campus, and then right at the statue of Artemus. That'll take you all the way into Bradenton Falls."

"Gotcha."

They hardly spoke on the drive into town. On the way she pointed out Marca's house and told him a little of Marca's history. He commented on the quiet and contrasted the darkened road to the omnipresent lights on most California highways.

"Take the second right," she said when they reached the main street. "It's the last building on the left, the one with the green awning in front."

Gallagher's on Pine had a reputation for offering man-size steaks Cajun style at a decent price. The parking lot was packed. Only two places were available, both posted with the distinctive blue sign. Scanlon slowed, then swung a fast right into the closer space.

"The guy at the DMV where I got the handicapped plates kept telling me how I'd lucked out," he said when he caught her quick glance. "No more circling for a place to park like all you ordinary folks."

"Lucky you," she said before she thought.

He grinned, but his eyes held an instant of pain. "Yeah, ain't that the truth."

While he got himself out of the car, Carly gave herself a short pep talk. About kisses, mainly. Drugging, dangerous kisses. Of course he'd come on to her. It was his pattern, wasn't it? The way he'd run his life. One big party, a string of one-night stands interspersed with TV interviews and talk show appearances. What was one more woman in one more town? Nothing, that's what. No more than a diversion. An antidote for boredom. A convenient receptacle for his sexual release. It was all so easy for him.

Or was it?

Glancing sideways, she saw that he'd pushed himself to his feet and was reaching behind the seat for his crutches. How could anything possibly be easy for him now? a tiny voice questioned.

The answer was obvious. It wasn't.

But that didn't mean he deserved to be forgiven for what he'd done, she told herself firmly as he came around to open her door. For the first time in seventeen years, however, the anger that she had always summoned so easily whenever she thought of that night in the desert refused to ignite.

Chapter 6

The scrape of silverware on china and the low hum of voices greeted them as they walked into the cozy restaurant. Placards from the various plays put on by the college over the years lined one paneled wall, while insignia from the fraternities and sororities lined another.

It was a lively crowd, and most of the tables were filled. Carly grabbed two menus from the stack near the door, explaining as she scanned the darkened interior, "Gallagher's is 'seat yourself' if you can find an empty space."

"Looks like that might be a problem," Mitch told her, pulling a folded handkerchief from his back pocket to wipe the sweat from his brow.

"Hmm, there's a booth, near the back."

She led, conscious of the startled looks that came their way. Several faculty members spoke or waved as they passed, and Carly saw the sudden glint of recognition in the eyes of others.

By the time they reached the booth and she'd slipped into the red vinyl seat, she knew that Mitch Scanlon's presence in Bradenton would be the subject of many conversations over morning coffee, both in town and on campus.

Mitch had to work at it, but he managed to get himself seated opposite her with a minimum of fuss. "Interesting place," he said, stowing his crutches under the table. "Smells spicy, like this little bar and grill I used to like in New Orleans."

"That's probably because the owner, Mick Gallagher, is from Louisiana."

He lifted one eyebrow. "Sounds more Boston than New Orleans."

"Mick's mother was Cajun and not quite five feet tall, but a real disciplinarian. He told me once that she used to swat him and his brothers with a frying pan when they didn't behave."

Glancing up, she saw a strange, almost haunted, look cross Mitch's face before he grinned her way. "Must have been interesting growing up in that household."

"Yes. I'm always fascinated by big families."

He absorbed that thoughtfully. "How'd he end up here?"

"His wife is an Oregon native. She was a navy nurse, which is how they met. Mick was working shore patrol, got beaned by a beer bottle, and swears he fell in love with her the minute she told him to stop moaning and take his 'stitching up' like a man. When Mick retired, she talked him into giving Oregon a year. They've been here six."

Carly unfolded the oversize cloth napkin and carefully spread it over her thighs. Though the booth was tucked into a dark corner, she couldn't fail to notice the curious looks coming their way.

Gallagher's blue eyes held a hint of that same curiosity as he barreled over to take their order. A giant of a man, with an unruly thatch of dark red hair and a booming laugh, he and his wife, Doreen, had six kids, all grown now, and four foster children of varying ages and physical disabilities, two of whom were currently attending Bradenton on full scholarships. Only Carly and the financial aid officer knew that she personally was paying the bills.

"Soup de jour is barley rice, only between you and me, I wouldn't recommend it," Mick informed them in his gravel-voiced version of a whisper. "Stuff's bad for the digestion, but the missus makes me put it on the menu. Claims it helps keep a person's arteries unclogged, or some such."

"Last year it was oat bran," Carly informed Mitch somberly before tuning to study the list of specials on the chalkboard over the bar.

"Dorrie damn near had me putting it in the whiskey," Mick groused.

Carly grinned. "Be honest, Mick. Dorrie's not quite that bad."

"Well, almost." Grinning self-consciously, the big Irishman pulled a pad from the pocket of his spotlessly clean white apron with one hand while retrieving a pencil from behind his right ear with the other.

"What can I bring you?"

"Blackened T-bone, rare, thickest one you got, and a double order of French fries," Carly said with a hint of defiance in her voice.

Gallagher regarded her approvingly. "Dorrie wanted to rip out the deep fryer, too, but I put my foot down," he grumbled as he scribbled on his pad.

Chuckling appreciatively, Mitch ordered the same and a glass of burgundy.

"Good choice, Mr. Scanlon, and by the way, welcome to Gallagher's. Me and my boys have been fans for years."

So much for anonymity, Carly thought with a silent groan as Gallagher cocked an eyebrow her way. "You want the usual to drink?"

She nodded. "Double lime."

"Comin' right up." Gallagher lumbered to the bar, returning immediately with the drinks before disappearing into the kitchen with their dinner order.

Mitch tasted the wine and found it surprisingly smooth. "Come here often?" he asked, watching her stir her mineral water. She seemed as much at home in this no frills place as she did in the manor house on the hill. It was a knack he'd noticed in others who were secure in themselves and their birthright. Mongrel bastards like him would never have that inner serenity, no matter how successful they became.

"Not often, no." She lifted the glass to her lips and sipped. Watching, he felt desire take hold and swell. "The last time we were celebrating Tracy's birthday. Since the year she turned four, I've allowed her to pick the place where she wanted to have her party. This year she picked Gallagher's because of the band."

Mitch glanced around. In one corner of the room a couple of long-haired rockers were setting up their equipment. "She must like metal."

"I'm afraid so." The soft smile flirting with her lips spread into a rueful grin. "I had a headache for a week afterward. Fortunately, the music isn't generally quite that earsplitting." She watched a couple of students walking past arm in arm before returning to the rapt study of her drink. "Tracy got a little carried away making requests, and in her opinion, the louder and more jarring, the better."

Mitch grinned. "She must have liked growing up here. Since she's not going away to college, I mean."

"Actually, we lived in Providence until she was nine. I was on the faculty at Brown."

Mitch took another sip and decided it fit—upper-class school, upper-class lady.

"And then you moved back here?"

She nodded, and the overhead light was trapped for an instant in her hair, turning it a lush velvet brown. "To become Dean of Women. My father had had a series of small strokes and let it be known that he expected me to return."

Mitch shifted, tried to get comfortable. "Did you always do what your father expected of you?"

"No, not always," she said in a curiously flat voice that spiked his interest. He waited, but it was clear from the sudden compression of her lips that she intended to say nothing more.

"I've always wondered what it would be like to live in a small town," he said, leaning back. Because he had secrets of his own too painful to share, he respected her need to keep hers. "As a kid I used to read stories about Norman Rockwell communities where people left their doors unlocked and the keys in their cars." His mouth slanted. "It never seemed real to me. Where I grew up, there were a saloon and a couple of working girls on every corner."

Carly acknowledged that with a brief smile. She knew the bare bones of Scanlon's impoverished childhood, but not the details. "Things have changed in the last few years, but basically Bradenton's exactly like one of those Rockwell paintings. At Christmas the youth choir from the Community Church goes caroling door to door, and every Easter, local civic groups take turns hiding eggs for the kids in Centennial Park.''

''What, no drive-by shootings or gang warfare?''

''Not yet, but we do have far too many cases of spousal and child abuse. And, of course, problems relating to alcohol and drug use.''

''By the students?''

She drew a breath. ''Even though we hit pretty heavy on the problems caused by substance abuse during freshman orientation, we invariably have that about twenty percent who don't listen.''

''How about you, Dr. Alderson? Were you one of those twenty percent when you were a coed?''

Though she knew he was teasing, Carly felt her blood turn cold. ''I've only been drunk once in my life,'' she said evenly. ''It wasn't a pleasant experience.''

''It rarely is.'' Mitch took another sip and thought about the first time he'd gotten drunk. He'd been six and thirsty. The kitchen tap had been broken, so he'd done what he'd seen his mother do countless times and downed an entire can of beer. Deathly sick for two days, he'd sworn he would never drink beer again. But he had, too many times to count. The last time had been the worst.

He moved restlessly, suddenly uncomfortable at the memory of that week in the desert, and let his fingers toy with the stem of his wineglass.

''This is just a guess, but I have a hunch your last coach, Parisi, didn't work real hard at enforcing training rules.''

Carly was taken by surprise. ''Why do you say that?'' she asked, leaning forward slightly to hear his answer over the rising noise level. The movement of her breasts beneath the black linen drew his gaze for an instant, sending a subtle shiver of awareness skittering through her.

''Higher than average absentee rate for Monday practice. My guess is a third of the team was hung over.''

She sat back, watching his eyes. They stayed level on hers, with only a hint of a smile lurking in their golden depths. ''What about you, Mr. Scanlon? If you were coach, would you enforce the training rules?''

''Absolutely.'' His mouth slanted. ''You look surprised.''

"I am surprised. From all I've heard about the great Mitch Scanlon, following rules seems out of character for you."

"I've broken my share, and every time, the team paid the price. Turned out I hated losing more than I liked going my own way."

Settling back in his seat, he let his gaze wander. As far as he could see, every table was taken, and several couples were hovering hopefully in the small foyer. By the time Gallagher came out of the kitchen with their order in hand, the band was starting to tune up. Mitch hoped there were no young people in the crowd tonight with Tracy's taste in music.

"Here you go, folks. Still sizzlin' and guaranteed to curl your toes or your money back." The burly Irishman braced the huge tray on the edge of the table and proceeded to deal out plates with the deftness of a Vegas cardsharper.

"What else can I get you?" he asked when the tray was empty.

"Catsup and another mineral water would work fine for me," Carly said, already cutting into her steak.

"Rare enough for you?" Gallagher asked when blood oozed onto the plate.

"Perfect," Carly all but cooed. "You get my vote for chef of the year."

Gallagher grinned. "I'll tell Dorrie you said so."

Mitch followed her example and took a bite. It was just hot enough to tease his tongue and spicy enough to bring tears to his eyes. He told himself it was just as good as sex and almost believed it. He finished first and pushed his plate away.

"Mr. Scanlon?" The kid who seemed to appear from no-where was about ten, with a Charlie Brown awkwardness about him, and big blue eyes filled with hero-worship. The Raiders T-shirt he was wearing was two sizes too big and faded nearly to gray.

"How's it going, son?"

The boy fumbled with the napkin in his hand. "Uh, my dad, he said not to bother you when you were eating."

"I appreciate that."

"Yeah, well, since you're done now, I mean, is it okay...can I have your autograph?"

Mitch smiled. "It would be my pleasure."

"Killer!"

Grinning from ear to ear, the boy handed over the napkin. "It's clean. I borrowed it from an empty table."

"You didn't happen to borrow a pen, too, did you?"

Looking stricken, the boy shot a fast glance over his shoulder. Uh, maybe, my dad—"

"I have a pen," Carly said, leaning forward to place it next to the crumpled napkin.

"Thanks." Picking up the pen, Mitch wondered how many autographs he'd signed over the years. Hundreds? Thousands? A lot, anyway. Somehow, though, he'd never gotten over the thrill of being asked.

"What's your name, son?"

"Kenny."

"Good name for a quarterback." The spark in the boy's eyes told him he'd guessed right. Grinning, Mitch scrawled a personalized message and signed his name. "Here you go, Ken."

The boy took it as though it were gold. "Uh, could you do another one for my brother Jimmy? He's real sick and can't get out anymore."

"Sounds rough. What's wrong with him?"

A sad look passed over the boy's face. "He has cancer. It's in his back now, and he can't sit up anymore, so my mom stayed home with him, but I know he'd be real upset if I came home with just an autograph for me and not one for him."

"I think you're right." Mitch started to ask Gallagher for another napkin, then thought better of it. Leaning forward, he hooked his wallet from his back pocket and extracted a grubby scrap of yellow notebook paper.

Carly saw his face change and wondered what was written on that much-handled piece of paper. Tempted to lean forward to peek, she took a sip of water instead and watched Scanlon turn it over and scrawl his name.

"Got this when I was about your age. I like to think this brought me luck when I needed it. Maybe it'll help your brother."

"Whose name is on the back?" Ken asked, turning it over, but before Scanlon could answer, the boy's head shot up. "Did Johnny Unitas really sign this?"

"He really did."

"Wow!" Ken stared at the faded signature with awe. "Jimmy's gonna split a gut when he sees this."

"You tell him to hang in there, okay?"

"I sure will." The boy's face changed, and his eyes fell. "And I'm real sorry you got crippled like it showed on TV."

"Yeah, so am I." He reached up to ruffle the boy's hair. "Keep rooting for the Raiders, okay?"

"You bet." Still grinning, the boy carried his prizes back to the table, where he showed both to his father, jabbering excitedly. The man's head came up, and his smile was shaky as he gave Mitch a thumbs-up.

Carly felt her throat tighten. "That was very generous of you," she murmured when Scanlon returned her pen.

He moved his shoulders. "Seems wrong somehow that they pay guys like me big bucks to play a kid's game, and scientists who really do some good have to beg for money." His mouth took on a mocking twist. "And before you say it, yeah, I took the money."

"Something tells me you also gave some away."

He glanced Kenny's way for an instant. "Not enough."

She watched his jaw tighten and wondered why she'd thought he had no depth. "I can't help thinking of Jimmy's mother. I can't imagine anything worse than watching your child suffer and not being able to take away the hurt."

He tipped his wineglass a little and stared into the ruby-colored liquid. "There was a kid in rehab with me, just turned fourteen. Broke his neck in a surfing accident, and the only thing he could move was his eyes. It was never going to get any better for him, and he knew it. His parents were great people. One of them was always with him. With his mom, the kid used to make jokes and laugh. He was trying to make her feel better."

His gaze came to hers briefly, before he returned to his study of his wine. "Kept telling her how he was going to marry this cute little candy striper and give his mom a house full of grandkids."

"And did he?"

"No." He poured the rest of his wine down his throat and shrugged. "One night he just stopped breathing. Nurse came in the next morning to give him his meds and couldn't wake him up.''

Something in his face touched her deeply. ''I'm sorry.''

''I told myself he was better off. Sometimes I even believed it.'' He frowned as the guitarist ran through a testing riff. Catching Gallagher's eye, he waved him over.

''How about some dessert?'' the Irishman coaxed, pencil already in hand. ''Got fresh peach pie tonight.''

''Another time,'' Scanlon said without consulting her. Just as well, she thought. She couldn't force down another sip of water, let alone more food.

Not since she'd held Tracy in her arms for the first time had she felt such turbulent, contradictory emotions. She hadn't wanted to spend any more time than necessary with Scanlon, but she'd done it for Bradenton. Then, damn him, he'd somehow finagled it so that she'd actually enjoyed talking with him. But this? She gazed down at the napkin crumpled in her hand. How could the man who'd just shared a little bit of his soul with her be the same man she'd met in Palm Springs?

''Sure you two don't want to stay to listen to the music? Them boys don't look like much, but they're good musicians.''

''Another time,'' she said, watching as Gallagher totaled the check.

''I'll hold you to that, Carly,'' Mick promised, dropping the check on the table between them. Before she could react, Scanlon's big hand flattened over it.

''Good to see you again, Carly,'' Mick said, watching the by-play with obvious interest.

''You, too, Mick. Give my best to Dorrie.''

''Will do.'' Instead of leaving, however, Gallagher shifted his gaze Scanlon's way. Even though the lighting was dim, she could have sworn his florid face had grown even redder.

''It sure would make me a hero to my boys if I came home tonight with Mitch Scanlon's autograph,'' he said in an un-characteristically tentative way.

Mitch slanted him a thoughtful look. ''Guess it wouldn't make me look too good in front of the lady if I turned you down, huh?''

''Hell no. Make you look damn bad, in fact.''

"Can't have that." Glancing her way, he lifted one eyebrow. "May I borrow your pen again, please?"

The grief was gone from his eyes, and his grin was a little on the cocky side. For a moment she wondered if she'd imagined the aching sadness she'd heard in his voice when he'd spoken of that young surfer. And then she realized he'd just tucked his sorrow inside again where no one could see it.

Wanting desperately to comfort him, she managed a smile as she opened her purse. Handing over her pen again, she found herself wishing he was a stranger instead of a very complex, very attractive man she was doing her best not to like.

Mitch drove home at a leisurely pace, enjoying the sense of intimacy provided by the car's confines. Usually he was bone tired after a busy day, but not tonight. He'd been too busy trying to coax a genuine smile out of her to pay more than fleeting attention to the pain in his legs.

The campus was still surprisingly busy, though most of the lights in the buildings had been extinguished. The rain had held off, and the stars were bright overhead. On the eastern edge of the residential area, a party was still going strong at one of the fraternity houses. Instead of the togas he remembered from his partying days, sarongs and loincloths seemed to be the costume of the day.

"When did college kids get so young?" he asked with wry amusement when he caught Carly's glance.

"I've been wondering the same thing lately," she admitted with a brief smile. "Fortunately, we have enough older undergraduates to keep things from getting totally out of hand."

"Coach said something about special programs for displaced timber workers?"

"We were the first to recognize the need," she said, her voice reflecting a quiet pride. "Several of the graduates from the pilot program are now teaching what they learned to others." Shifting, she crossed her legs, giving him a flash of silky calves and one trim ankle.

"Very impressive," he said, his voice scratchy and a couple of tones deeper than usual. He'd learned a lot about self-denial in recent years. Things he could no longer manage he'd made himself stop wanting. Things that took more effort generally took more time, so he planned his days—and nights—accordingly. Discipline was the key—that and a brutally honest acceptance of the difficulties and frustrations forced on him by his paralysis.

Making love took more than extra effort these days. It also exposed the very awkwardness and vulnerability he tried so hard to keep from showing. As soon as the bedroom door closed behind the lady of his choice, he felt the same clammy fear he'd felt the first time he stepped into the huddle as a professional. Outwardly calm, even cocky, he'd been a wreck inside, his guts churning so hard it had hurt to breathe. And his hands had been sweat slick from panic at the thought of the humiliating mistakes he was bound to make. But damn, it would almost be worth a hefty dose of humiliation to feel Caroline Alderson's soft body moving against his.

"Oh look, there're Tracy and Nigel," she said, leaning forward to peer through the windshield. They caught up to the MG at the mansion's driveway. The top was still down on the roadster, and Tracy was bundled against the night air in a bright yellow parka and stocking cap. Scanlon tooted, and she lifted a hand in the air and wiggled her fingers.

"Nice kid," he said, glancing Carly's way. "For what it's worth, I admire you for doing such a great job raising her."

"To tell you the truth, I'm not sure who raised whom." A gentle smile played over her lips, and he drew a hard breath. "She's told me more than once that it's just as difficult being an only child as it is being a single parent."

Glancing his way, Carly saw his jaw grow taut and wondered if he was thinking about his childhood. "Does she see much of her father?" he asked without looking at her.

"Tracy's father is not a factor in her life," she said carefully and calmly.

That brought his gaze her way, and she saw that he was surprised. "His choice?"

"Yes," she said, because any other answer would lead to questions she wouldn't—couldn't—answer.

"Man's a damn fool," he declared, his tone a little rough.

Carly stared straight ahead, stunned by the depth of emotion she'd heard in his cryptic words. She'd been so sure he wouldn't want the baby, so sure he would try to pressure her into an abortion, perhaps even offer her money. Convincing herself that a man that callous, that selfish, didn't deserve to know he'd become a father had been easy.

She tightened her hands around her purse and tried to level her suddenly erratic heartbeat. She was still trying when Scanlon made the turn onto the circular drive; ahead, Tracy drove straight through to the detached garage beyond the house.

The mansion's grounds were as brightly lit as the campus, but most of the windows in the big house were dark. "Looks like your mother's turned in for the night," he said as he parked in the same spot by the front walk.

Tracy was already out of the car and walking toward them by the time Carly left the Jag. "Hi, Mom," she called gaily. "Nigel's all tucked in for the night, safe and sound."

Carly smiled. "I wasn't worried." She slipped an arm around Tracy's shoulders for a quick squeeze. As always, she felt emotion swell in her chest whenever she touched her daughter. "Did you have a good time?" she asked, releasing her.

"Terrific, until Nigel ran out of gas."

Carly sighed. "Sweetie, I distinctly remember telling you—"

"I know, but I forgot. Anyway, it worked out."

"What did you do, call the auto club?"

"Not exactly. Ian flagged down a passing car, and—"

"What do you mean, *Ian* flagged down a car?"

"Now, Mom, don't get excited, okay? He just happened to be at the bowling alley, and one thing led to another. I drove him back to campus is all." She broke into a brilliant smile. "Hi, Mitch!"

"Made it back safely, I see," he said, nodding toward the garage.

"Yep. Not a scratch." She slanted her mother a quick I-told-you-so glance that had Carly wanting to strangle her only child then and there.

"We'll talk later," she promised.

Sighing loudly, Tracy returned her attention to the man at her mother's side. "Mom didn't tell me you were famous," she said with a good try at righteous indignation.

"Probably because I'm not anymore."

Tracy passed that off as not worthy of comment. "All the guys on the team are talking about you, and when I told them you were going to be the new coach, they nearly busted a gut."

"Tracy Alderson, you had no right to tell them any such thing!" Carly exclaimed, frowning.

"Why not? It's true, isn't it?"

"It is *not*. Nothing's been signed."

Tracy's breezy grin disappeared. "Oh. That's too bad, because the guys were really excited. Especially Ian." She shifted her attention to Scanlon, her face lighting up again. "He thinks you walk on water."

His grin was rueful. "I admit I've learned to do things differently these past few years, but I can't even begin to think how I'd manage that."

Tracy giggled. "Where'd you guys go, anyway?"

"Gallagher's," Carly interrupted, anxious to head off a budding friendship between Scanlon and her daughter. "And it's late. Shouldn't you be catching up on all the sleep you've lost studying late this week?"

"Sounds like a plan," Tracy said, glancing from one to the other.

"Night, Sweetie," Carly murmured. "I'll be right up."

"Oh, that's okay. I'm really tired, so I think I'll just go right to bed. But you take all the time you want." Tracy bent to kiss her mother's cheek before aiming a dimpled smile in Mitch's direction.

"Night, Mitch."

"Good night, Tracy," Carly repeated, more firmly this time.

Tracy's expression said she got the message, thank you very much. "See you tomorrow," she tossed at both adults before skipping off like a five-year-old who was delighted with herself and the world around her.

Scanlon watched her for a long moment, a strange, almost wistful look in his eyes. "Ian doesn't know it yet, but he's in for a hell of struggle with that one."

Carly inhaled swiftly, but before she could blast him, he suddenly turned her way and grinned. "Don't fuss, Mom. I'm not criticizing your little girl, just stating facts. She's got a mind of her own. Like her mother."

"If you mean I've raised her to think for herself, yes, you're right. She's very independent. Most only children are."

"Why do I get the feeling your mother raised you to be just the opposite?"

"Because she did. I was supposed to follow her example and become the perfect 'woman behind the man.' It was a terrible disappointment to her when she realized she wasn't going to have a son and I was going to have to take over for my father someday."

He leaned against the fender of the Jag, and she wondered if he was tired. "Is that why you're always so serious?"

"You make it sound like a crime."

"No crime. I just like the way you smile." He touched his finger to the corner of her mouth. "I wish you'd do it more often."

"Don't," she grated.

Mitch saw confusion cloud her eyes. No, not confusion, he decided. There were shadows in her eyes, the kind he'd seen too many times before in the eyes of paraplegics not to recognize the pain. This woman had been badly hurt. Perhaps not physically, but hurt all the same. Mitch knew from experience that the only way she would ever come out a winner was to confront her demons, which in this instance seemed to be him.

"How about a nightcap?" he found himself asking on impulse, something he rarely did these days.

"No, thanks. I think I'll call it a night." She marched past him toward the house. Chuckling, he followed at his more deliberate pace. Stopping a few feet from the door, she opened her bag and felt for the house key she was certain she'd put there earlier.

"Problems?" he asked, coming up to her.

"No, I—"

"Good evening, Dr. Alderson." The man came out of the shadows, startling her into dropping her bag. It was Chad Duncan.

Mitch moved to stand between them, saying with deceptive softness, "A little late for a social call, isn't it, friend?"

"Good to meet you, Mitch," the guy said, holding out his hand. "I'm Duncan, *Bradenton Falls News-Times*."

Mitch acknowledged the outstretched hand with the quick lift of one eyebrow. "Something we can do for you?"

"An exclusive would be nice." Shrugging, Duncan lowered his outstretched arm. "Something along the lines of an unofficial announcement of your appointment as Bradenton's new football coach."

"Can't announce what hasn't happened."

Duncan's grin flashed. "Hey, I understand. You want to save if for the press conference."

The illumination from the security lights cast hard shadows on Scanlon's face, but Carly was suddenly certain that the dangerous glint in his eyes came from within. "What press conference?"

"The one Marca Kenworthy is so busy setting up. According to my inside sources, she's hoping to invite reps from the major networks and—"

"As Mr. Scanlon's already said, we haven't a clue what you're talking about," Carly interrupted. "And forgive me for pointing it out, but you're trespassing, Mr. Duncan."

Even though she'd spoken pleasantly, the reporter's expression turned ugly. "Don't play lady of the manor with me, Carly. I knew you way back when, remember? And just because I work for a hick paper doesn't mean I don't have contacts all over the country. Soon as I heard the bad boy of the NFL was up here getting the VIP tour of the campus, I knew. Good old Brady is about to get itself a real high profile, honest-to-God football coach."

"Even if you guessed right, no one much cares anymore about what I do or don't do," Mitch said with an easy shrug. "So if I were you, I'd check out those *inside* sources of yours again, Duncan. Sounds to me as if somebody somewhere is trying to set you up for a bad fall."

Duncan struck a cocky pose. "No offense, Scanlon, but you're bigger news now that you're crippled than you ever were healthy. People these days love stories like yours." He directed a pointed glance toward Scanlon's legs. "Bet those braces get damned heavy by the end of the day." He snapped his fingers. "Now that's a lead for you. A real tearjerker, if I do say so myself. Probably sell every damn paper we print."

Carly felt Scanlon stiffen, but his expression remained un-ruffled. "No comment," he said when Duncan arched an in-quiring eyebrow.

"Too bad. Guess I'll just have to go with what I've got."

Grinning smugly, he started to walk away, only to stop short when Carly called his name. "Perhaps we can find some com-mon ground, here," she said, all but choking on her words.

"I'm always willing to listen. What do you have in mind, sugar?"

"How about a broken nose, for starters?" Scanlon said even more quietly.

"Hey, no offense, big guy. Just trying to make a living here."

Carly laid a hand on Scanlon's forearm. "It's okay, Mitch. Chad and I go way back. He was the editor of our high school paper the year I graduated." Without giving him time to react, she turned again to Duncan. "Come to my office tomorrow at two. I'll arrange for Dr. Kenworthy to be there, as well."

"No can do, Carly. My deadline's noon."

"Ten o'clock, then. That should give you plenty of time."

His expression said he didn't like it. "I guess that'll work," he said grudgingly. "See you then."

Carly managed a polite smile, for once grateful to her mother for training her to be gracious under pressure. As soon as Duncan was out of sight, however, she let her smile fade.

"I see what you mean about the press," she muttered as soon as she heard a car start somewhere below.

"Proud of yourself?"

Needing time, she bent down to retrieve her bag. Without looking at him, she found the key and slipped it into the lock. She looked at him, then wished she hadn't.

His face was hard, his eyes cold. A shiver of fear sliced her spine, but she managed a small, defiant smile. "We'll talk in-side."

Safely inside, she left her bag on the foyer table and headed for the parlor, flipping on lights as she went. Her heels made a hollow sound on the hickory flooring, and her pulse thun-dered in her ears.

It was cold in the small room, and she opened the fire screen and used the poker to stir the ashes, hoping for a spark of life. It didn't surprise her when she found the fire had burned itself out. Giving up, she leaned the poker against the brick and turned to look at him.

"Okay, so we kept a few things from you."

"A few? Now that's rich. In spite of all those fine sounding words you threw at my head, you don't really give a damn about my coaching ability, do you? It's the name you want, not me. Isn't that about the size of it?"

She managed a quick breath. She was risking everything on these next few minutes. "You don't have coaching experience," she explained without audible emotion. "Without the name, there's no credibility. Surely you can see that."

"Funny thing about being screwed, Carly. Sometimes you enjoy it, and sometimes you don't."

Her skin paled. Her lips seemed to lose all color, as well, but her eyes held steady on his. "Bradenton's in trouble. Whatever I have to do to save it, I'll do."

"You're up front, I'll give you that." He leaned a bit on his crutches and studied her with deceptively lazy eyes. Like a big cat who knows his own power, she thought, he was taking his time coming in for the kill.

"Does Coach know about this scheme of yours?"

Carly swallowed. "Yes, he knows, but that wasn't why he suggested you for the job. He really thinks you'll make a terrific coach."

"And if he thought I'd make a lousy one, would you still have wanted me?"

It was on the tip of her tongue to offer a quick "no," but she knew him well enough to realize he wasn't the type to be easily misled. She settled for telling a half truth. "Our long-term goals require that we hire an excellent coach. Bradenton's Wolves need to *win*, Mr. Scanlon, and they won't accomplish that with lousy coaching."

He conceded the point with a nod. "But coaching skill alone isn't all you're looking for, is it?"

Carly swallowed again, this time around a lump of guilt. "No, not all," she admitted. "We need a big name, as well. I just said as much."

Scanlon's gaze held hers for a long, tense moment before he smiled coolly. "Were you going to tell me about this news conference you have planned, or just let me walk in cold with the cameras already rolling?'' His voice was that same rough purr she would always associate with him, but this time it sent chills skipping along her vertebrae.

"It's traditional to announce the hiring of a new football coach at a press conference—once the contract has been signed and witnessed." She refused to make excuses. He might not like what they had planned, but there was nothing illegal or immoral about it. Quite the reverse, in fact. What they were doing would benefit more than a few individuals.

"You're saying that Duncan was just blowing smoke? That this is just local, no national coverage, no big-name sports reporters? Nothing that would make a guy like me feel he's being put on display?''

Carly took a deep breath. It pained her to accept the brutal directness of his gaze, but she forced herself. "We need publicity to fill the stadium. I haven't lied to you about that, or about anything else. Bradenton's in serious financial trouble. I won't bore you with the details. Just believe me when I tell you our situation is critical.''

He looked disgusted. "Maybe what you need is an accountant, not a coach.''

"What I *need*, what *Bradenton* needs, is a way to make a lot of money fast. Traditional ways of raising capital take too much time, time we don't have. Marca and I were brainstorming one night, and then all of a sudden, it came to us. For four years every school in this part of the country has been ridiculing the Wolves. Everyone expects us to lose, even the players. What if we hired a high-profile coach, then snapped that losing streak and started winning? Wouldn't that cause a lot of talk? Wouldn't that arouse interest in football circles and in the press?''

He flexed his tired shoulders and wondered why he'd suckered himself into thinking this evening might have had a different ending.

"I've seen your team's stats, Carly. Knute Rockne himself couldn't work that kind of miracle, not even with Vince Lombardi and Iron Mike Ditka helping out.''

"No, but a lot of people would pay just to see Rockne or Lombardi on the sidelines." She paused to lend her next words emphasis. "Or Mitch Scanlon. And if we make enough on gate receipts and concession stand sales, we can buy the time we need to come up with a viable plan to restructure our debt." She needed a breath and took it. "If we can generate enough excitement, we might even have a shot at TV revenues."

Mitch went icy inside at the very thought of TV cameras following his every move.

"If you want excitement, you'll have to look someplace else," he told her coldly. "I'm not in that business anymore."

Carly felt her heart pounding. She didn't want to see the raw pain in his eyes. She didn't want to feel the terrible frustration eating at him. Right now, she had to think of Bradenton. Next to Tracy's safety and happiness, it had always been her number one priority. And Bradenton needed this man.

"Remember how Ian reacted to meeting you?" When he didn't answer, she laid a hand on his arm. "Didn't you see the respect in his eyes? You heard what Tracy said. The players are excited at the idea of Mitch Scanlon becoming their coach. That team needs someone like you to make them want to win."

For a moment he wanted desperately to believe her. No one had needed him in a long time. Not on the field. As rewarding as he found his work with the handicapped, it couldn't negate his love of football. No matter how many years he spent away from the sport, there would always be a side of him that yearned to be a part of it again.

Afraid to let himself want something that badly, Mitch straightened his shoulders and forced himself to think rationally. Dreams were fine for those who had some hope of attaining them. He didn't. Football was a part of his past. He had long since accepted that it could not be a part of his future. Why was he allowing this woman to make him start wishing differently? He shook off her hand. If she touched him again, he wanted it to be with affection, not because she wanted something from him.

"I'm not a coach. I'm just a guy who used to play football."

She drew a breath. "If you want more money—"

"I've got money." Though his voice was controlled, his hands were white where they gripped the crutches, and she realized that he had a far greater capacity for violence than she'd wanted to acknowledge.

"The challenge, then."

"Getting my pants on over these braces every morning, then off every night, is a challenge. Carrying a cup of coffee from the counter to the table without scalding myself is a challenge. And stairs, now there's a *real* fun challenge for you. In fact, I'm full up on challenges. One more doesn't hold much appeal."

Carly winced at the cold, factual tone. "Name your terms, then," she said, with as much composure as she could summon.

His slow grin mocked her. "Now that has possibilities. Let me give it some thought and get back to you."

Her eyes, usually so calm, blazed suddenly. "You do that," she shot back, her control finally stretched beyond all limits. "And while you're thinking, think about this. You have no coaching experience. Zilch. And you've been away from the game for almost six years. How many other offers have you had to coach lately?"

"You play dirty. I'll remember that."

"When I have to." She curled her hands into fists again, ignoring the stinging sensation of her nails scoring her flesh. "Time is short, Mr. Scanlon. You have until nine fifty-nine tomorrow morning to accept our offer. After that, I intend to tell Chad Duncan that you are no longer under consideration for the coaching position."

Without waiting for a response, she walked past him and out the door.

Chapter 7

Carly was exhausted, as emotionally spent as an accident victim after the blessed numbness of shock had worn off. Yet she couldn't sleep. No matter how tightly she tried to weld her eyes shut, they kept popping open.

Giving up, she switched on the light by the bed and picked up a book. If she couldn't relax herself into sleep, she would read until her eyes crossed and her mind shut down. Five minutes later, she closed the book and returned it to the night stand. Instead of words and phrases, she'd seen sorrow shimmering in a pair of golden brown eyes. Eyes with lines of pain and suffering etched into the corners, eyes that rarely smiled and never really lost their shadows even when they did.

And such sorrow, so deep, so raw, for a boy he'd known, sorrow for a boy he would never know, both of whom had somehow touched his heart.

As Mitch had touched hers.

It was such a little thing, really, just a much-handled scrap of cheap yellow paper with a name penned on one side. A boy's priceless treasure and, she suspected, as precious to the man that boy had become.

Why he'd kept it all those years didn't matter, though she was far more curious than she should be. What did matter was the unselfish generosity he'd displayed in giving it away.

Rubbing her stinging eyes with tired fingers, she tried to merge the image of the caring, sensitive man she'd glimpsed tonight with the picture of a soulless, unfeeling rapist, but the images refused to mesh.

Still, he had raped her. Hadn't she been helpless, trapped beneath his hard, massive body, pinned to the mattress by tough sinew and heavy muscle? And hadn't there been pain and blood? And a terrible feeling of humiliation?

It had taken long and tortuous months of therapy before she'd been able to let anyone touch her again. More months before she could date again. And still, there had been nights when she'd lain awake, rivers of tears flooding her eyes until they were swollen and stinging.

Hugging her knees, she drew a shaky breath and, for the first time in seventeen years, let her mind run freely over that night in the desert.

Yes, he'd been drunk, but he'd also been solicitous, even though he'd thought her far more experienced. Yes, his eyes had glittered with sexual hunger, yet his smile had had a shy curl when he'd asked her gruffly to go with him to his room. She'd been the eager one, the one to agree without hesitation, the one to lift her face to his for that first frantic kiss. A kiss that he'd quickly gentled as though he didn't want to rush her. And when he'd framed her face with those large powerful hands, she'd been astonished to feel them tremble.

It was only when she'd actually felt the insistent prodding of his hot, rigid body against her virginal flesh that she'd tried to push him away.

Of course, it had been too late.

Carly rested her chin on her knees and stared at the framed lithograph of a mother and child hanging on the wall. How could she have been so blind? So stubbornly sure she'd been the only victim in that steamy room?

She was a social anthropologist, for pity's sake. A woman who had studied the history of social customs and mores. A woman who had refused to see the truth when it was right in front of her.

Mother Nature had given the male primate more than a strong, willing body with which to woo the female of his choice. She'd also given him a blind, unthinking drive to consummate the sexual act no matter what. At eighteen, Carly had been hopelessly naive to think a young and virile man caught in those last, frenzied agonies of sexual excitement would even hear her anguished cries, let alone find the strength to stop, while millions of years of instinct were urging him on.

Carly cringed inwardly and, sitting straight and stiff, rubbed her hand over her suddenly hot cheeks. All those years, she'd thought him vile and disgusting, the worst sort of man. A monster.

"Oh no, no," she whispered, her voice raw. Such a simple little word, but she'd said it too late. Too late for Mitch, too late for herself—and too late for Tracy.

"Oh, baby, I'm so sorry," she whispered, turning to gaze at her favorite picture of Tracy when she'd been a toddler, wearing most of the chocolate cake Carly had made for her second birthday and grinning with pure joy into the camera. Tracy had been only a few months old when Carly had first seen reminders of Mitch on that tiny face. When Tracy had smiled for the first time, really smiled, Carly had seen echoes of Mitch's carefree grin, and she'd cried.

She cringed to remember how sorry she'd felt for herself, how she'd castigated him to her therapist in that oh, so self-righteous tone. It had been his fault, she'd cried, his selfishness. His insensitivity.

Of course he didn't deserve to know he'd become a father. Of course he didn't deserve to be a part of his daughter's life. The other women in her therapy group had wholeheartedly agreed.

"Dear God, what have I done?" she whispered, her voice raw.

Two seconds later she was up and out of bed, too wrought up to rest. Crossing the room, she slipped out of her nightshirt as she went, letting it fall to the carpet in a heap. She would swim until she was too tired to lift her arms. Perhaps then she could lose her guilt in the oblivion of sleep.

Since her tank suit was still in the downstairs bathroom, she would make do with her ratty old bikini, the one with the frayed straps.

She went down the back stairs and through the kitchen, her bare feet as silent as Tabitha's on the tile. The French doors were unlocked. Passing through, she left them ajar. Inside, the windows were steamy, turning the area around the pool into her own private haven.

She thought briefly of switching on the underwater lights, then decided that the gothic atmosphere of the outside lamps shining through the fogged windows suited her mood.

Dropping her towel on the table, she padded to the pool's lip. Crouching, she scooped water into her cupped hand and let it dribble through her fingers. The water was bathtub warm, its slight odor of chlorine oddly comforting. She'd worked out a lot of demons in that pool.

"Having trouble sleeping?"

She gasped, her gaze wildly searching the shadows at the far end. She saw him then, chest high in the water, arms stretched wide along the lip, half standing, half reclining. His crutches and braces were lying nearby, next to a blue robe.

"I didn't see you," she said, easing into a sitting position with her feet dangling over the side.

"Or you wouldn't have come in?" The flat, slick surface of the water gave his voice a vaguely hollow quality.

"I'm not afraid to face you, Mitch." She kicked at the water and watched ripples spread toward him. "Contrary to what you may think, I've been up front with you from the start." She let that hang there a moment, then decided that now probably wasn't the time to take up where they'd left off. He didn't seem so inclined, and she felt too emotionally battered to press. "What about you? How come you're not asleep?"

"Needed the exercise." His tone didn't invite comment. Relieved, she took a deep breath and slipped into the water. She clung for a moment to the lip, then pushed into a crawl. It took her almost half the pool before she found a rhythm she liked. Even then, her muscles were too tense to allow her to relax into it.

Usually she swam mindlessly, picturing herself as pure fluid energy. But tonight she was hard-pressed to do more than cut her way through the warm water. Because the six-foot wide pool was enough to accommodate only two lanes, she soon realized that Mitch was swimming laps along with her. She was faster, of course, but then, he had only those steely arms and strong chest muscles to pull himself through the water.

Finally winded beyond her lungs' ability to compensate, she stopped, gasping for air, her fingers splayed against the tile while her feet settled to the bottom.

The pool was designed for exercise, not play, and the depth was a uniform four and a half feet. When she stood erect, the water lapped at the swell of her breasts, and she shivered as the cooler air hit her bare shoulders.

Gradually the burning in her chest stopped, allowing her to breathe normally. Lifting her head, she saw that he had also stopped and was sitting on the steps in the corner, looking dangerously appealing with his hair slicked down and water beading on his wide, tanned chest.

He'd been lean in his playing days, his muscles sharply defined, his chest wide, his belly flat. Since then, he'd packed more bulk onto his large frame, especially in the shoulders and upper arms. Imagining herself wrapped in those big arms had her growing warm inside before she locked down the thought.

"I owe you an apology."

Carly could only stare at him, the quiet *slap-slap* of the small waves the only sound in the enclosure.

"Apology for what?" she asked warily.

"For blowing up at you earlier. I acted like a spoiled kid who got mad because Santa only brought half the goodies he asked for." He moved closer, the water, stirred by his body, washing over her breasts.

She held on to the side and let her body float. "It seems to me we both want the same thing. You want to coach, and we want you to coach."

He acknowledged that with a nod. "This place must mean a lot to you."

"With the exception of my daughter, it's the most important thing in the world to me."

"Because it was founded by your family?"

"Partly. And partly because it's a very special place. People really care about each other here. They always have, which is one of the reasons we don't have oodles of money in the bank. We had a day-care center for faculty and students before any of the big colleges. And we had wheelchair ramps and special accommodations for the blind way back when I was a student here. It's not just the tangible things, either, but the sense of community we have.'' She drew a long breath. "If I could coach the team myself, I would. I'd even put on pads and play, if that would fill up all those empty seats, but it won't.''

"I'd come.'' His grin was restrained, scarcely more than a brief curving of those hard lips, and yet it had butterflies taking flight just below her sternum.

For an instant she felt as young and giddy as Sarah—until she reminded herself that Sarah had existed only in her imagination. Carly, the person she actually was, didn't indulge in flights of fancy.

"I had a phys ed teacher once tell me that I had the worst case of left-footitis she'd ever seen.'' She wiped the water from her face and ran her fingers through her dripping hair. "Swimming's the only thing I can do sportswise that doesn't cause people to fall down laughing.''

His mouth moved. "Life can be a bitch when you're a kid.''

"It wasn't fair, that's for sure. I was trying as hard as I could, and still I never once got above a C in P.E. Kept me from getting a 4.0 and the sports car my father promised me.''

Mitch watched her eyes cloud and wondered why. "So you bought your own.''

"Eventually—after I paid back all my student loans.''

He glanced around pointedly. "Cash flow problems?''

"No, Father and I had a difference in priorities.''

He took a chance and guessed. "Tracy?''

She glanced down, smoothing the water with a quick nervous movement of her hand. "He wanted to hide me away someplace until I had the baby, then give her up for adoption.''

Following her example, he stretched his arms along the lip of the pool and let himself float. Since he'd been at Bradenton, he'd missed his twice-daily swims in the spa pool. It felt good to get out of the braces and still be able to move around.

"How old were you when you had her?''

"Eighteen.''

"Must have been rough,'' he said, damn sure he wouldn't have had the guts at eighteen to do what she'd done.

"More like traumatic," she said, her voice flavored with humor. "I was extremely emotional in those days."

"And now?"

"And now I'm the serene, unflappable Dr. Alderson who rules Bradenton with a fist of iron," she murmured, only half kiddingly. She did have a reputation as a hardnose when it came to standards and discipline.

"A fist of iron, huh?" Reaching out a hand, he took hers and balanced it on his palm. "No, I don't think so," he said, curling his fingers around hers. "More like velvet."

Her mouth dropped open, and he chuckled. "Didn't know I was a poet, did you?"

He tugged her closer. Carly knew that to resist him would reveal just how vulnerable she felt.

"I still don't," she muttered.

His shout of laughter reverberated around the enclosure, and she felt her heart take an extra beat. "Looks like you're determined not to be impressed, no matter what tack I try with you."

"I've been swept off my feet before," she said with perfect honesty. "It's not an experience I care to repeat."

"Then I'm the guy for you, because there's no way in hell I can do that."

"Somehow I think you'd find a way if you really wanted to."

He grinned, but his eyes were shadowed and somber. "Cards on the table, Carly. Does my being crippled turn you off? Is that why you keep putting up a big Off Limits sign around me?"

Because he didn't wince at the term, she didn't either. "No, your being crippled doesn't bother me."

His gaze didn't waver. Hers did, but not for the reason she knew he must think.

"That's not what I asked," he said, a slight edge to his voice this time. She knew exactly what he was angling for, but she also knew that to tell him the truth would take them in a direction that terrified her.

"No," she stated flatly, tugging her hand free. Only a romantic fool would feel disappointed that he let her go. And she was no fool. "Your disability doesn't turn me off, but your lifestyle does."

"I won't deny I had a good time when I was a kid. More than a good time. I've grown up some since then." He splayed one large hand over his heart and looked boyishly contrite. She wasn't fooled. Scanlon was all man, and she was far too aware of the response he seemed capable of stirring in her.

"You've gotten older. There's a difference between that and growing up."

Again he laughed. "There'd sure as hell better be. I'd hate to think I was still the same horse's ass who bought into all the hype."

"Ah, so that's your excuse. You were just a naive kid?" Even as she spoke, Carly hated herself for her mocking tone. Who was she to be snide? God knew, she'd made her own share of mistakes, and most of them could be laid at the door of inexperience.

"No excuse. Fact." He studied her face intently, a frown slowly gathering in his eyes. "But I can see you don't believe me," he said slowly, as though feeling his way. "And I'm beginning to think that has more to do with you than me."

His hand came up to cup her waist, and she flinched. "Don't," she whispered.

"You don't like to be touched?"

Wary of revealing too much, she settled for saying, "That depends, I guess, on who's doing the touching."

He slid his hand to the small of her back and pulled her closer. "If I look hard enough, I can still see that scared eighteen-year-old unwed mother in your eyes."

"I doubt it," she murmured. Her nerves were humming. He was getting too close. Too personal.

"Why didn't you get Tracy's father to marry you?"

"None of your business." She brought a hand to his chest, determined to push him away. It was time they ended this game they were playing. But his chest was immovable, a wall of steely muscle and unyielding sinew.

"Did you love him?" he asked softly, his expression taut, as though the answer really mattered.

"Even if I did, he didn't love me. And I knew he never would." Admitting that aloud hurt, even now.

"And you were too proud to live with a man who didn't love you." He smiled. "I don't blame you. Charity's hard to accept under the best of circumstances."

Her senses were beginning to fog. It wasn't a comfortable feeling. Or particularly safe.

"Mitch, it's late."

"I have this problem, Carly." His hand tightened, and then, before she could guess his intent, she found herself sitting on his lap. "I've tried to shake it," he whispered, "but so far, no luck."

She didn't like the glint in his eyes, and for sure she didn't like the warm little waves of longing that assailed her senses. "I think I heard that before."

He gave a low laugh, but its husky vibrancy did little to lighten the tension. "Really?"

"Really. I believe I suggested a cure."

"Castor oil? No way." His mouth found hers, and her mind went blank, all her senses retreating in protective shock. And then, like a sleep-numbed limb coming alive, she felt everything at once. Not the pain or the fear and shame she might have expected, but a white, hot insidious desire she seemed powerless to resist. Not when there was so much hunger in his kiss. So much wild, sweet yearning in her body.

Shivering with pleasure, it took all her concentration to brace her hands against his massive chest to push him away. Then, as though they had a will of their own, her fingers curled over his broad shoulders. In the back of her mind, she knew history was repeating itself, and what was even worse, this time she couldn't blame her response to him on beer. She was perfectly sober, nearly two decades more mature, and, God help her, she still couldn't resist him.

Did you love him, Mom? Tracy's question whispered through Carly's mind as she pressed closer to the warmth of Mitch's body. Earlier this evening, when Tracy had asked that question, she'd felt so distanced from the naive, eighteen-year-old girl she'd once been. Now, encircled by this man's strong arms once more, the years seemed to fall away. Overwhelming attraction? The right chemistry? Rationally, Carly knew it could be nothing else. But that didn't lessen the impact Mitch had on her senses. Love at first sight existed only in fairy tales.

She would be the first to admit that. But neither could she deny that some feelings defied explanation.

He drew a hand up her side, his fingertips tracing each of her ribs and searing a path over her skin. Without realizing it, she must have stiffened, for he froze suddenly and whispered huskily against the corner of her mouth, "Carly? Are you all right?"

Taking on light from the windows, his eyes seemed to glow as he searched her gaze. Carly had a feeling he could see far more than she wanted to reveal. A word from her was all it would take, and he would release her. But was that what she wanted? Or did she want more of his drugging kisses? More of those tender caresses?

Shifting the position of his hand on her face, he lightly dragged his thumb over her mouth, his gaze fixed on the sensitive flesh at the inside of her bottom lip. When he slowly lowered his head, she knew he meant to kiss her again.

One heartbeat, two heartbeats. If she meant to protest, she had to do it now. No waiting this time until it was too late. She'd learned the hard way that with Mitch, you shouldn't play with the fire unless you expected to get burned.

"Ah, Carly..." he whispered in a gravelly voice. "I don't know what that bastard did to you, but, trust me, I won't hurt you. I swear I won't, sweetheart. Just relax."

She closed her eyes at the sensation of his mouth on hers, unable to breathe, unable to think. Memories, the present. The two swirled inside her mind, entwining, becoming a jumble. There was a part of her that couldn't entirely forget the past. The pain, the fear, the sick feeling of helplessness. But there was another part of her that was very much anchored in the present and filled with a wild, sweet yearning that only this man could slake.

When his mouth retreated, she murmured a dazed protest. At the sound, his eyes heated, and then, before she quite guessed his intent, his hand was against her spine, urging her closer, then closer still, until she was pressed intimately against him. His body was lean, hard where the muscles had been honed to springy steel, his skin radiating masculine heat more seductive to a tired body and soul than the heated water.

Like a man starved too long to ration himself, he explored her throat, her shoulder, the upper swell of her breast, his mouth hot on her skin. At the same time, he was painstakingly gentle, his callused palm making lazy circles on her belly until her skin was quivering beneath his. Methodically, relentlessly, he was building fires faster than she could put them out.

Summoning her voice to protest, she heard herself moaning instead, lost in the exquisite sensation of his hungry mouth on her hot skin. Nearly mindless, she arched back suddenly, needing air. His mouth skimmed her cheekbone, her temple. When his tongue plunged into her ear, she caught her breath and moaned again.

Suddenly the wall of the pool was at her back, and the breadth of his chest held her anchored.

"Tell me you want me," he demanded hoarsely, his eyes nearly bronze in the dim light. Unable to speak, she stared up at him, her heart pounding.

Against her thighs, she felt the hard bulge of his arousal. Heat, an insistent pressure. Oh, dear God... Only the cloth of her suit and his separated them. What had been pleasure an instant ago now turned to terror.

Panic burst someplace in her head, and then she was struggling, pushing hard at the arms that encircled her. Instantly, he relaxed his hold, but not before her nails raked his biceps, drawing thin bloody lines against the deep tan.

No! Don't, please, don't.

Mitch jerked backward, his passion-drugged mind struggling to make sense of her reaction. Seizing her by both arms, he held her away from him, his gaze searching her face.

Her eyes glittered like a wild woman's—not with tears, but rage. "I said no," she ground out, her voice trembling violently. "I meant no."

He stared at her, not quite believing what he was seeing. Or hearing. His own temper spiked, and then he saw the black terror behind her rage. Ready to slam something, anything, to ease the frustration raging inside him, he forced himself to grow calm.

"Think a minute," he said, his voice rough, but quiet. "Did you say no, or only think it?"

She stared at him, her eyes slowly regaining their focus. Like a sleepwalker, she shook her head, realizing too late that she was confusing the past with the present. What to say? She hadn't had a panic attack in years. But then, she hadn't come this close to having sex in years, either.

"I . . . you're right," she admitted, her voice quavery. "It was—I let—you were just—I let you think—"

He touched a fingertip to her mouth. "Carly, don't. It's all right, really. And it sure as hell isn't your fault. A woman has a right to change her mind. It happens."

She flinched, her thoughts turning chaotic again.

"Want to talk about it?"

"There's nothing to talk about. I changed my mind, and he . . . didn't."

"The bastard raped you?"

She heard the horror in his tone and felt a rush of emotion—some of which she could identify, some of which she could not. Not trusting her voice, she nodded.

"Tracy's father?"

She nodded again, then added tersely, "Please don't ask me any more questions, because I don't want to talk about that time—or that man—ever again."

He accepted that unquestioningly. "Want a hug?" he asked with a hint of humor in his deep voice.

"No, I want to sink under the water and drown," she murmured with absolute sincerity.

"No you don't, honey." His smile was so gentle she could only stare. Who was this man?

"Come here. Let me hold you a minute." Before she could answer, he put his fingers very carefully against her lips again. "I know, you don't want a hug, but I do."

Maybe, just maybe, she could have ignored the words, if only he hadn't smiled quite so self-consciously as he held his arms wide. But the need for human warmth, for an undemanding touch—those she understood.

"Just a tiny one, okay?"

Mitch heard the faint tremor in her voice and wished to heaven and hell he had five minutes alone with the guy who'd done this to her. Instead, he swallowed the questions that would only have her diving into that polite shell he was coming to hate.

"Your call all the way." He watched her eyes and saw the infinitesimal change that said she'd decided to trust him just a little. His breath hitched in his chest as he guided her head to the hollow of his shoulder and closed his arms loosely around her small, soft body.

At first she held herself stiffly, refusing to yield to the temptation to snuggle against him. But his warmth and the slow, even, undemanding cadence of his breathing lulled her into relaxing bit by bit until she was leaning into him, supported only by his wide chest.

She sighed, and the soft curling hair on his chest fluttered. "Tickles," he murmured over her head. "I like it."

Gingerly she touched the scratch marks she'd left on his muscular arm. "I'm sorry, really sorry," she said achingly.

"Some guys get notches on their bedposts. I get battle scars." He let that hang there a second. "Be honest, all right? Do you think it's my technique?"

She chuckled, then let her eyes fall closed. "I'd say it was more just bad timing."

"Bite your tongue. I've had some extremely knowledgeable people tell me that my timing is faultless."

"With a football, maybe," she came back with another laugh.

Only then did his big hand begin to stroke her back in a slow, reassuring rhythm. "Like that?" he asked in a low husky tone that rippled like pleasure through her.

"Mmm."

She heard him chuckle, but she was too drowsy to do more than curve her lips in a smile she knew he couldn't see. He nuzzled her hair with his chin, then tucked her more firmly against him and began to talk about growing up in California, learning to surf and the countless times he'd been dumped by a wave too big and too wild for his skill. About the fear and exhilaration of tumbling over and over in the same wave, not knowing whether he was up or down, and nearly drowning a time or two, before he'd been able to stay on the board. "Looking back, I can't count the times, about halfway through a wave, that I wished I'd never waded into the water," he admitted with a rueful chuckle.

He ran his hand up to her nape and stroked the hair there, his fingertips dragging lightly on the silken curls. "There's nothing quite like the panic a person feels when they're caught up in something frightening and discover they're helpless to make it stop."

Carly squeezed her eyes more tightly closed, suddenly and acutely aware that he was trying in the only way he knew to let her know he understood how she'd felt a few moments ago. An aching lump lodged itself in her throat. "I'm sorry," she said in a thin, taut voice.

"I don't want you to feel sorry." He cupped her chin and lifted her face. After searching her gaze, he said, "I never would have ridden a big wave clear to the finish if I hadn't forced myself to climb back on my surfboard, Carly."

She felt her mouth quiver as she said, "Sort of like climbing back on the horse after it throws you?"

He flashed a sheepish grin. "Something like that, only somehow I don't think riding a horse can compare to topping a wave and flying with the wind. By the same token, I don't suppose flying with the wind can compare to making love."

The promise in his eyes was unmistakable, and something within Carly responded. She wanted so badly to ask him to show her how glorious making love could be, but she didn't have the courage.

In the end, he settled the matter by dipping his head to kiss her again. Lightly, cautiously, keeping his hold on her relaxed. The fact that he was taking such care not to alarm her was reassuring. Against her better judgment, she rested her weight against him, and once again, his hands began to caress her skin, tantalizing her senses, making it difficult for her to think.

As he traced burning kisses over her throat, he whispered to her, talking about the surf and how terrified he'd been to try another wave, how he'd taken to floating on the board, letting the swells lull him, reacquainting himself with the water until he felt comfortable with it again.

Only fools got themselves in too deep. Into dangerous waters. Suddenly, like a wisp of warm air, the past slipped away, and she opened her mouth to his kiss, no longer capable of holding herself back.

She expected him to immediately deepen the kiss, to take what she offered with hungry urgency. But instead, he lulled her until she felt comfortable, surrounding her with warmth, lightly teasing her skin with his fingertips, carefully exploring the recesses of her mouth. His fingers curled around hers, and his thumb rubbed her wrist.

"I can't guarantee exhilaration, Carly. But I can promise I won't do anything to make you regret this."

She felt her lips tremble into a smile. "I'll settle for that."

He kissed her again, giving her time to retreat. Only she didn't want to. Not when his mouth was doing such sweet things to hers.

She felt him move, felt him lean backward slightly to use the steps behind him as a support. And then, slowly, his hands slid up her arms to frame her face. He lifted his mouth one more time, as though savoring the taste of her. When his lips settled over hers again, there was no hesitation. His mouth took hers completely, drawing in the taste of her breath by breath.

Afraid that her knees would buckle, she clung to his shoulders and felt the burning fatigue in her muscles fade as pleasure washed over her, as heady as anything she'd ever experienced.

She was no longer a giddy small-town girl grasping for a dream. And he was no longer that selfish, careless boy without a worry in the world. Her body trembled as it strained against his. The doubts in her mind slipped away. She would think later. Much later.

Mitch knew the moment she decided to completely trust him. Her body lost the last of its resistance, melting against his until he was certain she had to feel the pounding of his heart. Like a drowning man losing his last hold on the sky, he was being pulled down into her until all he felt was her warmth, her softness.

Years of self-discipline, of loneliness, of doubt slipped away into the vortex of need inside him. Holding her, losing himself in her sweetness, he felt whole again. Invincible.

A shudder ran through him, and he knew that he was close to the edge. Close to feeling an emotion he'd never felt before. Too close. But he couldn't seem to let her go. Not when it felt so good to hold her.

Suddenly she was aware of the extent of his need, not so easily hidden as hers. Nor as easily denied. But it was exultation that filled her, not fear. It was different, somehow, feeling him through the material of his trunks. More erotic.

She moaned, feeling a sweet, unfamiliar pressure building inside her. He touched her everywhere, his hands gentle, his concentration absolute. She arched and twisted, sensation building upon sensation, her hands clenching in his hair.

The water slapped the tiles, and the scent of chlorine teased her nostrils with every gasping breath. With every stroke of his fingers, every erotic pressure of his mouth, he was sensitizing her inch by inch, until she was mindless with the deepest, warmest pleasure.

Like a dance for perfectly mated partners, he took her soaring, stripping her out of the bikini top between long drugging kisses. And then, like an artist suddenly confronting a masterpiece, he stared down at her, his face tortured with emotion. Without hesitation, she lifted a hand to his face and caressed his cheek until the worst of the tension eased.

Mitch kissed the corner of her mouth and felt her tremble. He had no words to describe the feelings running through him. He only knew he was slowly, surely losing part of himself to her with each kiss, each sigh. Feeling her sweet, trusting response had him dizzy with emotions so powerful he was stunned. It was such a precious gift, her trust, especially since he knew how dearly it had cost her.

"I'm losing ground fast," he murmured, his voice thick with passion. "I want to make love to you, but I didn't exactly come in here prepared for this."

"You're not the only one," she whispered, her smile shaky.

"I can't make you pregnant, and I don't have anything you can catch, but if you want me to use a condom, tell me now while I can still stop."

His face was tight, his eyes dark with a need so strong it seemed to reach out to her. If, in those long-ago nightmares, she'd been afraid of him, that fear was gone now. And when she'd been so busy hating him, she'd been hating someone who didn't really exist. He had made some mistakes, yes, but so had she. They were both older and wiser now.

Even so, she had to be crazy to want this man, she told herself through a haze of desire. Crazier still to think that the history between them no longer mattered. She couldn't love him. She *wouldn't* love him. But perhaps allowing herself to feel pleasure at his touch was the last little bit of healing she needed to put the past behind her once and for all.

"Carly? Do you want me to stop?"

In answer, she offered her lips, greeting the thrust of his tongue with her own. And then his mouth was skimming her throat, his tongue trailing fire over her skin.

Slowly his hands stroked her thighs wider, her small eager gasps filling the lonely places inside him. His fingers dipped beneath her bikini bottom to tangle in the wet ringlets between her thighs, and just as she had earlier, she cried out at the pleasure.

"Easy, sweetheart," he murmured, his voice thick with strain and his own need to be touched. She clung to him, her head thrown back, her throat creamy in the hazy light. He didn't want to frighten her again, but, God help him, he couldn't stand much more of this.

He maneuvered until she was riding his hips. His body was already engorged and ready as he pushed aside the material of his trunks.

Her skin was hot where he pressed, and slick from the water and her own arousal. Watching her face for any sign of panic, he eased into her, so ready it took all of his control and force of will to keep from burying himself inside her with one hard thrust.

Carly leaned forward, her fingers clutching his shoulders for support as a new and unbearable ache built inside her. He was filling her slowly, inexorably, and she loved the feel of him inside her. She couldn't breathe, couldn't think, couldn't feel anything but the glorious spiraling pleasure.

And then in one blinding, cataclysmic moment, she was filled with him and the world was spinning in a vortex of sensation and joy. The climax took her by surprise, and she cried out as wave after wave of pleasure shuddered through her. She was spinning, soaring, and then she was being crushed against him.

His body shuddered. Clinging to him, she pressed her face against his strong throat and wrapped her legs around him.

Melted against him like this, she knew what rapture meant for the first time. Pure, delicious, enveloping bliss. She was at peace, the shame and humiliation and heartache forgotten. She wanted to laugh and cry and hug him so tight he would never get away.

"Oh, Mitch..." She wanted to tell him how sorry she was for having misjudged him for so many years, but to do that would be to draw back curtains on a truth she wasn't quite ready to discuss.

He murmured her name in response, his face against her throat, his skin damp and hot, his hand stroking her back. She listened to the sturdy thud of his heart as their breathing slowly returned to normal. Then she drifted, too spent to move, utterly relaxed. She felt safe, and so marvelous, so cherished. The surprise came slowly, like the first breath of a spring breeze. He was holding her as though she were precious to him. As though he couldn't bear to let her go.

A smile curved her lips, and she heard him murmur her name again. "Mmm?"

"Much as I hate to let you go, I think it's time you scooted upstairs." She sighed, knowing that he was right. Just because she was blissfully unaware of the passage of time, that didn't mean it had come to a stop. She had no idea how long they'd been lying there, buoyed by the gently lapping water, but she guessed it had been quite a while. Thirty minutes, possibly even an hour. Every second she lingered here, there was a greater risk of discovery. In spite of that, she couldn't quite bring herself to move.

"In a minute," she murmured, snuggling closer.

Mitch felt a lump the size of a regulation football in his throat. He'd made love to a lot of women, but he'd never felt such contentment afterward. It was as though he'd finally come home after a lifetime of searching, and he didn't want this closeness to end any more than she did.

Shutting his eyes, he pulled her nearer and wished that he could magically be whole again. Just long enough to carry her to his bed. Not to make love, but to sleep together, wrapped in each other's arms. The mere thought of holding her all night long had him aching inside with need.

"Carly, don't fall asleep on me, honey. It's only a guess, but I don't think your mother and Tracy are ready for that kind of a wake-up surprise."

Carly sighed and sat up. She couldn't resist kissing the corner of his mouth, so controlled now. "I have a feeling you're right about that," she murmured, winning a lopsided smile that had her heart turning over.

With apparent reluctance, he let her go. Just as reluctantly, she moved off his lap and looked around for the top to her bikini. It took her a moment to snag it.

Quickly, aware that he was watching her with an absorbed look on his face, she put it on, her fingers fumbling with the hook in the back.

"Very nice," he said, his eyes smoldering. "If you ever get tired of running Bradenton, you can always start a second career as a swimsuit model."

"No thanks," she said, leaning forward to kiss him. "I'm happy where I am."

He held her shoulders and kissed her a half dozen times. "Good night, sweet Caroline. Pleasant dreams."

He let her go with a hesitancy that disarmed her, then watched while she hoisted herself from the pool to pad across the tile and collect her towel. Without looking back, she pushed through the French doors and disappeared.

Chapter 8

Mitch had been deep in a dream of Carly when he woke to hear banging at his door. "It's open," he mumbled into his pillow. When the pounding continued, he called more loudly, "It's open, damn it."

The door swung inward, and Carly stalked in on bare feet, waving the portable phone at him. "For you," she muttered, handing him the receiver. Her hair was tousled, and she had the sleepy-eyed look of an extremely annoyed lady. He was pretty sleepy himself, but not sleepy enough to keep from noticing how desirable she looked.

"Who is it?" he said, pushing himself to a sitting position with his free hand.

"Someone named Scott. He didn't deign to give me a last name, just ordered me to 'give that no-good SOB a nudge and put him on the phone.' Obviously he has an utterly erroneous impression of our sleeping arrangements. And another thing, how did you get the number of my private phone?"

"From Tracy. I was using the phone in the kitchen when she decided to raid the refrigerator. Seems she was cramming for a final exam, poor kid." Mitch glanced at the clock, saw that it was half past five and figured he'd managed three hours of sleep. "I've pulled a few all-nighters myself—not that it helped much." He grinned at the memory of those late-night study sessions. He'd slept more than he'd studied, sitting up at the desk with his book open in front of him.

"You still haven't told me why Tracy gave you my private number," she said impatiently, clearly unimpressed with his former study habits.

"Seems to me that's a question you'll have to ask her."

Her mouth firmed. "Scanlon, I have limited patience under the best of circumstances, which these most definitely are not."

Mitch relented. "When I was talking to Scotty—this was around two a.m., you understand, and I'd gotten him out of bed—he asked for a number where he could reach me, and since there wasn't one on the phone I was using, I asked Tracy."

"But—"

"Later." Mitch cleared his throat, pressed the button and spoke into the receiver, his gaze never leaving hers. Carly in a temper in the morning was almost more than one lovesick guy could handle.

"You better have good news, old buddy." As he listened to the caller's reply, his grin spread, and Carly could see that he was clearly pleased with what he was hearing.

"Yeah . . . okay, wait, I'll find out." His gaze met hers, and she felt a definite shiver. "Where's the nearest TV station?"

"Medford.

"How far from here?"

"Twenty minutes south. Why?"

"In a minute," he promised, before repeating what she'd just told him into the phone. "How the hell do I know? Hang on. . . ." Frowning, he looked at her again. "Call letters?"

She had to think a minute, then recited them slowly. As he talked, it dawned on her that he was talking to the guy on the other end about giving an interview.

Her heart started racing, and her mouth went dry. By the time he hung up after promising to call back within the hour, she was biting her lip.

He tossed the phone to the foot of the bed before using both hands to hitch himself higher against the headboard.

"Scott who?" she asked.

"Scott Bendix, CableSports. Ever hear of him?"

"Of course I've heard of him, Scanlon. Everyone's heard of him and his megamillion-dollar contract."

Grinning like a kid anticipating Christmas, he patted the bed beside him. "Make yourself comfortable, honey. Gives me a crick in my neck having to look up at you."

"If I do, will you tell me what that phone call was all about?"

"Cross my heart."

She snorted, but sat. "Okay, talk."

He intended to, but first he treated himself to a long look. She would be a dream to wake up with, soft and warm and just a little grumpy.

"I slept great. How about you, bright eyes?"

"Fine—until your buddy *Scotty* woke me out of a sound sleep. He *said* you'd told him to call early." She poked him hard in the chest, and he winced.

"You know how those guys on the East Coast think—everyone should run on eastern time. Give him credit for waiting until it was eight-thirty in New York to call." He kept his gaze lowered while he idly played with the sash of her robe and wondered what she had on under it.

"I'll give you a cracked rib if you don't tell me what's going on."

Making a mental note to wake her up early again some time when he could put that feisty temper to better use, he relented.

"Here's the way I figure it. Duncan's going to break the story anyway, so we get a jump on him by giving Scotty an exclusive. He figures he can clear air time at noon their time." He grinned. "Nine our time, in case you're confused."

"An interview about what?" she asked cautiously.

"About Bradenton and the farsighted, brilliant decision made recently by the administration."

"You mean the one about trying to save Artemus's beloved elevator?"

His mouth slanted. "No, Ms. Smarty, the one about hiring one Mitchell Steven Scanlon as head football coach, effective immediately." He indicated the contract on the nightstand, the one he'd signed before he'd turned in. "Scotty thinks you should be interviewed, too, along with Coach, of course."

She had a moment of pure relief before she managed to corral it behind a thoughtful frown. "Certainly Coach should be with you, but I fail to see the reason for my presence."

"Moral support?"

"Are you kidding? If Coach can turn my mother into jelly with his gift of gab, he can talk to God himself and never flinch."

His mouth twitched. "Not for Coach. For me."

Carly made a very unladylike sound that had him lifting one eyebrow. "We've already discussed the kind of moral support you want."

He clucked his tongue. "Carly, you wound me. Here I am, admitting to a bad case of camera fright, and you belittle me. Shame on you."

She managed to keep her lips from curving. "How many times have you been interviewed on TV?"

"A few."

"Dozens? Hundreds?"

He cursed himself for starting this. She had a way of making him go too far, too fast on a lot of things against his better judgment.

"Never kept track."

She arched an eyebrow. "You mean you don't have row after row of videotapes of yourself?"

"Used to. Gave 'em all to UCLA. I hear they use 'em to show rookie quarterbacks what *not* to do."

"You mean you gave them copies."

"Nope. Originals." He lifted a hand to flip a curl away from her cheek.

"Why would you do that?"

"'Cause I like to touch your hair. It's soft. Smells good, too."

She frowned. "No, why did you give your tapes away?"

His gaze dropped, and he ran one hand lightly over his thigh. She couldn't help noticing how pitifully thin his legs looked under the sheet. Catching her looking at his legs had his mouth tightening.

"When I finally got it through my head that I wasn't going to play again, I put that part of my life behind me. Moved out of the media fishbowl to a quiet little suburb of Sacramento, started my business with Dante. Tried to forget all about football."

"You really didn't watch the Super Bowl, did you?"

His eyes grew cool. "Did you think I was lying to you?"

"I thought you were being a smart-ass," she admitted, wishing she'd never initiated this line of conversation.

His grin flashed, catching her by surprise. "I *am* a smart-ass. Picked up the habit as a kid. I've tried to kick it, but no luck."

She couldn't quite prevent her lips from curving this time. "At least you admit it. That's a start."

"So they tell me."

Mitch glanced at his travel alarm. It was getting close to six. He needed to get his butt out of bed and into the tub. He had a fleeting urge to ask her to join him before reality intruded.

"By the way, I don't recall getting a good morning kiss," he said, letting his gaze rest on her mouth.

"Mitch, about last night, I'm not usually so impulsive." Carly kept her gaze fixed on the small silver medal dangling from a heavy chain around his neck.

"Okay."

She nudged her gaze higher. Dark with stubble, his strong jaw had more than a promise of stubbornness, and at the moment, those brooding eyes had a rogue's twinkle. "What I mean is—"

"I know what you mean." He tugged on her sash and earned himself a fast little frown. "You found yourself attracted to a man you're not sure you even like all that much. It's got you spooked, and you want to back off. Is that about it?"

She blinked. "Well, yes...no. I mean, I want you to back off. I don't have casual affairs."

"Caroline, believe me, there's nothing casual about you. Or, for that matter, about how I feel about you."

"You don't even know me, Scanlon." Because she had her mind made up to be friendly but cautious, she smiled. "And I don't know you."

"Only my reputation, remember?" His voice was gently rebuking. "But that's okay. We can deal with that." As he took her hand, he fought down a need to pull her closer. "And now, bright eyes, you'd better get the heck out of here and into something presidential for the camera."

"Now, Mitch—"

"Waste of time arguing with a man who's working hard at being a gentleman, which is damn near impossible when he's sitting buck naked in bed with a very sexy lady less than an arm's length away."

She fought a sudden rush of heat. "I'll meet you out front at seven-thirty," she murmured. "Don't be late."

"Call Coach, okay? Fill him in."

Nodding, she got to her feet, and though he'd told her to leave, he let her go reluctantly, his fingers trailing along her arm like a caress.

"Hey, Alderson," he called, when she was about to reach for the door handle. "Here, catch."

The phone came arching toward her a split second before she saw it. Somehow she managed to pluck it out of the air before it hit the floor.

"Good hands, but the attitude could use a little work."

She couldn't resist a smile, so she didn't. "I'll keep that in mind . . . Coach," she said, and then left.

Mitch felt the laughter in his mind fade as quickly as it had come. It wasn't easy to accept the power she had over him. Nor to admit that there were major obstacles to be overcome before he could find out how far he could travel this particular road.

His friend Dante had told him that he would turn a corner some day and come up against a woman he wouldn't be able to blast out of his mind.

"Take my word for it, Scanlon, you'll be in for the biggest fight of your life, trying your damnedest not to fall in love with her for her own good," Jess had said with that smug look on his face. "Only it won't work, not if she's the right one, so you might as well save yourself a lot of sleepless nights and enjoy the ride."

Easy for Jess to say, with a wife like Hazel snuggling up against him every night and a house full of kids climbing all over him when he came home after work.

Leaning forward, he touched his toes and felt the tight muscles of his back give centimeter by centimeter until almost all of the tension was gone. Crutch walking was harder on the back than most people knew. Hard on the ego, too, he thought, straightening slowly.

No sob stuff, he'd warned Scotty.

Agreed. But people will want to know how you're doing, Mitch. It's the flip side of the cheers.

Scowling, he tossed off the sheet and stared at his legs. He'd almost gotten used to the scrawny look of his body from mid-thigh down. Maybe that was why he'd let himself forget how repulsive he could be to a woman.

In spite of the pep talk he'd given himself after Carly had left the pool, he still wasn't all that sure she could handle every aspect of his handicap. He'd seen the way her eyes had slid away from his legs only a few minutes ago.

Hell, maybe she should have caught him struggling into his braces when she'd walked in. Given her a good look at just how helpless he really was. And given him a chance to watch her reaction.

It might almost have been worth the slam to his ego to find out now if she couldn't deal with the daily struggles and indignities he'd been forced to accept as part of his life. Put the poor smitten bastard out of his misery.

Knowing he shouldn't, he took a deep breath and put every scrap of concentration he could muster into making those wasted muscles move. Fists clenched and teeth bared, he stared at his feet. Move, damn you. Move.

Please.

By the time he gave up and dragged his legs to the edge of the bed, he was drenched with the sweat of failure.

"This is pretty much the final proposal, subject to your approval, Madame Prez." Grinning like a Cheshire kitten, Marca handed Carly the sheaf of papers she'd just taken from her briefcase.

Carly scanned the neatly typed pages, clicking off points in her mind. Marca was meticulously and totally professional. Her hopes climbed higher.

"The press conference is all set to go?"

"Friday at three."

Carly nibbled her lower lip. The rest of the plan was pretty straightforward—a gala for the alumni to meet the new coaching staff, a virtual blizzard of press releases, even local TV spots to hype the exciting new look of the Wolves.

"What's this about new uniforms?"

"New coach, new uniforms. It's a psychological thing."

"It's also more than we can afford." Carly ran a line through that paragraph, drawing a dramatic sigh from its author.

"Okay, I'll give you that, but no way will I compromise on the T-shirts."

"Now Marce—"

"Trust me on this, okay? At the first game we'll give them away free with every ticket purchase, and then, when the team starts to win, we'll sell them at a huge profit." Her eyes gleamed with excitement. "Whoever invented logos should be enshrined in the advertising hall of fame as an authentic genius. Not only are jackets and shirts and hats free advertising, but the licensing fees are pure gravy."

It was all part of the public relations game, Carly reminded herself, reading on, just as the faculty teas and trustee stroking were part of hers.

"I had no idea TV time was so expensive," she murmured, glancing up.

Marca shrugged. "Local time costs peanuts compared to network air, which is why that ten-minute interview with Scott Bendix this morning was twenty-four karat."

Carly initialed the proposal before returning it to Marca's open case. "You know, Marce, I really think this might work."

"You bet it will. I checked with the public information office downstairs before I came up, and they were already swamped with calls from the media wanting interviews with Mitch. I'm thinking about holding the conference in the stadium. That way we can show off our new look at the same time."

"Sounds okay." Carly was about to ask Marca if she wanted to grab some lunch and conversation when Sandy buzzed.

"Yes, Sandy?"

"Please tell Marca that Mr. Scanlon is here to take her to lunch."

Carly shot a glance at Marca's guileless face before murmuring an assent and hanging up. "Your lunch date is here."

Marca bounced to her feet and closed her briefcase. "Great! I'm going to brief him on the campaign and talk about the press conference. Anything else you'd like me to cover?"

"Can't think of a thing," Carly said, reaching for her stack of phone messages.

"Want to come along?"

"No, publicity is your department."

Marca collected her things, then paused to give Carly a thoughtful look. "Something's happened."

"Pardon?"

"You look different somehow. Softer." Her eyes grew round, and her mouth popped open. "You and Scanlon, you've made love, haven't you?"

Carly drew a long breath and nodded. She felt her face warming—blushing at her age, she thought. What next? Borrowing his handkerchief to put under her pillow every night so she could breathe in the musky scent of his after-shave?

"I don't know how I could have been so impulsive, Marca. All these years I've organized my life so carefully, never doing anything on the spur of the moment, never even buying so much as a pair of pantyhose with considering my options."

She dropped her pen and pushed a shaky hand through her hair. "I keep telling myself it's just physical, some kind of irresistible chemistry between us, but, oh God, Marce, I think I'm in love with him." Agitated, she waved a hand. "Oh, I know, it's just puppy love. Sort of a delayed adolescence. Not much more than lust, really."

Marca drew a slow breath. "Is that so bad?"

Carly glanced around the office that had always been a part of her life. Up here in the tower, she could look down and feel distant from all the pain she'd left behind.

"I don't know, Marca, and that's the truth. You know how I feel about affairs between faculty members."

"C'mon, Carly. It's not against any rule I know of."

"No, but it's not good policy either. And what about Tracy? I can't tell you how many times I've preached to her about the need for love and commitment to make sex more than a physical mating. If she finds out her mother is having an affair with—"

"Her father?" Marca interrupted softly.

Carly nodded, her face suddenly ice cold. "That's another problem I'm not sure I'm ready to face." Her gaze flickered to the plaster cast of a small hand on the polished desk. Tracy had been a wide-eyed kindergartner when she'd given that to her for Mother's Day. For Father's Day, Tracy had made a similar cast for her Granddaddy Alderson, the only male role model she'd known.

Marca waited until Carly looked her way again, then asked in an understanding tone, "Do you plan to tell Mitch the truth?"

"Oh, Marca, I don't know!" Carly cried before rising abruptly to cross to the window. Across campus the rare elephant ear magnolia was coming into bloom. Nearby, the flowering plum she'd planted to celebrate Tracy's birth was already covered with pink blossoms. She still remembered the feel of that shovel in her hands and the burn of tears against her wind-chilled cheeks. In her mind the beautiful plum would always be Tracy's tree. It had blossomed seventeen times since then, growing tall and sturdy. Like Tracy herself.

"I never wanted Tracy to grow up without a father, but things just turned out that way. I always tried to fill in, but there were times when she missed having a daddy around to tell her how beautiful she was and how special and, oh, I don't know, do all the things fathers do with daughters."

"Are you saying you think that Mitch would have done all those things?" Marca asked as she joined Carly at the window.

"A month ago I would have said absolutely not and meant it. Now I'm not so sure." She rubbed a smudge from the pane with her forefinger before adding softly, "When he talks to Tracy, even about the most inconsequential things, she glows. At first, I thought she might have a crush on him—"

"Maybe she does," Marca said.

"Maybe, but I'm beginning to think it's more than that," Carly sighed. "She asks his opinion about her clothes and her hair—and boys."

There was an abrupt rap on the door an instant before it opened and Mitch came in. He'd removed the tie he'd worn for the interview, but he was still wearing his blazer and a blue-and-white striped shirt. His eyebrows lifted at the sight of the two of them sitting frozen, as though caught in some guilty act.

"Am I interrupting something important?" he asked, glancing from one to the other. "I can wait outside if you want."

Carly shook her head. "No, we were just finishing."

Marca picked up her briefcase and her purse, then offered Carly a coaxing smile. "Sure you don't want to join us? Scanlon's buying."

"I am?"

Carly heard the laconic humor in his tone and had a terrible urge to run into his arms. "No, thanks. You two go ahead. I have a pile of phone calls to return."

"Have fun," Marca said before she walked past Mitch into the outer office.

"Meet you at the elevator," he told Marca before closing the door.

"Something wrong?" Carly asked, glancing up in surprise.

"You asked me that once before, remember?"

She tapped her pen against her pursed lips. "Mm, no, I don't think I do, actually."

He approached the desk in his deliberate way. Seeing the heated look in his eyes had her pulse rocketing. Instead of stopping on his side of the desk, he came around to her side. One by one he rid himself of his crutches, then leaned against her desk and grinned crookedly.

"Okay, I'm ready," he said, folding his arms over his chest. She had to struggle to keep a straight face.

"So I see. The question that comes to mind, however, is ready for what?"

"For my attaboy kiss."

Carly blinked. "Perhaps you might explain that further."

"It's an accepted practice that when someone does you a favor, you thank them in some appropriate way. I broke one of my rules for you when I let myself be interviewed on the tube, and it was damn hard work, let me tell you. In return, I think I should get a reward, don't you?"

"Aha, now I understand." Reaching out, she pulled her crystal jar of lemon drops closer and took off the lid. "Take as many as you want."

His mouth twitched. "I can see this calls for tact and diplomacy." His hand tangled in the soft floppy bow at her throat and tugged.

"Scanlon—"

"You owe me, bright eyes."

Laughing in spite of her uncertainties, she let him pull her up and into his arms. "I offered you lemon drops."

"I want a kiss."

"I've always said a woman should pay her debts. And if that's what you want..." She focused her gaze on his mouth and felt him shudder. She saw his eyes warm a split second before his mouth covered hers.

The heat was instantaneous, exploding in her blood, then melting into her bones. Instinct had her clutching those wide, unyielding shoulders while her senses spun in a wild spiral.

His mouth was warm and moist and provocative, taking hers repeatedly, as though he couldn't get enough of her. When his tongue parted her lips, she sighed in welcome, her senses swirling faster and faster.

Mitch groaned and pulled her closer, her breasts soft against his chest. His palms flattened against her spine as desire took him to the edge of reason.

Dimly, through the haze of her own desire, Carly heard him groan. A shiver ran through her, and then, endearingly, through him, and then he was wrenching his mouth from hers.

Reluctant to let her go, he held her close for as long as he dared, then gently moved her to arm's length. "Talk about lousy timing," he murmured hoarsely, and she managed a sound halfway between a laugh and a moan.

Her face was flushed, her eyes cloudy and shaded toward a smoky gray. Her lips were still slightly parted and kissed to a rosy fullness.

"Sure you don't want to come with us?"

"I'm sure."

He played with a lock of hair that clung stubbornly to his fingers. "Meet me at the pool tonight," he murmured, his voice raspy with a need he could only partially hide.

"Tracy's having a sleep over. She and her friends generally end up in the Jacuzzi before the night is over."

He drew a deep breath. "Guess that's a no on you and me taking a midnight swim," he drawled, his grin lazy.

"Yes, that's a definite no." She rubbed a trace of lipstick from his mouth, and he tried to bite her finger. "And you'd better get going, or Marca's going to come in here and drag you out kicking and screaming. She can be very impatient."

"She's not the only one who has a problem with patience." He offered her a lazy smile before retrieving his crutches. "Don't worry, bright eyes. Even if she throws herself at me, I'll resist. My heart belongs only to you."

She knew he was teasing, but for a moment the thought that he might really love her had her emotions tumbling wildly.

"Get going," she muttered. "Some of us have work to do."

By the time he'd closed the door behind him, she had already dialed the number she needed and was on hold. But she was thinking of him.

Chapter 9

Just as Marca had predicted and Carly had hoped, the news that Mitch Scanlon was coming out of retirement to coach at a no-name college in Oregon had produced a media circus. Carly had never seen so many Minicams and microphones in one place in her life.

Because of threatening rain, they'd moved the conference from the stadium to the largest classroom on campus. Every seat was filled, and the aisles were packed.

To her astonishment, she'd discovered that Mitch truly did suffer from camera fright. She'd surprised him standing alone in one of the offices, his face gray. His eyes had been closed, and he'd been talking to himself. Psyching himself up the way he'd never had to do before a game, he'd admitted with obvious embarrassment.

Deeply touched that he'd agreed to what was in essence an ordeal for him in order to help Bradenton, she'd proceeded to kiss him exuberantly and so thoroughly that his face had turned from ashen to flushed, and his eyes had lost all sign of fear.

His grin had been cocky when he'd taken the stage after Marca's introduction, allowing everyone to see the extent of his disability as he'd approached the podium, dragging his dead legs a rigid thirty inches at a time while the cameras recorded every torturous inch.

At first the questions had been stilted, even diffident, but when it became obvious that Mitch was willing to answer even the most personal questions, the reporters began clamoring for his attention, shouting and waving their arms to draw his gaze. After that, the conference became more like a party, with Mitch cracking jokes that had everyone laughing, including him.

Carly left before the end with a lump in her throat and tears in her eyes, and was waiting for Marca and the others in the office Marca had appropriated for the occasion. Coach came in first, his seamed face alight and his eyes glowing. Scanlon followed, looking emotionally drained and physically weary—and thoroughly masculine in chinos and a pale blue shirt with a button-down collar and sleeves he'd rolled nearly to the elbow. As of two days ago, he had officially become Bradenton's head football coach with the rank of full professor and all the perks that went with that position. The contract signed in his self-assured scrawl was now on Carly's desk, along with all the other papers required of a new faculty member.

"This calls for a celebration," Coach boomed, already stripping the cellophane from the biggest cigar Carly had ever seen.

"Don't even think of it," Carly warned, snatching the matchbox from his hand before he'd even gotten it open.

"Tyrant," Coach muttered, his expression mutinous as he looked to Scanlon for support.

Scanlon's grin flashed, and Carly wondered if she was the only one to see the subtle signs of strain in his face. "Don't look at me, Pete," he drawled. "I'm not about to take her on when she gets that determined glint in her eyes."

Coach scowled. "Damn it, Mitch, I thought you'd be on my side."

"Hey, I don't want you dropping dead on me—at least, not until football season's over. You promised to help me get the hang of this coaching thing, remember?"

Carly saw the mixed emotions on Coach's face and fought an urge to laugh. Gotcha, you old finagler, she thought as Marca came bustling in and closed the door.

"Kudos all around, guys and gals. On a scale of one to ten, we just pulled off a twelve, publicity wise." She circled the desk, sat down in the chair and produced a magnum of champagne from someplace on the floor.

"Somebody open that," she muttered before diving below the desk again for glasses. "Pretend these are Baccarat crystal," she said as she plunked a stack of plastic cups on the table.

Mitch leaned against the desk and propped his crutches next to him before reaching for the champagne. Carly watched his hands expertly manipulate the cork and thought about the feel of those long, supple fingers against her breast. It had been three days and nights since they'd made love.

He hadn't suggested another midnight swim, and she told herself she was glad. Too many things had happened too quickly, and she needed time to sort out her emotions.

The cork came out with a satisfying pop, requiring a cheer from the assembly. Carly found herself looking into Scanlon's eyes and smiled. His gaze dipped to her mouth, and she felt a flurry of need.

"Marca's right. You were great."

"Talk's easy," he said with a shrug, as though he hadn't been to-the-bone terrified to make his way to the microphone. "Let's see what all those football experts asking the questions have to say after the season."

While he poured, Marca launched into a sprightly analysis of the conference, including pithy comments on some of the more prominent attendees. When all the glasses were filled and in hand, she got to her feet and looked at Carly.

"All kidding aside, if Bradenton survives, it will be because Carly refused to let Old Brady sink without a fight. I won't go into all the reasons why these past weeks have been difficult ones for her, but I will say that I admire her tremendously, and for her sake, I hope the darn team wins every blasted game it plays." Grinning, Marca raised her glass. "To Carly."

Carly had never been comfortable as the center of attention. Now, with Scanlon's lazy gaze leveled on hers and the strain of too many hectic weeks thrumming in her head, she felt almost giddy. Because she had to, she summoned a smile and murmured her thanks.

Beaming at her like a worn-at-the-edges uncle, Coach downed his champagne in one swallow, then smacked his lips. "Not bad for a start. I'll buy the next round at Gallagher's for anyone interested."

By the time Carly and Mitch left Gallagher's an hour later, she was tired of talking. It seemed that everyone she knew had stopped by to meet the new coach. Driving them home, Mitch took the long way through campus, and she was nearly asleep with her head on his shoulder by the time they returned to the mansion.

He parked the Jag in the spot he'd come to consider his own and killed the engine. Before she could move, he had his arm around her and was pulling her across his lap for a long, leisurely kiss. By the time it ended, they were both breathing hard, and Carly was realizing that she wasn't as tired as she'd thought.

"It's been a long time since I necked with a pretty girl in a car," he said, kissing the tip of her nose. "Too bad there's not a drive-in movie around here so I could have an excuse to do more of it."

She took his hand and threaded her fingers through his. "I forgot to mention it to you when you signed your contract, but here at Bradenton we expect our professors to refrain from all public displays of affection. Sets a bad example, you know."

Mitch nuzzled her hair, and the light, whispery scent of her tempted him to do more. "I gotta tell you, Carly, since I've been on campus, I've seen things going on in broad daylight that even made an old guy like me blush."

She rested her head against her shoulder and inhaled the clean smell of his skin. "That's only because the weather's nice. In the winter they do those things inside."

She heard him chuckle. "I'm planning to head back to Sacramento sometime before Memorial Day weekend. There are things I need to do, arrangements I need to make, before I can move up here permanently."

Carly wondered if he would miss her while he was gone. She already knew how *she* would feel. "When do you plan to start practice?"

"Middle of June. I figure I'll let the guys blow off steam for a couple of weeks after classes end before I introduce them to my way of doing things."

"Which is?"

"Which is what I'd better be figuring out between now and then."

She drew back far enough to show him an ominous frown. "That definitely doesn't sound reassuring, Professor Scanlon."

He raised his eyebrows, giving him the look of a mischievous little boy. "*Coach* Scanlon to you, lady. I've even got the whistle to prove it."

"You do?"

"Yep. Coach gave me his. Said it had brought him luck, and since we both know I'm going to need plenty of that..." He let the thought dangle while he nudged her chin a little higher with his knuckles.

He smiled even as his mouth covered hers. He felt her soften, and he buried his fingers in her hair, feeling pure softness swirl around his fingers. Her scent spun in his head until he felt disoriented, like a man who'd just had the wind knocked out of him. Even though he knew they were sitting still, he felt staggered. Humbled.

He'd dreamed of this night after night, lying alone in a room in her house, imagining those soft lips yielding to his. Longing to feel her body against his, her soft breasts pressed against his chest.

He tasted her slowly, his tongue running along the curve of her mouth until he was nearly crazed with desire. He tasted her more deeply, moaning as her tongue touched his, then darted away.

Drawing back, he kissed each corner of her mouth, feeling her smile, and then slowly, indulging himself shamelessly, he trailed kisses along her throat until she moaned.

"Come inside with me," he murmured against her silky, perfumed skin. To his room, where the bed was soft. And it was dark. "Please, Carly, let me make love to you again."

He felt her go still, and he lifted his head to look at her. Her eyes were slumberous, her lips slightly parted. Slowly her brows drew together in a frown. When she looked up at him, he braced himself for the gentlest of noes.

"I'm . . . scared."

Something tore inside him, and he bent to kiss her very gently. "I'll tell you a secret, honey. So am I."

Her lips trembled into a smile. "If I change my mind . . ."

"If you change your mind, we'll stop."

"Promise?"

"Promise."

She searched his eyes, looking for something he hoped to hell she would find, and then she nodded. "Let's go inside," she murmured, leaning into him to kiss his throat. "I like touching you without all these clothes in the way."

Mitch felt a moment of raw fear. Then, before he could change his mind, he bent to kiss her one last lingering time.

"C'mon, sweet Caroline," he said, smiling down at her. "Let's take this party inside, where it belongs."

By the time they reached the guest suite, Mitch had gone quiet and his jaw had taken on a hard tension. Carly felt a flutter of nerves as he opened the door for her, then stepped back to let her enter first.

"I used to love to come in here when this was Grandmama's room," she murmured. "She always had time to listen to my stories."

"Stories?" He pulled his wallet and keys from his trousers and dropped them on the table.

"More like fairy tales, I guess. Princes on white chargers type of thing. I was very romantic in those days."

He took an awkward step forward until they were very close. She had to tilt her head back in order to meet his eyes. "And now?" he asked, his tone showing that he really cared about the answer.

"Now I still believe in happily ever after for the damsel in distress, but I think she has to make it happen herself."

He reached out to touch the garnet teardrop dangling from her ear. The back of his thumb rubbed her jaw, and she took a stuttering breath.

"Are you living happily ever after, Carly?"

"I'm content, yes."

His hand tangled in her hair. It smelled like sunshine on a meadow and twined around his fingers seductively. "But not happy?"

"Sometimes I am."

"How about now?"

She had to think about that. "More like surprised," she admitted.

He lifted an eyebrow. "Where did that come from?"

Needing to touch him, she ran her hand over his arm and felt the promise of power in the hard muscles. "Never in a dozen lifetimes did I expect to find myself here with you alone, with a bed only a few feet away."

Gazing into his eyes, she saw a sudden wariness cloud the golden irises. "Why are you here?" His voice carried a tension that hadn't been there moments before. And his jaw was suddenly tight. What had she said, she wondered, to put him on guard all of a sudden?

"Because I choose to be," she murmured, needing him to know that she walked her own path. "Because it's what I want."

"Couldn't be you've decided to make me into another of your charity cases, could it?" His tone was icy now, his hard mouth biting off the words.

Carly knew an instant of confusion before his meaning sank in. "I'm not even going to waste energy answering that," she declared softly, turning away.

He caught her hand and pulled her back. "Stay," he said, his voice rough.

"Why should I?" She hated this mix of emotions he could arouse in her. One minute he was vulnerable and charming, and the next he was pushing her away with hard cynicism.

His smile was part cajoling rogue, part vulnerable man. "Because you have a generous nature, and because you believe in giving a guy who might just be a little more sensitive than he should be a second chance."

"Sensitive? You?"

His neck turned the color of old brick, and a muscle spasmed along the hard line of his jaw. "Not everyone can handle sex with a paraplegic."

She drew her eyebrows together. "I don't remember complaining about your paralysis the other night in the pool. In fact, I don't remember giving it much thought."

His mouth moved. "It's easier for me to move in the water. Easier to pretend I don't have to do things differently these days."

Suddenly his meaning was as clear as one of the auditor's printouts. It had been nearly dark in the pool, and the water had blurred the image of their bodies. But here in his room, with the lights on, he was afraid she would be revolted by the sight of his nude body, by his wasted legs.

Very carefully, she skimmed her hand up his arm to his shoulder. "I have my own insecurities," she murmured. "For example, I always need to be on top."

A flame leapt in his eyes at that, and she hid a smile of deep satisfaction. "Any particular reason?" he asked, his voice still tense.

"Yes, but it's private. Are you okay with that?"

Mitch searched her eyes for the pity he'd been half certain he would see there, but instead he saw a shadowed image of the scared eighteen-year-old girl who'd suddenly found herself alone and pregnant.

"I'm okay with that." Desperately needing to touch her, he lifted a hand to her face. Smiling, she nuzzled his palm with her cheek, and like a floodgate suddenly letting go, his need poured out, nearly taking him under.

He touched his lips to hers and felt her shudder. Her arms hooked around his neck, and she strained against him. "Whoa," he murmured, smiling when she drew back and squinted at him, her eyes already cloudy with desire. "How about we continue this over there?" he said, jerking his head toward the bed.

She smiled and nodded, but before she let him go, she kissed the tension-hard corner of his mouth. They walked together to the bed. He stripped back the covers with an impatient jerk, and she laughed.

"Tilly's going to have a fit if you tear her favorite duvet," she murmured.

"I'll buy her another one," he said with an impatient glance at the satiny cover.

"Don't think she won't insist on that."

While she slipped out of her shoes, he unlocked his braces and sat down. After stowing his crutches out of the way under the bed, he took her hand and pulled her toward him. "Now, you were saying?" he said, his grin slanting crookedly.

She kissed him, then reached for the top button of his shirt. "I remember seeing you play," she murmured. "I thought you were gorgeous then. You're better now."

His hands were busy undoing her belt and sliding down the zipper of her slacks, but his eyes smiled up at her. "Thought you said we'd never met." Her slacks whispered down her legs, revealing a wisp of purple satin and lace almost too small to be called panties. He drew in a harsh breath, trying to hold on to his control.

"Didn't you say you would remember a name like mine?" she challenged softly, busy tugging his shirt free of his trousers.

He started to say something, but the sudden slide of her hands over his now-exposed chest had him sucking in hard. And when she slipped his shirt over his shoulders, then traced the line of his collar bone with her tongue, he groaned.

"Does that feel good?" she murmured.

"God, yes," he said, his voice thick. Wrapping his arms around her waist, he pressed his face to the warm hollow of her belly and waited out the violent need to hurry. She was so warm and sweet and adorable, and he was drowning in her.

He wanted her—no, he *needed* her—the way a man needed to feel cool sheets against his body when he was worn out at night, or to fill his empty belly when he'd gone too long without food.

He kissed the marble-white skin below the lace edge of her bra, then hooked his thumbs under her panties and slipped them over her hips. She was perfect, he thought. Nicely rounded and soft. He ran his hand along a faint white scar just above the wedge of soft brown hair, and she stilled.

"From your baby?" he murmured, and she nodded. Glancing up, he saw a shadow pass over her face, whether pain or pleasure he couldn't tell. Either way, he found himself intensely moved. "I bet you were spectacular with a big belly, sweet Caroline."

He felt her tremble and bent to kiss the scar. Her hands tangled in his hair, and she moaned softly. He held her tight for a long moment, then set her away from him. "I think I'd better get my pants off while I still have come coordination left," he said, working up a smile.

"Anything I can do to speed things along?" she murmured, tracing the line of his cheek with a fingertip.

"Yeah, lights out would help."

"All right." She reached over to turn off the lamp. The room darkened, but light from the outside streamed through the windows. Knowing instinctively what he needed, she went to the window and pulled the drapes, taking her time. Even with the drapes drawn, some light still filtered through, enough so that when she turned, she could see him silhouetted against the lighter texture of the sheet. He was lying flat, his spine arched up while he worked his trousers and briefs together over his hips. She heard the rustle of fabric, the muted sound of steel against steel, as he sat up to finish ridding himself of his clothes.

While she was slipping out of her blouse, he was wrestling with straps and cuffs. While she was placing her clothing neatly over a chair by the window, he was twisting to put his braces on the floor, near at hand.

Taking a silent, deep breath, she climbed in next to him and let him draw her back against the piled pillows. "You smell good," he murmured, cradling her against his big chest. "Very classy."

She rubbed her cheek against his shoulder and felt him tremble. "Do tell, *Coach* Scanlon, what does 'classy' smell like?"

"Like flowers and candlelight and sex." He tipped her head up and covered her mouth with his.

Though the kiss was tinged with impatience, he forced himself to go slowly even as her hands were racing over his skin, touching him everywhere, her fingers eager and testing, until he was slipping fast toward the already splintered boundaries of his control.

He tasted her need, and his own spiked hot, bringing a shudder to the parts of his body that could still feel pleasure or pain. "Tell me what I can do to make you feel good," she murmured, her breasts soft, her nipples pebbled.

"Anything you want," he managed to get out before a groan shook him.

Taking him at his word, Carly let her hands roam over the hard planes of his chest, molding her fingers to the contours of powerful muscle and lean sinew until his breathing was tortured and her head was swimming.

She loved touching him. She loved hearing him groan as her fingers found yet another sensitive area. She moved lower, aware of the heat of his skin and the extent of his arousal.

She straddled him, and he cupped her breasts in his hands, the glitter of need in his eyes visible through the charcoal darkness.

"Carly," he murmured, his tone strangled. "I can't wait much longer." He framed her waist with his hands and guided her to him.

She gasped at the hot pressure, her mind swirling and her body consumed in an age-old need to be filled. Clutching his shoulders, she let him take over. His hands were gentle but urgent, caressing her, positioning her. He thrust upward slowly, inexorably, sliding into her with steady, hot insistence until he was sheathed inside her and she was soaring.

Mitch fought for sanity, blood roaring in his head, and the pressure building in his body screaming to be released. Her fingers dug into his shoulders, her soft frantic moans driving him mad. He began to move, thankful for the hours he'd spent strengthening the muscles of his belly and the still functioning muscles of his hips and thighs.

He felt her tremble, her breath coming in helpless little gasps. He was breathing just as hard, his chest hot, his groin a pool of searing need. And then she was crying out, a long, sweet gasp of pleasure that brought tears to his eyes. He waited... waited....

At last, feeling her relax slightly, he gritted his teeth and thrust hard again and again until pleasure exploded in him in a powerful, exultant rush. Spent, he collapsed against the pillow and pulled her close. Her skin was dewy, her hair a soft tumble against his cheek. Closing his eyes, he luxuriated in the feel of the warm weight against him. Gently, rhythmically, he trailed his fingers along her spine, loving the silky feel of her.

She sighed, and the soft curling hair on his chest fluttered. "Still tickles," he murmured over her head. "I still like it."

She smiled and let her eyes close. "Mmm."

She heard him chuckle, but she was too drowsy to do more than curve her lips in a smile he couldn't see. He nuzzled her hair with his chin, then tucked her more firmly against him.

Gradually his heartbeat settled to a more normal rhythm, and he found himself drifting, so comfortable that he never wanted to move again.

Carly was gloriously drowsy, wrapped in a state approaching bliss, conscious only gradually that he'd stopped stroking her and gone stiff.

"Mitch?"

"Ah, honey, I need to move you a minute." His voice was raspy with pain.

She rolled away from him and sat up. His breathing was ragged as he grabbed his left thigh with both hands and kneaded the hard knot steadily until slowly, imperceptibly, he relaxed.

"What was it, a cramp?" she asked when he settled back again.

"Yeah. Happens now and then. No real reason, just crossed wires." He reached out to stroke her breast. "I need to hold you again," he murmured. She went into his arms eagerly, full of emotions and feelings that she would need time and distance to sort through. For the moment she was greedy for the warm, sweet feeling of safety she'd found in his arms.

They rested quietly while the big house settled around them. His chest rose and fell steadily under her, and her legs tangled with his. The powerful muscles that had allowed him to elude countless tacklers were gone, but the spirit that had driven them seemed even stronger to her now.

Gradually she became aware of the steady thudding of his heart beneath her ear, and she eased her head up.

"Hmm?" he murmured.

"I thought you were asleep," she whispered.

"Not a chance," he said with a smile in his voice. "I was just working up the courage to ask you to stay with me tonight." He rubbed her shoulder with the flat of his hand, and she shivered.

"Okay, but set the alarm for five," she said after thinking it through.

"Now that sounds like something a man can look forward to." He sounded so boyishly eager that she laughed. "Don't get too excited. All I'm going to do is get up and go back to my own room."

"So that you don't have to answer embarrassing questions?"

"So that we both don't." She ran her hand over the contours of his chest. Finding the small silver medal, she touched it gingerly and asked, "Is this something special?"

"St. Christopher's medal." He hesitated, then covered her hand with his. "Remember that boy in rehab I told you about?"

"The surfer?"

"His name was Franco. The medal was his. His father gave it to me after he died."

She drew an unsteady breath. "I'm sorry."

"So am I. But, simplistic as it sounds, I believe he's happier now."

"It's not simplistic," she chided softly. "And I have the same feeling."

She lifted her head, trying to see the expression in his eyes. He took advantage of her nearness to kiss her. It was a long, draining kiss that left her breathless.

"No more questions, bright eyes. It's late, and since you insist on hauling your cute little tush out of here at the crack of dawn, I think we'd better get some sleep."

Reluctantly she agreed and pulled out of his arms. "Grab Tilly's precious duvet while I set the clock," he ordered, switching on the light.

She winced as the light blinded her for an instant. By the time the alarm was set, the light was out again and she was tucked up tight against him, she had quietly, inevitably, accepted the fact that she was indeed in love.

Carly heard the alarm and for a minute was disoriented. She usually woke to the sound of music on her clock radio. Still half asleep, she managed to shut off the annoying buzzing without waking Mitch.

Accustomed to sleeping alone, she'd awakened several times in the night to find herself held tightly against him. He was a heavy sleeper, scarcely moving, his breathing deep and measured.

Lying quietly in the hazy light of dawn, her face only inches from his, she watched him sleep. His face had become so dear to her, not only because the hard angles and strong bones were beautifully formed, but also because of the strength she saw there. Unable to resist, she gently smoothed the tumbled hair from his forehead, loving the soft coolness of the dusty blond thickness. No matter where they went from here, she'd had this one glorious night.

Inching closer, she gently pressed her lips against his, and he frowned. His lashes fluttered, then slowly opened. Surprise surfaced first in the depths of his tawny eyes, then a smile slowly kindled, stirring her heart. "Thought I was dreaming," he murmured, his voice rusty.

"It's five past five," she whispered. "I have to go."

He drew his eyebrows together. "Kiss first," he ordered. He pulled her close and covered her mouth with his.

When his blood started to heat, he reluctantly ended the kiss and let her go. Her cheeks were pink, and her eyes were soft with the same need he'd seen in his dreams. Hungrily he watched as she slipped from the bed and dressed hastily. After slipping into her shoes, she bent to kiss him one last time.

"I'll see you later," she murmured, hating to leave.

"Tonight," he ordered, hooking a strong arm around her neck and pulling her down for one last, lingering kiss that left them both flushed and breathless.

"Tonight," she promised before slipping away, leaving him alone.

Crooking an elbow, he slipped his hand under his head and closed his eyes. His body was sore, but he would trade a few aches and pains in private places to hold her again.

Damn, he felt good, he thought, sighing heavily. His dream had been erotic and detailed, and his heart was still running a little fast. He smiled as he remembered a particularly steamy part, his mind playing over the details. Suddenly he realized that he'd been wearing his braces in the dream, and his stomach thudded. It was the first time since his injury that he'd seen himself as he was now in his dreams, rather than strong and whole, the way he wanted to be again.

Slowly he drew a ragged breath. Until this moment he'd always harbored a secret belief that someday, somewhere, someone was going to come up with a miracle cure for his kind of paralysis. That hope had gotten him through some tough times.

But now he had Carly, and maybe that was what his subconscious was trying to tell him. That maybe it didn't matter now that he was never going to move his legs again—not when he had his very special lady sleeping next to him.

Chapter 10

Carly sat back and swiped her bedraggled bangs out of her eyes with the back of her wrist. She'd been working in her flower garden for almost two hours, and it was finally beginning to shape up. If she worked fast, she might even get the rest of the petunias into the ground before it got too dark to see clearly.

Frowning, she studied the pattern of color. Something wasn't quite right. Maybe more white next to the purple and pink? "That should do it, don't you think, Tabby?" she said to the cat stretched out on the warm earth. Tabitha regarded her with bored green eyes before opening her little pink mouth in a huge yawn.

"Thanks for that vote of confidence. Just for that, you can just move those lazy bones of yours so I can put these pretty flowers in the spot you kept all nice and warm for them."

Lifting Tabitha to her lap, she took time to rub the cat's ears. Instantly a low rumbling purr broke the tranquil silence, and she laughed softly. "At least *you* didn't desert me tonight," she murmured, bending to rub her cheek against Tabitha's soft fur.

It was Tilly's day off, and she had gone to Medford to visit her sister. Coach had talked Felicity into going out to dinner, and Tracy was working the four to twelve shift at the movie triplex in Bradenton Falls. As for Scanlon, she never knew when he would be home.

He was scouting the local high schools, talking to the coaches about prospects other colleges might have passed by. It was a long shot, he'd explained to her and to Coach, but worth the time and trouble, especially if he came up with a talented kid or two.

They'd made love twice more in the last week, once in the pool, once in his room. Remembering those times in his arms had her smiling at odd moments and forgetting her train of thought in meetings. Even Sandy had remarked on her absent-mindedness.

"I'm in love, Tab, and I'm scared," she murmured to the little cat who blinked up at her with haughty indifference. Laughing softly, Carly rubbed Tabitha's belly, and the low rumbling purr intensified. "My conscience tells me I have to tell him the truth. Everything I believe in tells me I should. But it's so hard to know how to tell him. Or even when."

Last night, when she'd been nestled against Mitch's warm broad chest and he'd once again mentioned the nagging feeling that they'd met before, she'd nearly blurted out the truth. Only uncertainty about his reaction had stopped her.

"I'm afraid he'll hate me for not telling him about Tracy," she whispered into the cat's fur. "Or maybe I'm afraid he won't believe me. And what about Tracy, Tab? Should I tell her the truth, or shouldn't I?"

Tabitha regarded her lazily, looking bored, and Carly sighed. "If only my life could be as uncomplicated as yours, Miss Pampered Cat," she said, giving the cat a final nuzzle before setting her aside.

Carly was watering the last of the transplants when she heard the Jaguar pulling into the drive. Still on her hands and knees, she quickly gathered her gardening implements and stowed them in her tool caddy.

She glanced over her shoulder and waited until he was closer before smiling a welcome. It was obvious from his expression that he was surprised to see her.

"So you're the one who's into flowers," he said, glancing around meaningfully. "I wondered."

"I call it my hobby, but I suspect it's more in the nature of therapy. Working in the dirt tends to ground me."

"Sounds dangerous to me." He stopped at the edge of the walk and squared his shoulders. To relieve the tension in his overworked arms and back, she suspected. "Got a minute for a tired coach?" he asked when she scrambled to her feet.

"Only if he doesn't have a problem he needs solved immediately." She wiped the dirt from her hands and shoved them into the oversize pockets of her khaki gardening shorts.

He smiled then, but the tired look around his eyes remained. "Sounds like you've had your quota of problems for today."

"And then some. How about you? Find any hot recruits?"

"One. Kid named Henry Williams. He and a bunch of other guys were playing pickup basketball on the courts behind the student union when I stopped for coffee. He's got the perfect build for a quarterback."

"But Ian's our quarterback."

"Ian's graduating in another year. Williams is a freshman, although he looks older."

"He is. Henry's one of the boys from the 'Youth at Risk' program. He spent last year at McLaren."

"What's that?"

"Juvenile hall. He belonged to a gang in Portland and got mixed up in a shooting, although he was only charged as an accessory."

He looked thoughtful. "Any reason why he can't go out for the team?"

"None that I know of. Is he interested?"

His mouth slanted. "Yeah, he's interested. Turns out he's a big fan of the Jacks."

She pushed back her hair. "Most folks are around here."

"That's why I figured an exhibition game between the Jacks and the Wolves might draw a pretty good crowd. I called in a few favors and arranged for some of the guys from Portland to drop around for a pick-up scrimmage before the season starts. We settled on the first Saturday in September."

Carly felt her excitement growing. "The *NFL* Lumberjacks?"

"Right." The barest hint of a smile tugged at his mouth.

"The same Portland Jacks that went to the Super Bowl last year?" She knew she sounded incredulous and she didn't care. This was almost too good to be believed.

"Seems to me someone told me that not too long ago, yeah."

She choked back a laugh. "How . . . what favors?"

"Actually, it was more like blackmail. I just reminded J. C. Cobb of how good I used to make him look, and how if I hadn't, he wouldn't be coaching those same Jacks. It took him a while, but he finally admitted that I was right."

She drew a quick breath, but what she really wanted to do was throw herself into his arms and hug the dickens out of him. "I can't believe it. The Jacks."

"Not all of them," he hastened to remind her. "Just the guys who hadn't already made other commitments. Mostly rookies and second-string guys."

She bit her lip, a list of things to be done already started in her head. "I'd better call Marca first. We'll need massive publicity and special tickets. Maybe some of those T-shirts she's so high on."

"Whoa, hold on. I had to do some horse trading for this deal, and I thought I'd better check with you first before things got out of hand."

"What kind of horse trading?"

"Since the guys don't get paid extra for this kind of thing, J.C. and I came up with the idea of making it a benefit for the Jacks' scholarship fund. We donate all the proceeds from the ticket sales in return for the players' services."

She felt a pang of disappointment before shrugging it away. "That seems fair. After all, the purpose is really to inspire our players and get some publicity for the team."

She felt Tabby's warm body rubbing against her ankle and glanced down. The fat cat's bushy tail waved in the air like a plume, the tip jerking back and forth.

"Go catch a mouse," she muttered, drawing an impudent meow from Tabitha and a startled look from Scanlon.

One side of his mouth moved. "Hey, wait a minute. You're talking to my roommate. I'm not crazy about waking up to find she's brought a dead body to bed."

Carly blinked. "So that's where she's been. I wondered why she hadn't been sneaking into my room lately."

"She followed me in three nights ago and wouldn't leave. I woke up in the middle of the night with her draped around my neck and damn near threw her across the room before I figured out I wasn't being strangled in my sleep. Now she sits by the door and waits for me to come home. She looks so pathetic that I haven't been able to turn her away."

Carly laughed. "I know what you mean. She's a cuddler from way back. Comes from being separated from her mother too soon, or at least that's what Tilly claims. We found her on our doorstep one morning, and she's been ruling our lives ever since."

Carly pulled her hands from her pockets and bent down to rub the cat's ears. The security lights had yet to be turned on. The light from the terrace was too distant to provide much more than a faint glow, but it was enough to enable her to see the smug look in Tabby's eyes.

"Spoiled, aren't you?" Carly murmured, straightening. As though aware they were discussing her, Tabby sashayed between them, stepping daintily over Scanlon's size twelves before rubbing against the backs of his legs.

"If she bothers you, just throw her out," Carly murmured. "She's used to it."

"I'll keep that in mind. Right now we have an understanding. She keeps my neck warm, and I sneak treats in for her every night."

She glanced up and found him watching her with a brooding look in those dark eyes. The teasing comment she'd been about to make vanished, her thoughts scattering like so many fallen petals. Even though he hadn't moved, even though they were nearly an arm's length apart, she felt as though she was being slowly seduced.

"I . . . this is certainly good news. About the Jacks."

"There's one more thing," he said, forcing his mind off the memory of her soft body curled into his and on to the reason he was in her life at all.

"What's that?"

"I agreed to TV coverage by one of the Portland stations. Seems they cover all the preseason games before hooking into the usual network coverage."

She moved toward him. "TV? That's fantastic! How much will they pay, do you think?"

"Not a lot. It's local, remember?"

"You're right. For a minute I got so excited I forgot."

Mitch was suddenly aware of a soft quality to the air and the quiet that seemed to wrap around them. Freeing a hand, he smoothed her hair. She smelled like the flowers she'd been planting, and there was a smudge of dirt on her chin.

"Someone from the Jacks organization will be contacting Marca tomorrow or the next day, unless you'd rather he called you directly."

"No, Marca's the expert, but I'll let her know they'll be calling."

Backlit by the glow from the porch, her face seemed more lovely than ever. But it was her soft pale lips that drew his attention.

"Don't I get a kiss for being such a good boy, bright eyes?"

"One thing you are not, and that's a boy." She let her gaze linger on those wide shoulders for a beat longer than courtesy demanded and felt desire stir to life in secret places.

"Can we try for good?" Very slowly, he bent his head toward her and heard her breath hitch. Covering her mouth with his, he luxuriated in the softness of her lips and the warmth of her breath on his face. Need rushed through him like a drug suddenly shot into his veins. He swayed, then found his balance and pressed a hand to the small of her back, steadying them both.

"Gardening must be hot work," he murmured, kissing a smudge of dirt on her cheek.

"Oh, it is," she murmured, shivering. "Very." Drawing back, she smoothed a finger down the shallow crease in his cheek before allowing herself the pleasure of tracing his lower lip with that same fingertip. "Recruiting must be hot work, as well," she murmured, loving the sudden glint of need in his eyes.

"Sweaty, too," he agreed, then groaned as she pressed closer. "How about a swim?" he managed to get out between kisses.

"Sounds wonderful," she answered a little breathlessly. "Especially since no one else is home."

Mitch allowed himself one last kiss before drawing back. Unfortunately Tabby chose that moment to come between them. Startled, Carly moved, and, caught by surprise, he felt his balance shift and tightened his grip to keep her from falling. Somehow, though, her feet tangled with one of his crutches, and the two of them went down together.

Mitch lost his crutches, one of which hit Tabby on the head, and the indignant cat yowled and took off running. Carly landed on top of Mitch, her hands still on his shoulders. "Talk about a passion killer," he muttered, and she pressed her face against his chest to keep from laughing.

"Are you okay?" he muttered, his voice a deep rumble in his chest. She lifted her head and looked into his eyes, where she saw a quick flash of anguish before the shutters came down.

"I'm fine," she murmured, a little breathless. "How about you?"

His mouth slanted. "I'm okay, but you'd better worry about that cat, 'cause I'm going to kill her as soon as I get myself out of this damn flower bed." She recognized a frazzled ego when she heard it, and she burst out laughing.

"Not if I beat you to it," she vowed shakily.

"We'll both do it, only you'll have to catch her," he said, rolling her to her back. She started to push him away, then realized that he'd angled himself so that he was lying next to her, not atop.

"It's a deal," she managed to murmur before his mouth covered hers again. His kiss was demanding, eager, his hands pushing into her hair, holding her as he kissed her again and again, each kiss more draining, more arousing, until she was aware only of the delicious sensations tumbling through her. Moaning helplessly, she opened her mouth to him, wringing a harsh groan from his throat as his tongue slipped inside, tentative at first, then hot and insistent.

Her hands kneaded his back, thrilled with the feel of hard muscle through the thin shirt, loving the sense of power and strength she felt there. Warmth spread over her skin as his mouth began a sensuous exploration of her throat, his breath hot and moist and arousing.

"Sweet Caroline," he murmured against her ear. "My shy little temptress."

Scanlon, my love, she thought, nearly mindless with swirling, consuming pleasure. The pain he'd caused her was forgotten, submerged in sweet desire. The last of her reservations slipped away, and she gave herself into his hands, lost in the orgy of new sensations.

He shifted to her side, one hand already tugging her shirt free of her shorts, his fingers warm and gentle as they slid over her rib cage. She gasped, arching backward as the sensations built to a nearly intolerable intensity.

His fingers slipped under her bra to stroke her nipple with the gentlest of friction until her breast was swollen and hot. Only then did he attend to the other breast, using the same sweet skill until she was writhing helplessly, awash in pleasure. His hand left her breast then, but only to push her shirt higher. She moaned as he brought his mouth to her belly, his teeth nipping gently at her skin, lower and lower.

Her hands tangled in his hair, her fingers lost in the golden thickness. His tongue lapped at her belly button until she cried out. Tiny spasms of sensation ran through her, stronger and stronger. Frantic now, she arched upward, whimpering helplessly.

"Easy, sweet, I'll take care of you," he murmured almost incoherently as he pushed himself backward, tugging her shorts lower on her hips as he moved. Cool air hit her skin, heightening the sweet tugging tension that was torturing her almost beyond bearing. Bracing himself on his elbows, he kissed the quivering flesh of her belly, then moved lower, his tongue trailing fire along her skin.

His hands were patient, his mouth hot. Sensations built until she was mindless. At the first jagged peak she cried out, and then she was tumbling, coming to earth slowly.

He murmured her name, his face pressed against her throat, his skin damp and hot.

"Mitch?"

He lifted his head and looked at her. "What can I do for you, honey?" he asked, his voice slurred and his eyes smoldering.

She smiled, so full of love it hurt. "I think I should be asking you that," she murmured, caressing his face.

"Next time," he replied, his tone husky and his smile drowsy.

"But—"

"Shh, it's okay." Tightening his arms, he rolled them over until she was cradled against him. "I think we just ruined a couple hours of work," he murmured, his deep voice touched with wry humor.

"It was worth it," she managed to whisper, so content she wasn't sure she would ever move again.

"Liked that, did you, sweet Caroline?" he asked in a low, husky tone that rippled like pleasure through her.

When she didn't answer, he tipped her face up to his. When he saw her lip clamped between her teeth, he swore an oath so ripe it had her jolting. "Baby, I'm sorry. I thought . . . hell, I don't know what I thought."

She let out a sound halfway between a moan and a laugh. "You idiot, I'm not upset. I'm happy. I feel as though that was my first time and you are my first lover."

His expression turned pensive. "Carly, I've done a lot of things that might shock you. I'm pretty beat up in the white knight department."

Her hand trembled as she touched his face. "Let's pretend the rest of our lives start now, this minute. The past doesn't matter."

For the first time in years Mitch felt the hard knot of tension in his belly ease. He kissed her gently, then brushed the hair from her face. It was trust he felt from her, trust that he planned to nurture with the greatest care.

He thought he'd known what needing was all about. Now he knew that he'd never needed anyone the way he needed her. Emotion filled him until he wasn't sure he could handle much more.

He growled something, then pulled her to him for a hard hug. "Now, get," he ordered, masking his frustration behind a lazy grin. "I know I can get up okay, but I'd just as soon not have an audience while I figure it out."

It was on the tip of her tongue to offer her help, but the look of fierce pride in his eyes stopped her. Leaning forward, she kissed him tenderly and then scrambled to her feet.

"Oh, and about killing the cat?" she said, watching him. "In my opinion, she deserves a nice big tin of tuna." She waited for the deep masculine chuckle she needed to hear before she turned and left.

Chapter 11

Tracy spooned sugar onto her already sweetened Crunchy Crispies before glancing across the table at her grandmother. "No way, Grandmother. Nothing pink, and definitely not organza, whatever that is."

Felicity dabbed her mouth with her napkin before reaching for her teacup. "Organza is a type of fabric, Tracy, and it's perfect for a graduation dress."

"No one is going to know what I have on under that long robe, so what difference does it make? Besides, it's going to be hot, and all the girls voted to wear shorts."

Her grandmother nearly choked on her tea. "Did you hear that, Caroline? Shorts!"

Carly glanced up from the morning paper. She had already had her swim and her coffee, and, since it was Saturday, she wasn't in her usual time squeeze. Besides, she and Tracy had a date to go shopping later, and the stores at the Medford Mall didn't open until ten.

"I'm sorry, Mother? What did you say?"

"Your daughter is planning to wear shorts under her graduation robe. What do you say to that?"

Carly met Tracy's gaze over the top of the sports page. "I'd say it's a darn good idea, actually. Should save me a bundle on a dress."

Tracy grinned, and for a moment Carly's heart all but stopped. It was Scanlon's grin she was seeing on her daughter's face, right down to the slight little downward hook at one corner. The same grin she'd just seen in the article on the sports page announcing the exhibition game set for the first week in September.

"Give it up, Grandmother," Tracy suggested, flipping her hair over one shoulder. "I'm incorrigible."

Carly ignored the distressed look her mother shot her. "Which reminds me, Mother, have you asked Coach to be your date for the graduation ceremonies? Ticket requests are due in by Wednesday, and I need to know how many to ask for."

"Caroline, I've told you this before. Peter and I are not dating. We're friends, and friends see each other occasionally for dinner or a movie, that's all."

"Fine, Mother. Are you going to be 'seeing each other' for Tracy's graduation and the reception afterward?"

Felicity's flawless complexion took on a pretty pink glow. "Yes, we are, but only because I didn't want him to feel slighted."

"That's very thoughtful of you, Mother."

"It is, isn't it?" Felicity said with the faintest of twinkles in her eyes, and Carly realized that she was liking her mother more and more these days. She liked *everyone* more these days, including herself.

Sunlight filtering through the tinted windows overhead felt wonderfully warm on her bare shoulders, and she lifted a hand to finger comb her still damp hair.

"Don't forget Tilly," Tracy mumbled, her mouth full of cereal.

"Of course not," Carly chided gently. "Tilly's family, just like Aunt Marca."

"And Mitch."

Carly closed the paper and folded it carefully into fourths before placing it next to her coffee mug. With each day that passed, she was becoming more and more convinced that Mitch had a right to know that Tracy was his daughter. But whether or not to tell Tracy the truth was an issue she had yet to resolve, and until she did, she didn't know exactly how she was going to couch her revelation to Mitch.

"Honey, it's very generous of you to include him because he's a guest," she said, feeling her way slowly, "but I'm sure he's not expecting an invitation. Besides, the seating is limited."

"Limit's six to a graduate. Six tickets, six guests. Works for me."

"Well, yes, but Aunt Marca might want to take a date."

"Aunt Marca swore off men after her divorce, remember?"

Carly wondered if Tracy remembered everything everyone said to her, or just the juicy parts. "She might have changed her mind."

"Too late. I've already invited Mitch."

Carly felt her jaw drop. "When?"

"A couple of days ago when Ian and I ran into him at the stadium."

Felicity lifted a perfectly shaped eyebrow. "Who is this Ian you keep talking about?"

"Oh, Grandmother, you know. Ian Cummings, the Wolves' quarterback? Coach Gianfracco and Mitch were discussing him the other day while Mitch and I were playing backgammon, remember?"

"Is that the boy who's in danger of flunking Spanish?"

"That's the one. Mitch offered to tutor him."

Felicity brightened. "Ah, indeed. He must be valuable to the team."

"Only the most important man on the field when our team has the ball."

"What did Mitch say when you invited him?" Carly asked, her voice only slightly strained.

"That he would be delighted to attend, provided he was back from Sacramento by then."

Inside the house proper, the phone rang suddenly, breaking off in the middle of the second ring, and Carly assumed Tilly had picked up one of the extensions.

"Sweets, I hope you won't be disappointed if he can't make it. After all, he's going to be very busy getting the team organized for the beginning of preseason practice."

"Not to worry, Mom. I'm not a baby, you know. If Mitch can't make it, I'm not going to cry every night into my pillow."

"Well, of course you're not, dear," Felicity murmured. "Tears are terribly self-indulgent, after all."

Tracy ignored her grandmother, concentrating instead on her mother. "But it would be nice to have a man around the house permanently, especially one as nice as he is." Her tawny eyes brightened as though she'd had a sudden inspiration. "Plus he has a great sense of humor. That's probably even more important at your age, right?"

"Oh, absolutely," Carly said dryly. "We old folks need a good laugh now and then."

"Oh, Mother, you know what I mean."

"Carly, have you seen Mr. Scanlon this morning?" Tilly came toward her, carrying the portable receiver from the den extension.

"Not yet. Is that call for him?"

The housekeeper nodded. "It's a Mr. Dante from Sacramento. I knocked at the door of the guest room, but he didn't answer."

"Maybe he's in the shower."

Tilly's eyes registered doubt. "I didn't hear the water running."

"Maybe he's out jogging," Tracy said, grinning.

"Tracy!" Felicity exclaimed, aghast. "That's not a kind thing to say, considering his unfortunate situation."

"Oh, Grandmother. He knows he's handicapped. Why should we try to pretend he isn't?"

Carly glanced at her daughter in amazement. For a sometimes flighty sixteen-year-old, Tracy sometimes showed remarkable wisdom.

Frowning, she rose and extended her hand for the phone. "Maybe I'll have better luck."

Tilly looked faintly relieved. "Find out when he'll be wanting his breakfast while you're at it."

"Will do." She cinched her robe tighter before rapping on the door leading from the terrace to the guest room. "Mitch, are you awake?" When he didn't answer, she knocked louder and longer.

"Mitch? Your friend from Sacramento is on the phone for you."

When there was still no answer, she turned the knob and inched the door inward. The light by the bed was still burning, although daylight was streaming through the windows.

He was lying on his back with the duvet bunched at his waist. His eyes were closed, his brows drawn, his face ashen under the morning whiskers. A worn notebook lay next to him, and she realized he'd fallen asleep reading.

"Mitch? It's Carly," she murmured, closing the door behind her.

He didn't respond. Swallowing a sudden jolt of panic, she hurried to his side. She touched his shoulder with her fingertips and called his name more loudly. His lashes fluttered, and he muttered something she didn't understand.

"Who should I call? Mitch?"

Suddenly she remembered the phone in her hand. Taking a deep breath, she punched the talk button and lifted it to her ear. "Mr. Dante?"

"Yes?" The voice that had answered was deeper than most and flavored with caution.

"This is Caroline Alderson. Perhaps Mitch has mentioned me?"

"He had indeed, Dr. Alderson. Where is the lazy so-and-so, anyway?"

"He's still in bed, and, Mr. Dante, he seems to be in severe pain."

"Muscle spasms in his legs?"

"Yes, I think so."

"Is he conscious?"

Carly glanced at Mitch's ashen face. "Not really."

"Okay, this is what you do. Soak a couple of bath towels in hot water, hot as you can stand it, and then wrap his thighs as tight as you can. That should ease the pain enough to bring him to long enough to shove a Demerol down his throat. You'll probably find the tablets with his shaving stuff. Got all that, or should I repeat it?"

"No, I've got it." She took a much needed breath. "I take it this has happened before?"

"A few times, yeah," Dante drawled in what she suspected was a major understatement. "One more thing, Dr. Alderson. Mitch hates for anyone to see him like this, and he hates having to accept help even more. Most likely he'll be in a vicious mood when he wakes up, so be prepared."

"I will, and thanks for the advice."

"You're welcome. Better take down my number just in case, though."

"Just a minute, let me find a pen." Glancing around hastily, she saw a gold pen on the dresser, along with a man's wallet, car keys and small leather notebook.

"Okay, shoot," she said when she'd grabbed the pen and torn a page from the notebook. Wedging the phone against her shoulder, she wrote down the number he gave her and shoved it into the pocket of her robe.

"Have him call me when he's up to it, okay?"

"Yes, I'll do that."

She switched off the phone and left it and the pen on the dresser before hurrying into the bathroom. She plugged the tub, turned on the hot tap full blast and impatiently waited for the tub to fill. When the steam was thick enough to raise a sweat on her skin, she tossed the two towels from the rod into the water and watched them sink before searching for the pills.

She found them tucked inside a worn leather shaving kit, just as Dante had suggested. A quick glance at the label gave her the dosage, two tablets as needed for pain. She pocketed the tiny bottle, then filled the glass she found on the sink with water and carried it into the bedroom.

He hadn't moved. Agony seemed an inadequate term for what he seemed to be suffering, she thought as she drew back the comforter.

The next few minutes were an exercise in patience as she managed to wrap one thigh, then the other, in the hot towels. By the time she finished, she was drenched in sweat, and he was groaning steadily as she covered him again.

Twenty minutes later she'd wiped his face a dozen times and checked the clock at least twice as often. He was still out, but his color was better, and he'd stopped groaning.

Closing her eyes, she flexed her aching back, then reached for the towel again. Before her hand reached his face, his hand came up to stop her. His eyes were open, but unfocused.

"Mitch, it's me," she murmured when pain shot up her arm from the pressure of hard fingers. "Let me go, Mitch. It's Carly."

"Sweet Caroline," he murmured as he eased the terrible pressure; then his fingers fell away. He looked exhausted, but alert enough to swallow the painkillers.

"Two, right?" she asked, reaching for the water.

When he nodded, she slipped the pills between his lips, then held his head while he swallowed. "You can go away now," he said, his eyes closed. He sounded perfectly reasonable, which surprised her, given Dante's warning.

"Will you be all right?"

"Just need to sleep," he managed to get out between gasping breaths. He'd gone through some bad times in the past five years, but he couldn't remember hating his disability more than he did at this moment.

Carly eased to her feet, careful to keep from jarring the bed, but the sudden clenching of his jaw told her that she hadn't been careful enough.

"Sorry," she murmured before bending to kiss his forehead. *I love you so,* she told him silently before leaving him to fight his way through the pain alone.

Carly stopped by Tracy's room to explain that she was running late, then went straight to her bedroom to call Dante.

"Are you sure he'll be all right?" she asked after identifying herself and giving him a quick run-down of what she'd done.

Dante's sigh was impatient. "Yes, I'm sure. He just needs to sleep off the medication."

Carly rubbed Tabitha behind the ears absently, her mind still on the suffering man one flight below. "Does this sort of thing happen often?"

"Often enough."

Carly drew a breath. "I'm sorry, I forgot to tell him you called."

"Don't worry about it. Next time you see him, tell him I've lined up a couple of prospects with executive experience in spa management for him to interview when he gets back next week. If he has any questions, he knows where to reach me."

They chatted for a few minutes longer, then hung up.

It was nearly four in the afternoon by the time Carly returned home. After their shopping spree, she'd dropped Tracy at Karen's and then worked for an hour or so in her office on end-of-term reports before heading home.

She was loaded down with packages and out of sorts when Tilly opened the back door for her. "I saw you coming," the housekeeper explained as she relieved Carly of two of the bulging shopping bags. "Looks like Tracy found a few things she liked."

"Just a few," Carly muttered, depositing the remaining bundles on the kitchen table. "I think we'll just leave all of these here and let her put them away."

Tilly nodded. "She'll want to show them off anyway, before she hauls them all upstairs."

Carly flexed her tired shoulders, then sniffed the air. "Is that gingerbread I smell?"

"It is. I was just getting ready to prepare tea for your mother and Mr. Scanlon, if he's up to it."

"How is he?" Carly asked anxiously. She'd worried about him non-stop all day.

"Truth to tell, Carly, I haven't seen him."

"Hmm, maybe I should check on him." She hesitated, not wanting him to think she was hovering. "I'll take him a cup of tea and a piece of gingerbread."

"Poor boy is probably half-starved," Tilly muttered, putting two squares of still warm gingerbread on a plate. "Big as he is, he needs lots of fuel."

Carly poured tea into one of the cups already waiting on the tray, added a slice of lemon to the saucer and then, remembering, spooned in two sugars. "He likes his drinks sweet," she murmured when she caught Tilly's eyebrows lifting.

"Noticed that, did you?" Tilly handed her a small wooden tray, a knowing look in her eyes.

"Of course I noticed," Carly said archly as she picked up the tray. "After all, I am my mother's daughter. We live to hostess."

Tilly shook her head, her eyes twinkling in her kind face. "Tell Mitch I'd be happy to fix him a steak if he can't wait until dinner," she called after Carly as she left the kitchen.

Mitch sat up in stages, his thighs screaming and his gut queasy from the medicine and pain. He hadn't had spasms that bad in months. He wouldn't have had them now if he'd chucked aside his macho pride and used the chair when he was tired.

Slowly, in the way he had to do everything now, he unwrapped the sodden towels from his legs and tried not to think about Carly's hands on his wasted muscles. Hell, he should be glad he'd been pretty much out of it, he thought as he piled the towels on the already damp sheet. Humiliation was something he handled better in small doses—when he was able to handle it at all.

It hurt to turn toward the clock, but he did it anyway. Seeing that he'd slept away a good part of the day, he scowled as he reached for his undershorts. He needed a hot bath and a shave before he went looking for coffee and something to fill his empty belly. If he was lucky, he wouldn't run into Carly until he'd had some time to patch up his battered ego.

The muscles he could still feel screamed in protest as he struggled into his shorts, then one by one his braces. He was strapping the last cuff when he heard a rap at the door, followed by Carly's voice calling his name. Before he could tell her to go away, she walked in, carrying a tray.

She was wearing tan slacks and a silky shirt the color of smoke. A gold locket on a simple chain nestled just above her breasts. She looked neat and stylish and just about as sexy as a woman can look in clothes. His pulse speeded up, yet at the same time embarrassment coiled in his belly. Even though he knew it wasn't her fault that she'd caught him at his most vulnerable, he found himself hating the fact that she had.

"Good, you're awake," she said as she balanced the tray she was carrying on one hand and closed the door with the other. "How are you feeling?"

Like a poor excuse for a man he thought before answering with a terse, "Okay."

"Before I forget to mention it again, your friend Dante wants you to call him when you get a chance. He said to tell you that he's lined up some prospects for you to interview."

"You talked to Dante?" he demanded too quickly.

She nodded, an uncomfortable look taking over her face. "That's actually the reason why I was in your room earlier—to tell you he was on the phone. He's the one who told me what to do to ease the spasms."

Her gaze jerked away from his legs, as though the sight of the braces disgusted her, and his mood turned ugly as heat climbed his neck.

"Sounds like the two of you had quite a talk. What else did my old buddy tell you about me?"

"Nothing more than I needed to know to help you," she returned with a poise that shamed him. He was being an ungrateful jerk, he told himself before clearing his throat and forcing out the words she deserved to hear. "Thanks for taking care of me. I owe you one."

Carly heard the stiff crackle of pride in his tone, which she'd expected. What she *hadn't* expected was the hint of vulnerability in the set of those huge shoulders and the way his big hands were clenched where they gripped the rumpled sheet. Realizing that he was embarrassed for her to see him at his most helpless sent a wave of tenderness running through her.

"Actually, I'd say we were even," she told him with a casual smile as she crossed the room to set the tray on the table by the bed. "You were there for me that night when I fell apart in the pool. I was happy to return the favor."

When he remained silent, she indicated the tray with a smile. "I figured you'd be hungry, so I brought you a cup of tea and some of Tilly's gingerbread. Also, Tilly said to tell you she'd be happy to fix you a steak if you're too famished to wait until dinner."

"Must be my lucky day. A pretty nurse hovering and room service to boot."

Carly caught a hint of sarcasm in his voice and reminded herself that he was more than likely still hurting.

"Would you like lemon? I couldn't remember—"

"You don't have to feed me, Carly," he declared in a cold voice. "It's my legs that don't work, not my hands."

"I know that, Mitch," she said quietly. "Just as I know you're upset because you hate to accept help, but we all need help on occasion."

His mouth compressed, deepening the lines that suffering had etched into his strong face. "It's not the help I mind. It's the pity that usually goes along with it."

"I don't pity you," Carly stated firmly.

His tawny eyes took on a bleak cast. "I've heard that before from a woman. Like the dumb jock I am, I even believed it—until I found out from some of my buddies in rehab that the lady in question was turned on by gimps." Her soft gasp was like a knife to his heart, and even though he felt as though he were bleeding regret, he made himself go on. For the sake of his pride he needed to know that the woman he was coming to care about so deeply wasn't playing that same sick game. "Seems it gave her a thrill to make love to a guy who couldn't move half his body, no matter how aroused he got." His mouth twisted. "She knew all the right things to say, I'll give her that, but then, so do you."

It took a moment for Carly to feel the hurt. When she did, something died inside. "If that's what you think of me, we have nothing more to say to each other." She turned to go, but he lunged forward and caught her hand, dragging her back. His fingers were steel, hurting her where they gripped. Though fear surged, she managed to fight it down because she sensed an inner agony in him far greater than the physical pain he'd endured earlier.

"Let me go," she said quietly, her gaze locked on his.

Though he eased his grip, he kept her prisoner. "Why did you let me make love to you, Carly? Was it because you felt sorry for me?"

Carly took a deep breath and reminded herself of the years she'd spend believing that no man would ever want to touch her once he'd found out that she'd been raped. In his own way, Mitch was feeling just as insecure about his sex appeal. "I made love to you because I trusted you not to hurt me the way I'd been hurt before," she said, smiling softly at the memory of exquisite tenderness that night in the pool.

"Which is just a diplomatic way of saying I'm safe, right?"

Puzzled by his words, she let her smile fade. "In a way, yes."

"Safe because I'm only half a man," he suggested in that same cold tone she was coming to dislike intensely.

"No, of course not!"

"Safe because I couldn't rape you the way Tracy's father did, even if I wanted to?"

Carly stared at him, unwilling to believe her ears. Could he really be that insensitive? "I'm not even going to dignify that with an answer."

Mitch heard the tremor in her voice and was suddenly ashamed of himself. "Hell, I don't know what I'm saying." He realized then that he was still clutching Carly's wrist and let her go. "Look, I'm sorry I blew up at you." He glanced down, his shoulders taking on a weary slump that tore at her soul. "I admit I've got more than my share of ego. Guess that's why I thought I was helping you heal."

"But you are!" she declared emphatically. "I realize now that what happened that night in Palm Springs was just as much my fault as yours, and—" Carly bit off the rest, but it was too late. Mitch's face had turned the color of wet ashes.

"Sarah?" he murmured, looking up at her in stunned disbelief.

"Yes, that was the name I used. It sounds silly now, but it made me feel more... interesting."

Though his face was still ashen, his gaze had narrowed, becoming accusing. "So you deliberately lied when you said we'd never met."

"Mitch, try to understand," she pleaded softly. "Coach invited you to visit while I was in the East, and when I walked into the parlor that night I wasn't ready to deal with the past. And when I realized you couldn't remember where we'd met, I decided not to... refresh your memory."

Reeling as though from a blindside hit, Mitch stared at Carly's face and tried to see a girl named Sarah. Once he'd been thankful to find his recollection of that night blurred, as though a curtain had been drawn over his mind, obscuring everything that happened from the time they left the bar until he woke up the next morning in a half stupor. Now he struggled to push past the fog, only to find the same scant impressions. So few, really. A feeling of soft skin against his, the taste of sweet kisses, an instant of the purest bliss as he'd plunged into her. And then, the next morning, those awful bloody sheets.

"You came to my room, you had to know that I wanted to make love to you," he said hoarsely.

"I thought I wanted that, too." Carly drew a shaky breath. "It was my first time, I was scared, and then . . ." She had to take another breath before she could continue. "It was as though, suddenly, I realized what was really happening, that I was making a terrible mistake."

She took a breath, realizing that the words she had to say would hurt. "You didn't give me a chance to beg you to stop, but. . . at the time I didn't understand how. . . difficult it would be for you to back off once you were excited. And you'd had a lot to drink."

"Don't sugarcoat it, Carly!" he commanded bluntly. "I was lousy, stinking drunk." He hadn't had a beer since, and only rarely had more than a glass of wine with dinner. "For what it's worth, I tried to find you later—after I'd sobered up enough to realize what I did—but you were gone. I knew I'd been a self-ish ass, but, God help me, I never for one minute thought that you might have been unwilling."

Suddenly he dropped his head and buried his face in his hands. His shoulders heaved as he drew a harsh breath before lifting his head again. "I know it doesn't mean jack to say I'm sorry, but you have to believe me, Carly, I've never regretted anything more in my life."

"I do believe you, Mitch—now. But it took me a long time to let go of my anger—and my guilt."

Mitch bit his lip, his eyes turbulent, his expression troubled. Finally he straightened his shoulders, then asked softly, "And . . . Tracy?"

Carly's mouth trembled, then firmed. "She's your child."

For a frozen moment Mitch couldn't breathe. His chest burned, and he felt lightheaded. Finally starved for air, he dragged in a harsh lungful and tried to make sense of chaos in his head. But his usually logical mind refused to move past a mercifully numbing shock.

"Why didn't you get in touch with me when you found out you were pregnant?"

"Several reasons," Carly admitted. "Primarily, though, I convinced myself that you wouldn't want anything to do with me or the baby."

"You were dead wrong," he said with rough emphasis. "I know what it's like to grow up without a father. I never would have wanted that for a child of mine."

"But I didn't know that!" she protested urgently. "How could I?"

"By giving me the chance to tell you!" he snapped, his eyes flashing as much in anger as frustration.

"Put yourself in my place, Mitch," she said as calmly as her thudding heart would allow. "You were already famous, and I was a nobody, just a girl who agreed to a one-night stand. You yourself say that you didn't even remember my face the next morning. What makes you think you would have believed my story, even if I'd come to you?"

"Damn it, Carly! I would have married you! Hell, I..." He stopped abruptly to pass a hand over his face. "Okay, let's forget the past," he said with a rare impatience. "But what about now? Why didn't you tell me that night in the pool. Or last night?"

Carly felt a stab of guilt. "I wanted to," she admitted softly. "Especially that night at Gallagher's. And then later, in the pool, I realized that I'd been terribly wrong about you. You weren't selfish or callous, just the opposite."

He lifted one eyebrow sardonically. "Are you sure you weren't waiting for the right moment to cut me off at the knees? Like now, maybe?"

"How dare you!" Carly exclaimed, her body beginning to shake.

"You lied once. Maybe you're lying again."

She drew a sharp breath. "I'm telling you the truth, Mitch. Believe me or not. It's your choice."

She turned stiffly and walked out, closing the door very softly behind her.

Jess Dante cradled his Scotch and water on his flat belly and watched his two-year-old son Tyler chasing a butterfly around the backyard of the old Victorian house in a Sacramento suburb where he lived with his wife Hazel and their two children.

Mitch sat nearby, cradling three-year-old Francey against his chest. Worn out from a wild game of soccer she'd had earlier with her Daddy, she had climbed into his lap for a victory hug and almost immediately fallen asleep.

Hazel had offered to take her inside when she'd gone in to tend to the arroz con pollo, but Mitch had claimed the little tike was sleeping too soundly to be moved. In reality, he'd been enjoying the feel of the small warm body nestled against him so trustingly.

Hazel had simply smiled that kind smile of hers, kissed her daughter on the top of her head, and then kissed him on the cheek before muttering one word. "Softy."

Not many people knew him well enough to know he'd always been a sucker for kids. For a lot of years, he'd always figured to have himself a house full once his vagabond playing days were over.

"I couldn't even face her the next day, Jess. Every time I thought about what I did to her, I got a bellyful of acid." He drew a hard breath. "Damn, I still can't believe I didn't recognize her."

"Eighteen years is a long time."

A burly, craggy-faced California native of Italian descent, Dante had been well on his way to becoming number one in Formula One racing when an accident had cost him his right arm. After a difficult recovery, he'd returned home to attend law school, becoming one of the most respected criminal attorneys in the state.

It had been his idea to join forces in the spa and half his money that had gotten it started. Along the way he and Mitch had become friends, closer, perhaps than most, because each understood the demons the other kept hidden from the world.

"I remember walking out of my motel room the next morning and heading for the nearest bar," Mitch confessed, fighting the sudden rush of shame. "Two days later I woke up in the drunk tank with the D.T.'s and some guy swinging a sledgehammer in my head."

Dante took a sip of his drink, his gaze on his son. "I've had a few headaches like that myself," he said in a voice that said he wasn't proud of admitting that about himself.

"As soon as I raised bail, I tried to find her. Went to every motel in Palm Springs, but there was no one with her name registered. Now I know why."

Mitch swallowed another mouthful of soda, then poured the rest onto the grass and crumpled the flimsy can in his fist. Since he'd gotten back to California, he'd been having trouble keeping much of anything down. He didn't even think about sleeping.

"Hey you two," Hazel called through the open kitchen window. "You've got ten more minutes to talk dirty before dinner's on the table."

Mitch watched Dante's face soften and looked away. "When's Hazel due?" he asked, watching Tyler's grubby hands flailing the air as the butterfly dipped and soared just out of range, as though playing tag with the giggling toddler.

"Second week in January." Dante drained his glass and set it on the table between them. "Another girl."

Mitch smiled. "Tyler's going to have a heck of a time holding his own."

Dante looked at his friend. "How's it feel to find out you have a half-grown daughter?"

Mitch felt the familiar thud in his gut. "Like someone came up with a cure for paralysis and then told me I didn't deserve to have it."

Dante's dark eyes flooded with sympathy. "Could be you're being too hard on yourself here, Mitch. Times were different when we were kids."

Mitch slanted him a hard look. "Tell me something, Jess. Did you ever force a woman against her will?"

Dante's face tightened. "No."

Mitch scrubbed his free hand over his face. "God, Jess. I keep seeing Carly's face when she told me. Her eyes. I should have known.... I even had this nagging feeling we'd met someplace." He gave a snort of self-disgust. "Even when we made love, it didn't connect. I thought it was some other bastard who'd hurt her."

"What are you going to do?"

"What *can* I do?" He'd asked himself that same question over and over. He still didn't have an answer. "All I know is football, so I'll do my damnedest to give her the winning season she wants, but that's not nearly enough."

He'd lain awake night after night since returning to California, imagining what the last seventeen years had been like for her. Suffering through childbirth at an age when most girls were going to dances and football games, hearing the gossip, seeing the stares, raising Tracy alone. Worrying about her, seeing her through the sniffles and the first day of school.

"Sometimes I think about all the times I felt sorry for myself these past five years. Funny thing, I don't think I'll ever feel sorry for myself again, not when I think about the hell I put her through. I deserve to be crippled. And worse."

Dante reached over and laid his hand on Mitch's knee. "I wish I could tell you it would all work out," he said before sitting back again. "But that would be a lie, and we both know it. Sometimes there's not one damn thing you can do to make things right."

Mitch lifted his chest in a breath so slow it didn't ruffle a hair on Francey's dark head, but he felt as though he'd just run a marathon. "I'm crazy about her, Jess. Ain't that a hoot? I want her so badly I'm damn near sick with it."

"Then fight for her, Mitch. Fight the way you fought to walk again."

"If I thought it would do any good, I'd crawl the length of the damn stadium to beg her forgiveness."

"Dinner," Hazel yelled. "Rustle those sexy buns, gentlemen, or I'll feed it to the chipmunks."

Dante called to Tyler, who came toddling over, a big grin on his face, his arms outstretched. Jess scooped him into a one-armed embrace and kissed his fat little cheek. Tyler giggled as Jess set him on his feet again, then handed him the empty glass.

"Here, tiger, take this in to mama while I get your sister, okay?"

"'Kay."

Tyler toddled across the patio, happily chattering to himself. Watching, Mitch felt pain squeeze his heart.

"Hang in there, buddy. I've never known you to quit yet," Dante said feelingly.

Glancing up, Mitch met Dante's compassionate eyes squarely. "There's always a first time." Careful not to wake Francey, he lifted her into her father's waiting arm.

"Shove that soda can in my pocket, will you?" Dante asked. "Hazel recycles everything."

Mitch did as he was asked before reaching down for his crutches. "How about ex-football players?" he asked, using the arm of the sturdy chair as support while he levered himself to his feet. "Think she can recycle me into something someone would want?"

Dante didn't smile. "I think that's something you're going to have to do for yourself."

Chapter 12

Carly cried at Tracy's graduation. Everyone assumed it was because her one and only fledgling was leaving the nest. Everyone knew how close they were, how fiercely she had protected her child from the moment of her birth. And that was part of it. But as she sat in the hard chair on the floor of the high school gym, she was also crying for the things her little girl had never had—like the joy of seeing her father's eyes light up with happiness the first time her tiny hand grasped his. Or the quiet security of knowing that she was loved by two parents who also loved one another.

Carly knew now that would never be, no matter how much she might want it to be. She had accepted that. She had made peace with it. She *had*.

If only Mitch hadn't sent the corsages. Three. One for each of the Alderson ladies. Only Tracy's had been signed with love.

"...and the requests for season tickets are running ahead of even my most optimistic projection." Marca tossed the report onto Carly's desk and sat back with a pleased sigh. "Lord, I'm good."

Carly broke off another square of chocolate from the half-finished bar and popped it into her mouth. "Don't break an arm patting yourself on the back just yet, Kenworthy. We're still a long way from solvent."

It was almost the end of July, and Alderson Hall was all but empty. Most of the department heads were on vacation, leaving the most junior members of the faculty to teach the abbreviated summer session. Tonight, as was her long-standing custom, Carly was hosting a reception for the incoming freshmen to personally welcome them to a week-long orientation period. Tomorrow she had meetings scheduled with the various department heads, and then, tomorrow night, she was leaving on a month-long alumni junket to Europe.

The trip she'd anticipated so eagerly a year ago was now a duty. Her bags were packed, her tickets confirmed and reconfirmed for the chartered flight she was to meet in Portland, her desk nearly clear. She would be returning a scant two weeks before classes began.

"Why do I keep thinking I shouldn't go on this trip?" She flicked a quick glance toward the window. It was raining again.

"Ever hear of a Superwoman Complex? Whoever came up with that one had to have you in mind."

"Don't be nasty, Marca. I know I can't do it all. I don't even try."

"That's true. You let Joe McNabb fix broken light sockets and cranky elevators, and so far you haven't subbed for Dr. Hong in Advanced Mandarin, although you've taught in just about every other department."

"I know my limitations."

"Uh-huh. What about last January, when it snowed so much none of the maintenance workers could get to campus, so you ran the snow blower? And then there was the time the flagpole rope got snarled and—"

"Enough!" Carly held up both hands, laughing in spite of herself. "I get the point. Maybe I'll admit I have a minor compulsion to handle the important things myself, but I don't have a problem delegating responsibility to people I know I can really trust. Like you."

"And, of course, you never check up on me or anyone else to make sure things are being handled properly, right?"

"Only in the course of my own responsibilities." Carly glanced sideways at the lengthy list of To Do on her daily planner, the one organized in five-minute blocks. "For instance, if I had any doubts at all, I'd ask you very discreetly if you've remembered to put the date and time of cheerleading tryouts on your calendar."

Marca sighed dramatically. "Don't worry, I'll be there, ready to offer a sympathetic shoulder if Tracy doesn't make the squad."

"I know you will. And I know I really didn't have to remind you. It's just that this is the first time I've left her for more than a few weeks at a stretch. And I guess I'm going through separation anxiety."

"She's a high school graduate now, and a duly enrolled college freshman. And in four months she'll be eighteen. In other words, she's a big girl. She'll be fine. It's you I'm worried about."

"I'm a survivor, you know that. I just hope Bradenton is." She sighed, then furrowed her brow. "How many tickets aren't sold yet?"

"I'm not going to tell you, because you'll only brood about it on the plane."

Carly wanted to argue, but she knew Marca was right. "You're right. I apologize for being a wet blanket," she said, rubbing her aching head. Two weeks ago she hadn't known a headache could withstand every remedy known to medical science and some she'd invented out of desperation. But this one had.

"I understand. You have your reasons." Marca helped herself to a double square of chocolate. "Have you heard from him?"

Carly glanced toward the black clouds outside. Appropriate, she thought with a ragged sigh. "Not a word. Not even a bread-and-butter letter thanking me for my hospitality."

"Under the circumstances, that might be just a little bit too much to expect, don't you think?"

"You mean because I lost my temper and spoke rashly and did all the things I've prided myself on not doing for so long? Or do you mean because he didn't even have the guts to say goodbye?"

Marca rubbed a finger over her nose. "Maybe he was bleeding too much," she said laconically.

"Thanks a lot, Marca."

"Hey, I'm here to serve!" Her smile flashed, but her eyes were troubled. "For the record, though, I think it's a good thing the history between you two is finally on the table. Keeping secrets can be a dangerous proposition, especially between two people who are sleeping together."

Carly opened a carefully marked folder and placed Marca's most recent progress report on top. A copy of Scanlon's contract was there, as well, along with a note he'd sent Sandy only a few days before, asking her to contact a real estate broker on his behalf.

"I keep telling myself he won't say anything to Tracy. That he has more integrity than that. More compassion."

"I agree."

Carly ran her fingertips over the folder. There was a buzzing in her head now, to add texture to the pain. "I understand that Coach has heard from him. Apparently he's due back on Saturday. He's a professional. He won't let his personal feelings interfere with his job."

Carly's eyes stung. She couldn't remember when she'd wanted to cry more than she did at this moment. But big girls didn't cry. Nor did college presidents.

"I hurt him, Marca. If I'd taken a knife and shoved it into his belly, I couldn't have hurt him more. He was feeling vulnerable, and instead of understanding, I pulled out all the old pain and humiliation and resentment and dumped it on him."

Marca drew a long, sad breath. "Oh, Carly, life can be a bitch, can't it?"

Thirty-one days later, Marca picked Carly up at the airport in Medford and they talked nonstop all the way back to the campus. Carly's first question was about Tracy and her giddy excitement at making the junior varsity squad.

"She's already got her uniform," Marca said with a grin. "I keep telling her she'll wear it out before the season starts if she doesn't stop trying it on three times a day."

Carly laughed. "I can't wait to see her. Has she changed?"

Marca shot her a quick look before returning her attention to the freeway ahead. "You've only been gone four weeks."

"Feels more like four years." Tired and already jet-lagged, Carly leaned back against the Bronco's high seat and closed her eyes. "How's Coach?"

"Impossible. The press loves him."

"And . . . Mitch?"

"He bought a small place in that new development across the river from me. Since it wasn't quite finished, he was able to have them customize it for his special needs. He moved in last week. Had some of the guys from the team helping." She hesitated, then added, "Tracy helped, too."

Carly sighed. "I know. She told me on the phone when I called two nights ago."

"It wasn't his idea," Marca hastened to explain. "I know, because I asked her in a roundabout way."

Carly nodded. "What about the team?"

"Improving every day. He's holding two practices a day, six days a week. Since today's Sunday, I can't drive you by the field to let you watch, but believe me, it's a sight to behold. All those muscular young bodies glistening with sweat. Wow!"

"Marca, behave yourself."

Marca grinned. "From what I've heard, Mitch runs a very tight program, all business. Seems he loaded them all into a bus the first day of practice and took them up to Portland."

"To see the Jacks practicing?"

"No, to a rehab center. Made them spend the whole day watching the patients going through all kinds of hell. According to Ian it made a big impact. Now, when someone starts to complain, one of the other guys just quietly tells him to shut up and get back to work." Her lips curved. "He's also got them on a strict regimen, no smoking, absolutely no drinking and an eleven o'clock weeknight curfew, which, I gather from the rumblings, is not all that popular at the moment."

Carly slitted her eyes and stared straight ahead. "I hate to admit it, but I spent the first part of my trip waiting to hear that he wasn't coming back from California."

Marca grinned, but sobered quickly. "This is just a guess, but I think he's put himself in a hell far worse than any you or I could ever have thought up for him as punishment."

Carly rubbed the spot just above her heart that had been aching since she'd left. The irony was inescapable. "Maybe he has company in that hell."

"Is that the way you want to leave things?"

Carly straightened and flexed her shoulders. "I had a lot of time to think on this trip, and I've come to the conclusion that I like my life the way it was just fine. I don't need Mitch Scanlon to make me happy or complete or more of a woman."

"Maybe you don't need him, but you love him, and I can't imagine how you can just slip back into your old workaholic life without missing him terribly every single minute."

"I can, and I will."

Marca shot her a quick look, then lapsed into silence for the rest of the drive. As soon as they reached the campus gates, Carly was suddenly wide awake and excited to be seeing her daughter again.

The campus looked as well kept as ever, with emerald vistas as far as the eye could see. In the bright sunshine, the buildings seemed more white than gray. The stadium was hidden behind a hill to her right, but she knew it was there. The first game was only three weeks away.

Her stomach knotted, and her throat hurt.

"Home sweet home," Marca murmured as she braked for the turn into the driveway. "How's it feel to be back?"

"I'll let you know tomorrow, after I've had a look at my desk."

Marca parked behind the MG and set the brake. "I'll help you with your bags, and then I have to split. I *know* what *my* desk looks like, and it ain't pretty."

Carly got out slowly, still stiff and achy from the long series of flights. "What time is it?" she asked, checking her watch. "The pilot told us right before we landed, but I just want to double-check."

"Four-oh-eight. What've you got, London time?"

"Don't ask."

Carly had traveled light, and between them, they managed the two suitcases and three huge shopping bags filled with treasures she hadn't been able to resist.

Tilly saw her first and hurried across the foyer for a hug. Carly set down her bundles and held out her arms. "Oh, Tilly, it's so good to see you!"

"Welcome home, Carly. We've all missed you."

"I've missed you, too. All of you."

Tilly stepped back and looked her up and down with all-knowing eyes. "You've lost weight, honey. Didn't they feed you over in those foreign countries?"

"Yes, but I ran it off."

"I'll just run these up for you," Marca said, moving past her to the stairs. "Go ahead in. I'll let myself out."

"Thanks for picking me up. I owe you one."

"Don't worry, I'll put it in the tally book. Right next to all the ones I owe you."

Tilly picked up the bundles and followed.

"I'll get those, Tilly. Don't bother."

"It's no bother. Besides, you'll be wantin' a private moment with Tracy and your mum. They're out on the terrace, having tea."

Carly straightened her tired shoulders and hurried through the house's air-conditioned rooms to the terrace. In her absence, maintenance had replaced the glass panels with the summer screens, and the scent of flowers mingled with the familiar tang of chlorine.

Her mother was sitting at the table with the blue-and-white umbrella tipped to put her into deep shade. While she sipped tea and paged through one of her expensive decorating magazines, Tracy was sunning herself by the pool. Her bright pink bikini was still damp, and she'd twisted her hair into a loose knot on the top of her head. Escaping tendrils curled in charming wisps around her face. She looked so beautiful that for a moment Carly could only stand and stare.

Sensing her gaze, Tracy glanced up, squealing with delight as soon as she saw who was standing there. "Mom!" In a blur of pink she was out of her chair and running toward Carly like an excited four-year-old.

A lump blocked Carly's throat as she gathered her daughter into her arms and hugged her tight. Her heart was racing, and she felt like crying, but she managed to keep it light as she held Tracy away from her to study her face.

"Yes, this is definitely my daughter the cheerleader."

Tracy beamed. "I kept thinking I'd get out there in front of all the judges and just freeze up."

"But you didn't, and I'm proud of you."

"Thanks." She shot a look over her shoulder, then grinned. "I'll go change into my outfit while you say hi to Grandmother, okay?"

"Very much okay." Tracy gave her mother a kiss on the cheek before heading inside at a very uncheerleaderlike lope.

"Welcome home, dear," Felicity said with what looked to Carly like genuine delight. "I hope you had a lovely time."

"Mostly it was hectic. I'm glad to be back."

"You looked tired, dear. Did you sleep on the plane?"

Carly shook her head. She hated to fly under any circumstances, but flying over water for hour after endless hour always made her tense. "Mostly I'm jet-lagged. I feel as though I could sleep for days."

Felicity looked dismayed. "I hope you're not too tired for the welcome-home dinner I've arranged. Now, don't get that mulish look, Caroline. It's very casual, just family. And Marca and Peter, of course. I invited Mitchell, as well. After all, he still seems like family, even if he's no longer under our roof. But he asked to be excused. Apparently he had made other plans for this evening."

Carly was too tired to feel more than a dull pain above her heart.

The last day of August set a high-temperature record. Outside the air-conditioned mansion, heat rose in shimmering waves, wilting the leaves of the trees and driving all but those with lizard blood inside.

Carly turned from the window to watch with mixed feelings as Tracy closed the box containing her books and other favorite things she intended to take across campus to her dorm room. The rest of her things were already in Felicity's sedan.

"Have you met your roommate yet?" she asked when Tracy straightened.

"Not yet. I hear she's from Tacoma."

Carly nodded. "How about blankets? Are you sure you don't want to take one more just in case that old boiler goes out again?"

"I'll be fine. Besides, I can always hunt up one of the guys on the floor and cuddle in with him."

Carly took a careful breath. "Does that mean you're over your infatuation with Ian?"

Tracy's gaze slid from her mother's. "No, but I have kept my promise not to date him."

"I wasn't asking, sweetie. I trust you, you know that."

"I know." Tracy glanced around the room, then nodded. "Guess that does it." She drew a long breath, then hunched her shoulders. "I hate to leave, and yet I can't wait. Does that make sense?"

"Absolutely," Carly said with only a faint tremor in her voice. "That's exactly the way it should be."

Tracy nodded, her expression turning pensive. "I was kinda hoping you and Mitch might hit it off, you know? Maybe even end up together?"

Carly managed a grin. "You know how it is with people our age. We're too set in our ways."

"He always asks about you when I run into him at the field."

"Does he?" Carly tried to make her question casual. The sudden glint in Tracy's eyes told her that she'd failed.

"The whole time you were gone, he would ask me if I'd heard from you, if you were having a good time, stuff like that, and then when I'd tell him, he'd get this sad look on his face. I think he missed you."

Carly drew a breath. "You like him, don't you?"

Tracy nodded. "I think he's just about the bravest person I've ever met, next to you, of course." She ended with a grin, which Carly managed to return.

"Of course," Carly teased, before sobering. "I'm curious, sweetie. What made you think of Mitch as brave?"

Tracy shrugged one shoulder as though embarrassed now that she'd initiated this topic. "When we're done practicing, some of the other girls and I usually hang around a while and watch the guys. There was this one time when Mitch was trying to teach Ian something about timing, you know, like leading the receiver, and Ian just couldn't get it right, so Mitch handed one of the guys his right crutch and took the ball himself. But when he tried to throw it, he lost his balance and fell down, right in front of the team and a lot of other people who were just hanging around watching, like Karen and me.''

Carly winced. ''Was he hurt?''

''Just his pride. His face got real red, and he sort of bit off his words, you know? Karen and I were about to cry, 'cause he was so helpless, and the guys just looked at each other like they didn't know what to do. And then Mitch just started to laugh. It was like he broke the tension, you know, and everyone else started to laugh, too. Ian and one of the other guys helped him up, and then Mitch ordered Jackson Finney to stand behind him so he wouldn't fall. Told Jackson his tail would be in a sling if he let the coach fall on his, um, butt, and then Mitch threw that ball right into the hands of Billy Randolph.'' She shook her head before reaching down for her suitcase. ''I gotta tell you, Mom, Mitch must have been some great football player.''

Carly busied herself checking the zipper on a large tote, her eyes swimming with tears she didn't dare shed. ''He was,'' she said softly, lifting the tote's strap to her shoulder. ''And I have a feeling he's going to be a great coach.''

Just as he would have been a great father.

They were two days into the fall semester when Carly ran into Mitch in the foyer of Alderson Hall. He was wearing an orange polo shirt with the Wolves' logo written across his broad chest in electric blue, and twill slacks, as though he'd just come from practice. He had just left the Dean of Men's office and looked preoccupied and tired.

He smiled a little when he saw her, but something in his eyes kept her from smiling back. He stopped as she neared, and she felt her pace slowing, though a part of her wanted to ignore the obvious invitation. Her heart still ached from the harsh words they'd exchanged the last time they were together. The last thing she needed now was another confrontation, especially in public.

''So, how was your trip? ' he asked after they'd exchanged stilted greetings.

"Exhausting," she replied, both relieved and disappointed at his impersonal tone. "It'll be a long time before I can get excited about fifteenth-century architecture and archaic plumbing."

His mouth slanted, but his eyes remained guarded. "Guess I probably shouldn't mention the problem McNabb has been having with the training room whirlpool to you right now."

"Not unless the building's in danger of falling down and I'm the only one who can save it."

His eyes crinkled slightly. "It'll keep till you've sorted yourself out."

Somehow she managed to work up a smile. Being near him, and yet so emotionally distant, was much harder than she'd anticipated. "Thank goodness. I knew I'd come home to a stack of paperwork. I didn't expect a mountain." But that was her problem, she reminded herself. "How about you? Are you and the Wolves ready to take on the Jacks on Saturday?"

"Ready as we'll ever be."

Carly felt a hole open in her stomach. They were conversing like colleagues who didn't know each other very well, using the stilted words that polite people used when they had little in common with one another. But we made a baby, she wanted to shout. And we made love.

"Think you'll win?"

He shook his head. "No, but that's not the point, is it?"

"No, I guess not." She shifted her briefcase to the other hand. She wanted to be in his arms, and, at the same time, she wanted to forget she'd ever met him. "Marca tells me it's a sellout."

"So I hear." He noticed that she'd changed her hair. Cut it, curled it, something, but it was still shiny and clean-looking and framed her face like a shimmery cloud. He wanted to crush it in his hands and inhale the scent of flowers he knew he'd find there. But during one of the endless string of nearly sleepless nights he'd endured these past three months, he'd vowed never to touch her again without her permission.

"I saw the interview you and J. C. Cobb did with Scott Bendix last Sunday. All three of you looked like you were having a good time."

"J.C. did most of the work. I played straight man."

Carly didn't agree, but the hard edge to his voice warned her to drop the subject. "Tell me about the team. Is it really shaping up to be as good as Coach says?"

He shrugged. "They're better than they were a month ago. Not as good as they should be." He shifted position, and she realized she'd never seen him looking so discouraged.

"Can they win? That's the important thing right now."

"Yeah, they can win—once they get it into their heads they're not still a bunch of losers."

"Everyone who's watched the scrimmages has raved about the great job you've done molding them into a team."

Mitch didn't bother to acknowledge the compliment. He knew how far the team had come and that he'd had a big part in that. But he also knew they were far from the championship team Carly wanted so desperately. Check that, he thought wearily. The team she *needed* if her plan was to succeed.

"A team that's still going to lose its first game against Beaverton unless things improve," he admitted to her—and to himself.

"There's still time. The season doesn't start for two weeks."

He nodded, then drew a deep breath. He wanted to touch her so badly he ached. If he could just hold her for a moment, maybe he could purge himself of the terrible pain in his soul. Maybe then, breathing in her scent, feeling her softness, he could find the courage to plead for her forgiveness. He knew he didn't have the right to ask even that much of her—not after what he'd done.

He glanced around. The administration building was always a busy place at the start of the term. He caught the curious looks directed their way and wondered if his shame was as obvious to everyone else as it was to him. Heat climbed his neck, as he forced himself to steady his gaze on hers.

"I, uh, see Tracy now and then at the field. Practicing with the junior varsity yell leaders."

"It's a wonder she doesn't sleep in her uniform."

"She tells me she's going to be living in the dorm."

Carly nodded. "It was her decision, and, I think, a good one. But that big old house will seem terribly empty once she's gone."

"She, uh, asked me to come to your welcome-home dinner, but I figured that I'd be the last person you'd want to see." Mitch realized that he was actually praying for her to contradict him. For the past two months he'd gotten the shakes every time he'd thought about seeing her again. As he watched her soft lips curve into a frown, he felt the same clammy chill in his belly.

"I'm sure Tracy understood why you refused," she said in that same coolly polite voice she'd used that first night in the parlor when she'd ordered him to call her *Dr.* Alderson. He knew then that he'd had his chance with her, and he'd blown it. Though he was standing perfectly still, he felt as though he'd taken a helmet in the gut.

"I hope you know I would never say anything to her. About my being her father, I mean. I know I don't have the right."

Carly felt a wave of sadness so intense she nearly cried out. "Maybe someday, when she's older," she murmured.

"Yeah, maybe then." Mitch knew he should leave, but he couldn't seem to make himself say goodbye. Seeing her again had sharpened the pain that had only just begun to dull, but being able to watch the small, familiar gestures of her hands and the sweet curve of her mouth when she spoke of their daughter was worth the torment he would suffer later.

"Carly, I was out of line that day in the guest room when you were trying to explain your reasons for not telling me about Tracy. Once I calmed down, I realized that you don't owe me anything, not even an explanation. I'm the one who owes you." He dropped his gaze, then lifted it slowly to hers again. "Is there any way we can get past this? Maybe talk it out and see if we can at least be friends?"

She drew a long, shaky breath. "Is that what you want? For us to be friends?"

He *wanted* to spend the rest of his life trying to make her forget the pain he'd caused her. He *wanted* her face to be the first thing he saw when he woke up every morning, and he *wanted* the taste of her lips to be the last thing he remembered before sleep claimed him every night. However, what he wanted and what he deserved were about as far apart as the goalposts at the stadium. "I know it's asking a lot," he said around the lump in his throat, "but yeah, I'd like us to be friends."

"I don't know, Mitch. Without trust..." She shrugged. "I'll have to think about that." The pressure in her chest was getting worse.

"I understand." He ran his tongue over his bottom lip. It was the kind of nervous gesture she'd never associated with him. "I guess what I *can't* understand is why you even talked to me when I showed up here last spring. Or... why you let me make love to you?"

It hurt her to hear the vicious self-hatred in his voice. She'd heard it in her own voice enough times to imagine the savagery of the wounds he'd inflicted on himself. Mixed emotions stirred inside her.

"I asked myself that same question," she said in a low, controlled tone. "The only answer that works is that I saw you as a different person. It was difficult, at first, to believe that. But I also know that when someone as active as you were suddenly faces total destruction of his self-image, it takes enormous strength and courage to survive, let alone become whole again. And you *are* whole," she murmured. "I admire you more than I can say." Her voice trembled, and she bit her lip. He reached out as though to touch her, then changed his mind and returned his hand to the handle of his crutch.

"Don't," he said in a raw tone. "Please don't hurt." A muscle pulled at the side of his jaw, and he swallowed hard. "Tell me what I can do to make this up to you, Carly. Anything you want you can have, only don't hurt anymore. I can't stand that."

"Oh, Mitch." Carly took a step toward him, only to stop abruptly when someone called out her name. Glancing in the direction of the voice, she saw the Dean of Women hurrying toward them.

His face changed. "I'd better take off. It's almost time for practice."

She sensed his torment and ached to reach out to him. But the stiffness of his spine and the rigid set of his shoulders told her more than any words could have that he would take that kind of simple human gesture as pity.

"Yes, I have a meeting of the Deans' Council in a few minutes myself."

"Take care of yourself," he said, his voice gruff.

"Always," she said, angling her chin a little higher. "See you around campus."

Chapter 13

Mitch watched his quarterback disappear under a crowd of
defenders and spat out a curse foul enough to curdle black
coffee.

"Damn it, Ian," he said, when the boy had extricated himself from the pileup. "How many times have I told you not to
telegraph your pass?"

Ian took off his helmet and wiped the sweat from his hot
face. "Sorry, Coach. I thought I had it that time."

"Son, I could have picked six people at random off the street
to line up opposite you, and you still would have been sacked."

Ian's eyes turned defensive, but Mitch wasn't in the mood for
excuses. The Jacks game was tomorrow, and one week later, the
Wolves played last year's conference champion in the first real
game of the season. "Look, Ian," he said, letting his impatience show, "a quarterback has to do more than throw a decent spiral and scramble when he has to. Sometimes he's got to
be a good actor, good enough to fool those big, mean-as-sin
guys on the other side of the ball into thinking he's going to do
one thing long enough to let his receivers find running room."

Ian stared at his cleats, a mutinous set to his jaw. Mitch
leaned on his crutches and bit down hard on the need to vent

his frustrations on the kid who was the cause of only the immediate one.

One more time, he thought. The kid has to get it sometime—if I don't wring his neck first. Glancing around, Mitch spotted Ian's backup leaning against the goalpost, flipping a football from hand to hand.

"Hey, Henry!" he called, aware that Ian had suddenly stiffened. "Come here a minute."

"What d'you need, Coach?" the backup QB asked eagerly, his grin as eager as a small boy's.

"You saw the play we just ran?"

"Yes, sir."

"I want *you* to run it."

Henry's dark eyes shifted nervously toward Ian, then snapped back to Mitch. Eighteen months ago a Portland judge had given the boy a choice, college or prison, and Henry had chosen college. He'd managed a C minus average his freshman year and had promised Mitch to do better this semester.

For the first week of practice Mitch had watched the youngster carefully, then decided to make him Ian's understudy. Henry had learned quickly, and although his passes were often off target, they had possibilities, and his footwork was nothing short of awesome. In another year Henry would have every pro scout in the country taking notice.

"Now?" Henry asked tentatively, as though he hadn't quite decided if Mitch was serious or not.

"Now." Mitch blew his whistle, and practice stopped dead as the other players on the field shifted their full attention his way. It had taken him two weeks to establish the kind of discipline he knew was necessary for a championship team, and another week to convince even the most rebellious of his squad that he meant it when he said he didn't give second chances.

One lapse of discipline, one broken rule or halfhearted effort, and that player was off the team. He'd had to cut three of last year's starters before the rest of the team paid attention. After that, however, he'd had little trouble.

With Ian, however, the trouble wasn't discipline. It was ego. For three years he'd been the best player on the field, and he knew it. Ian was still the best player, which was why he'd gotten it into his head that he didn't have anything more to learn.

"Same play, red 68," Mitch shouted. "And let's get it right this time."

The players lined up quickly, but when Henry took his place behind the center, Mitch caught the questioning looks sent his way.

"Pay attention, Cummings," Mitch ordered, ignoring Ian's furious expression. "Maybe you can learn something."

He hated to slice into the kid's pride, but he had to know now if Ian had enough fire in his belly to get the job done. He'd tried damn near everything else. Maybe the threat of replacing him with a green sophomore would kick start him into some much needed humility.

Henry wiped his hands on his butt, then took his position, legs planted squarely, head up, his hands snugged tight against Tom Pulli's thighs.

"Red 68. Red 68. Hut . . . hut, hut!"

Like a finely tooled machine, the play meshed flawlessly, just as Mitch had diagrammed it one late night while reviewing some old Raiders' plays. Henry tap-danced left, his shoulders signaling a cross-field pass. At the last moment, with the defenders moving left, he suddenly twisted right, cocked his arm and sent the ball zinging a full forty yards into the hands of the receiver—and out again.

Crestfallen, Henry came trotting up, his body language telling Mitch that he considered himself a failure.

"Damn good job, Henry." Mitch made sure his voice was loud enough to carry to the others, but not so loud that his intention was obvious. "Perfect misdirection, well-timed throw. Work on softening those bullets of yours next, okay?"

Henry's eyes lit up. "Sure will, Coach. Right away." He jogged off, his back just a little straighter. Ian watched him go, a muscle working in his jaw.

"He's not as good as you are yet, which is why you're the starting quarterback and he isn't," Mitch told Ian quietly. "It's up to you to make sure I don't change my mind."

Mitch didn't bother to wait for an answer. He had other things on his mind, like a place kicker who tended to hook the short ones left, and a secondary with holes like Swiss cheese. And a woman whose eyes haunted his every lonely hour, awake or asleep.

* * *

Ian kicked the left rear tire of his BMW and swore long and fluently.

"Ian, don't," Tracy pleaded, laying a hand on his arm. "You'll hurt your leg, and then you won't be *able* to play."

He shook off her hand, still furious at the humiliation he'd suffered at the hands of the man he'd idolized. "I'd like to knock Scanlon on his crippled ass, that's what I'd like to do. Hard-nosed bastard thinks he knows it all." He leaned against his car and ground his teeth. Not even Tracy's shyly eager kisses had been able to distract him.

"He's just doing his job, Ian," she said with that quick little rush in her voice that had first attracted him—as though she were in a hurry to say and do it all.

"Like hell. He's just got it in for me because I can do all the things he can't anymore."

"That's not true, and you know it. Mitch wants you guys to win, that's all. You said so yourself only a few weeks ago."

He scowled, wanting her to be wrong, but knowing she was right. A few weeks ago he'd been as excited as a five-year-old on Christmas Eve. But that had been before Coach Scanlon had started ragging on him. Now all he wanted to do was kick down doors.

"Yeah, well, if he wants us to win so bad, how come he's threatening to put Henry in my place just because I screwed up one lousy play? Tell me that, Miss Sunshine and Light!"

"I don't know, Ian. Maybe because he thinks you can do better."

Ian stared at her, his stance belligerent, his fists clenched, but the fury he'd carried with him from the field was ebbing away. "Well, he's right," he muttered. "I *can* do better than any of those guys."

"Then why don't you show him?"

Tracy's smile always made him feel special. Maybe that was why he'd broken his own rule about dating girls who didn't know the score. "C'mere, Sunshine," he ordered, his voice a low growl. "I'm tired of talking."

She went into his arms eagerly, love shining in her eyes. But it was the soft invitation of her sexy little mouth that he cared about most. Soon he would convince her to let him make love to her. Very soon.

Ian dropped Tracy off at the bottom of the mansion's driveway, and she walked the rest of the way. It was Friday night, and, since Ian had to study for an exam, she'd invited herself to dinner. Besides, her mother hadn't been herself since she'd returned from Europe.

Even so, as her short skirt swished against her thighs and her feet fairly danced up the drive, she felt slightly guilty for being so happy while her mother seemed more and more preoccupied. But life was so great! She was a Bradenton cheerleader, and Ian loved her.

Her mouth was still swollen from the kisses that got better each time he took her in his arms. A man's kisses, she thought, remembering the boys she'd dated in high school. Nice guys, sure. Especially Greg Hardesty. But Greg had never made her go breathless with a look the way Ian did. Or make her heart race just by touching her. It had been easy to keep Greg at a safe distance. A firm "no" whenever he'd pressured her to go all the way had been all it had taken.

It was becoming harder and harder to say "no" to Ian, especially when she wanted so desperately to say "yes." Still, she knew she wasn't ready to let him or anyone else make love to her.

"Tracy? Is that you, sweetie?"

Her mother's voice drew her to the back of the house. Trowel in hand, her mother was planting marigolds, still dressed in a linen business suit and low-heeled pumps.

"Hi, Mom."

Carly patted planting mix around the bright little flower before glancing up at her daughter's face. "I drove by the stadium to pick you up, but you were with Ian."

"We were just talking," Tracy hedged reluctantly. Her mother hadn't said anything when she'd admitted to dating Ian every weekend since classes had begun, but Tracy knew that she wasn't pleased.

Seeing Tracy's gaze slide away from hers, Carly put down her trowel and got to her feet. "Let's sit for a minute," she invited, indicating the granite garden bench by the birdbath.

"Uh-oh," Tracy said, sighing deeply as she moved toward the bench. "This sounds heavy."

Carly brushed the dust from the hard granite, then sat down and folded her hands in her lap. "I know you think I'm being overprotective, and maybe I am. It's just that you remind me so much of myself at your age."

"Is that bad?" Tracy asked as she sat next to her mother. The hard stone was cold against her bare thighs, and she shivered.

"I'm not sure it's good *or* bad, Trace. I just know I was inexperienced and far too trusting, and when I met a man I thought I loved, I ignored everything I'd been taught to believe in. It could have ruined my life."

"You mean because you got pregnant?"

Carly nodded. "Yes. I won't lie to you and say it was easy being eighteen and pregnant. But I was lucky, because I had a family who didn't turn me out, even though they were ashamed of what I'd done."

Tracy blinked. "Grandmother and Grandfather were ashamed of you?"

"Yes. I wasn't perfect, and that was difficult for them to swallow. I don't blame them, but losing their trust and respect hurt for a long time."

Tracy furrowed her brow, her golden eyes more thoughtful than Carly had ever seen them. "Mom, I'm not going to get pregnant," she said after a moment's reflection. "If I decide to have sex, I'll go on the pill first, just the way I always promised you I would."

Carly drew a long breath. "Sometimes, it's not always that easy, sweetie. Even on the pill, you have to protect yourself from AIDS and—"

"I know all about that, Mom. I'm not stupid."

Carly's smile was bittersweet. "Darling, Ian is a very charismatic young man. He's bright and sophisticated and enormously attractive, but he's not looking to settle down any time soon. More importantly, he doesn't strike me as all that responsible."

Tracy stiffened. "Are you forbidding me to date him, even though I'm in college now?"

Yes! Carly wanted to shout. But she knew that would be the worst possible thing she could say. "No, Tracy, but I'm asking you to go slowly. Give yourself time to settle into college life. Date other guys, too. Have a good time.''

''And don't have sex until I'm thirty-five, right?''

Carly saw the twinkle in her daughter's eyes and knew she'd made her point. Anything more would be counterproductive. ''Hmm,'' she murmured, pretending to think it over. ''Maybe twenty-five—if he's the right man for you.''

The light touch worked to perfection, and the stony look in Tracy's eyes melted away. ''It's a deal.''

Carly gave her daughter a one-armed hug. ''Now go say hello to Grandmother and Tilly. They've been looking forward to this evening all week.''

''Okay. See you at dinner.''

After Tracy left, Carly sat perfectly still, trying to rid herself of the sick panic churning her stomach. It was so hard to know how far to push her almost-grown daughter, what words to use.

When she'd seen Ian and Tracy kissing in the parking lot behind the stadium, it had been all she could do to drive on past when every maternal instinct she possessed had been urging her to snatch her daughter out of harm's way.

And then what? she asked herself. Have her hate me for the rest of our lives? The very thought made her shudder. ''Oh, Mitch,'' she whispered in a choked voice, lifting an anguished gaze to the overcast sky, ''I wish I were in your arms right now, listening to you tell me that everything was going to be all right with our daughter.''

Silence flavored with birdsong and regret answered her.

The game with the Jacks had been over for a couple of hours, and Mitch was tired. He'd left the party J.C. had thrown at Gallagher's after one glass of wine.

Even though the Wolves had played better than he'd expected, he didn't feel much like celebrating. Everyone else had been having a great time. Marca and Coach and his two assistant coaches. And Carly. Each time she looked at someone else with a smile in those bright eyes of hers, he wanted to smash something—or someone—only there was no one to blame but himself. A few years back he might have been tempted to drink himself into a stupor, or put the Jag into racing gear and red-line the engine until it exploded, anything to be free of the guilt that never quite went away, no matter how tired he made himself. Not even the increasingly frequent bouts of excruciating spasms had driven the shame from him for more than a few hours of oblivion. Tonight, each time she'd thrown her head back to laugh at one of Todd Winonski's lousy jokes, the knife had sliced a little deeper into his heart.

He'd given the team permission to stay out a couple of hours after curfew. They deserved it, after the yeomen's effort they'd turned in. He was proud of them. He wondered if he would ever be proud of himself again.

It was a little past midnight, and he was lying in bed reading when he heard brakes squealing outside, followed a few seconds later by a pounding on his front door.

"Give me a second!" he shouted, grabbing his sweat pants off his wheelchair and struggling into them, cursing steadily. The pounding abated only briefly before resuming. He transferred himself from the bed to his chair, then wheeled himself through the small house to the front door.

"Yeah, yeah," he said, flipping on the porch light before turning the bolt. Moving the chair to one side, he leaned forward and opened the door.

"What the hell...Tracy? Good God, honey, what's wrong?"

Still dressed in her cheerleading uniform, she stared at him with glassy eyes, her mouth swollen and her breath coming in visible jerks. "C-can I come in?"

"Yeah, sure." He took her hand and pulled her inside, then stuck his head outside, looking for Carly. He saw the MG angled halfway onto the curb, the lights still burning. His heart thudded violently and he tasted fear as he shifted his gaze to his daughter.

"What's wrong?" he said, still holding her hand. Her skin was so cold it scared him. "Talk to me, Tracy. Is it your mom?"

Tracy shook her head. Her face was paper white, with a sickly tinge of green around her mouth. She started to speak, then choked and pressed her hand against her lips, her eyes darting around desperately.

"The john's down the hall to the left," Mitch said, pointing.

She bolted from the room. He shoved the front door closed before turning his chair to follow her. The door to the bathroom was closed, but he heard the sound of violent retching from within. He waited impatiently until the terrible sounds stopped, then rapped hard on the door. "Tracy? Can I come in?"

When she didn't answer, he pushed open the door and wheeled inside. She was still crouching in front of the toilet, her head hanging and her arms folded over her stomach. Tears streamed down her face.

"Poor baby," he murmured, grabbing a washcloth from the rod. "Did you have too much to drink?"

He kept a close watch on her as he wet the rag in warm water. Leaving the water running slowly, he leaned forward to wipe her face. She flinched away from his hand, and he froze.

"Tracy?" He put just enough authority into his voice to startle her into looking at him again. "Honey, I can't help you if I don't know what's wrong."

She blinked, her eyes still glazed. "Ian," she whispered through bloodless lips. "He wanted to make love. I told him 'no,' but he wouldn't stop. I tried to scream—" She choked, and then she was crumpling forward. He caught her before she hit the floor and somehow managed to pull her onto his lap. She was all arms and legs, and because his chair was a modified racing design, it had no arms to support her. At first she held herself stiffly, but gradually she relaxed against him, drawing her legs into a fetal position and holding on to his neck tightly.

Sobs shook her, and tears wet his neck. "It's okay, baby," he murmured, trying to gentle his voice. He'd never felt so helpless. At the same time he was filled with a killing rage, and he was suddenly glad Cummings wasn't within range. Because he didn't know what else to do, he simply held her and let her cry until she was lying limp and drained against him.

"Hang on tight," he ordered in a low tone. "I'm going to take you for a little ride into the bedroom, okay?"

She didn't stir, but her hands tightened around his neck. He had to let her go in order to propel the chair, and she whimpered. "Hang on, baby. Just hang on."

Reaching the bedroom, he wheeled to the side of the bed, then brought his arms around her slowly. When she didn't stiffen, he held her close, feeling her heart beating as fast as a trapped bird's.

"Oh, Mitch, I was s-so scared," she cried, her voice muffled by his shoulder. "I'm still s-scared. I couldn't let Mom s-see me, and Aunt Marca wasn't home when I got there. I didn't know where else to go."

He started to ask how she knew where he lived, then remembered that she'd been with Ian and some of the other guys when they'd helped him move in. "I won't let anything hurt you anymore, I promise."

Tears stung his eyes, and he had to bite his lip to keep from saying all the wrong things. So he just pretended that she was three years old and needed a lot of hugging from her daddy. When he felt a deep shuddering sigh go through her, he nudged her chin up and wiped the tears from her cheeks with his fingers. "Better now?"

She tried to smile, and it broke his heart. "Don't tell Mom," she whispered brokenly. "She warned me. She s-said Ian was too old for me." Her voice broke, and fresh tears ran down her cheeks. "She'll hate me, I know she will."

"Tracy, listen to me. Your mother will never hate you, no matter what you do."

"She will, I know she will. She warned me and warned me. She told me I had to take responsibility for myself and my body. Sh-she told me a guy would take whatever he could, whenever he could." She shuddered, and her arms tightened. "But I trusted Ian. He said he'd take care of me. He didn't want me to come to his room because he wanted my first time to be special, so I borrowed Mom's car so we could go to a motel. He said he'd stop if it hurt too much, but he d-didn't."

She started sobbing, and he muttered a silent, helpless curse. There had to be more he should be doing for her, but he didn't have one decent idea of where to begin. He waited until the sobs had turned to jerky little sniffs, and then he eased her head up again. The anguish in her eyes scored his heart, but he managed to dredge up a reassuring smile that took some of the tension from her face.

"I'll tell you what. You lie down on my bed until you feel strong enough to decide what you want to do next, and I'll go make you some hot chocolate. Okay?"

She nodded like a docile five-year-old, but she was shaking so hard he had to half lift, half boost her onto the big bed. Silently cursing the arrogant little snot who had done this to her, he managed to get her covered up before her eyes closed.

He sat watching her for a moment, then scrubbed his cheeks with his hands before wheeling himself into the kitchen. He had to think a minute before he could recall Carly's private number. With each number he punched out, his heart thudded harder. He was still trying to find the guts to break the news to her when she answered.

Carly parked her mother's Buick next to the MG, collected the keys from the roadster and turned off the lights. Heart pounding, she hurried up the ramp built into the front porch of the small frame bungalow.

Mitch had been terse on the phone, telling her only that Tracy was at his place and needed her. "Don't bother to knock," he'd instructed after giving her directions. Her hand was shaking violently as she pushed open the front door and called his name. Glancing around as she hurriedly closed the door, she saw a sparsely furnished room and a stack of packing boxes in one corner. She closed the door and turned to find him sitting in a wheelchair at the opposite end of the small living room.

"You made good time."

"Where is she? What's wrong?" she demanded, her voice shaking almost as violently as her icy hands.

"She's asleep," he said, wheeling toward her.

"I want to see her." Before she could get past him, he grabbed her arm and held on.

"In a minute. We need to talk first."

She tried to jerk free, but a quick, painful tightening of his fingers told her not to waste her energy. "Please," he said, when she glared at him. "For Tracy's sake."

She bit her lip, then nodded. Relieved, he let her go. The last thing he wanted to do was use force on her. It had already cost him to touch her, knowing how she must hate to have his hands on her.

"Why is she here, Mitch?"

"She needed a friend. That's the short answer."

"And the long one?"

He drew a deep breath and asked her to sit down. He saw the hesitation in her eyes, but she did as he asked, perching tensely on the edge of the sofa cushion. "Okay, I'm sitting. And I'm giving you two seconds to explain before I leave this room to find my daughter."

He took a deep breath. "I don't know all the details, but apparently she had a date with Ian Cummings tonight." He saw the horror dawning in her eyes and knew that he wouldn't have to say the word he hated. But he made himself say it anyway. "Apparently he raped her."

She shook her head. "No, not that," she whispered hoarsely. "Anything but that."

He wanted to be somewhere else almost as much as he wanted to hold her. No, he wanted to be some*one* else. Not even the all-but-unbearable pain of retraining his traumatized muscles had hurt as much as the wounded look in her eyes. "She's okay—"

"No," she said carefully. "She's not."

He plowed his hand through his hair. "I meant physically."

She looked at him as though he'd just crawled out from a slime pit. "You think so? Well, I don't. Ian's a big man and very strong, like all athletes. In an hour or so she'll have bruises where his hands held her down. But that's not the worst of it. The worst is feeling as though you've been ripped apart inside." She took a quick breath. "Oh, there's not much blood, and torn tissue heals. In a few weeks only a doctor will be able to detect the physical evidence, but don't ever tell me he didn't hurt her."

Mitch was gripping the seat of his chair so tightly that his knuckles felt bruised from the inside, and he himself felt flayed, as though each word had stripped away his skin, leaving him bleeding and defenseless.

"Tell me what you want me to do," he said as calmly as he could manage. He needed to do something, anything, to keep his mind from splintering into madness.

"Call Dr. Robert Braddus. His number is in the book. Ask him to meet Tracy and me at the emergency room of County

General. And then just stay away from me and from my daughter. Just looking at you makes me sick to my stomach."

Carly saw his shoulders jerk and broke off, appalled at herself. "I didn't mean that," she said in a voice ravaged by the tears she needed to shed and couldn't.

"Yes, you did," he said, his face bleached white. "Tracy's in the bedroom, through there. He jerked his head toward the door.

"Mitch—"

"Take care of your daughter, Carly," he said in a low, harsh tone that somehow ripped through her own anguish. "You know what she needs. I'll call the doctor."

He turned his chair and wheeled toward the desk, his big shoulders stiff. Only the knowledge that Tracy needed her kept her from going to him to beg him to believe her when she said she hadn't meant the words she'd flung at him.

They would talk later, she promised herself, as she hurried in to her child.

"You wanted to see me, Coach?" Ian looked puzzled. He didn't look particularly worried. Mitch almost felt sorry for the boy.

"Close the door, son."

Ian shut the door behind him and took a few steps into Mitch's living room, glancing around curiously. "Looks like you've still got some unpacking to do."

Mitch leaned on his crutches and wished he had the next few minutes behind him. "I understand you had a date with Tracy Alderson tonight."

Ian grinned, but he was beginning to feel pretty uptight. He'd seen Coach Scanlon angry before. He'd seen him disgusted and kick-ass sarcastic. He'd never seen his eyes so cold and his face so hard.

"Don't worry, Coach," he said quickly. "I was in before curfew, honest. I was asleep when you called."

Coach's expression didn't change. "Did you have a good time?"

"Good enough, yeah. Why?" Nervous now, the boy shoved his hands into the pockets of his sweat pants and rocked back on his heels.

"First time I saw you, kid, I figured you and me were a lot alike."

"Yeah? That's good, huh?"

"I know someone who wouldn't think so." Coach took a couple of steps toward him. It still amazed Ian that Scanlon could get around as fast as he did sometimes, considering the crutches and braces and all.

"Uh, Coach, did I do something to tick you off?"

"That's one way of putting it." Scanlon's mouth slanted. Instead of relieving Ian's mind, the stiff half smile only made his heart race.

"Uh, do you want to talk about it, or what?"

Coach slipped his arms from the cuffs of his crutches and propped the crutches against a chair. "Let's work on the 'or what' first," he said, steadying himself with one hand on the back of the chair while the other reached out to Ian's shoulder in a fatherly gesture. Before Ian could take another breath, he found himself neatly pinned against the carpet by a wrestling takedown move he should have seen coming and didn't. He was dimly aware of the phone ringing shrilly as Scanlon's voice grated harshly in his ear. "You raped Tracy tonight, didn't you, son?"

"No, no," Ian cried, but his cheek was pressed against the rough nap of the rug, making it difficult to speak. "She wanted it."

"Way I heard it, she begged you to stop, but hell, you had that hot itch between your legs, right?"

"No!" Ian started to struggle, but punishing hands forced his trapped arm toward his shoulder blades a few inches more. Biting his lip to keep from screaming, he let himself go limp.

"What's it feel like, knowing you're helpless?"

"Please, Coach," Ian whimpered, so frightened he was close to passing out cold. "Please don't hurt me." The pressure eased off enough to allow him to catch his breath.

"Isn't that what Tracy said, right before you raped her? *Isn't it?*"

Ian nodded. He felt sick.

Scanlon rolled off him and sat up. Ian glanced at the door, but the look in Coach's eyes told him not to try it. Slowly he sat up, his arms tingling and his wrists aching where Coach's fingers had held him.

"Is . . . she all right?" Ian felt his face burning.

Scanlon reined in the need to vent his own shame and self-hatred on the kid and merely shook his head. "Her mom took her to the hospital. As far as I know, they're still there."

Ian's gaze fell away, and the boy's shoulders hunched. Mitch remembered the sick feeling scouring the lining of his belly when he'd seen Sarah's—Carly's—blood on his sheets.

"I don't know if Tracy will press charges. I hope so."

That brought the boy's head up fast. "You mean with the police?"

Mitch could only shake his head at the kid's ignorance. "Rape is against the law."

"But . . . I didn't mean to. I mean, things just got out of hand is all. You know how it is sometimes when a guy gets excited."

Nausea roiled in Mitch's stomach, but he managed to keep from retching. "Pay attention, Ian. I'm only going to tell you this once, and you'd better memorize every word. If Tracy doesn't press charges and the sheriff doesn't throw you in jail where you belong, you are going to become a model citizen. You'll go to class, do your homework, practice football and— *if*—I decide to let you play, run your butt off during the games. You will not date, you won't even so much as flirt with a woman until you graduate. Got that?"

Ian looked shell-shocked, but he managed to nod. "I'm sorry, Coach. Honest to God, I didn't mean this to happen. I like Tracy a lot, maybe I even love her." The boy's eyes pleaded with him to understand. "I just got carried away, you know?"

Mitch nodded. "I know, son. I wish I didn't."

Ian swallowed hard. "Do . . . do you think she'll ever forgive me?"

Mitch felt his stomach twist. "I don't know. If you're lucky, maybe."

"She said she loved me." Ian stared at the floor, his face growing redder and redder. "I guess maybe I ruined that, too."

Mitch closed his eyes for a second and summoned up the image of Carly's face. Instead of love in the bright eyes he adored, he saw disgust. "Yeah, kid, you ruined that, too." And so had he.

Carly turned away from the pay phone in the hospital lobby, a sinking feeling in her stomach. Mitch still wasn't answering his phone. She'd called the first time right after Dr. Braddus had taken Tracy into an examining room. That had been over twenty minutes ago, and she'd been trying to reach him ever since.

Too wrought up to sit, she began pacing the small room, oblivious to the sympathetic looks of the two other women seated nearby. One was waiting for her daughter-in-law to deliver a baby, The other was waiting for a friend, a fact Carly had overheard while listening to the endless ringing on the other end of the phone.

"Oh, God, Carly! I got your message. What's wrong?"

Spinning around, she saw Marca hurrying toward her. "Come out in the hall," she said, grabbing Marca's arm.

As soon as they were alone, she leaned against the wall and poured out the whole story. "Tracy's still in with the doctor."

Marca's fingers dug into Carly's arm, and the sudden pain was a welcome diversion. "Oh, God. Poor Tracy. Poor *you*."

"Oh, Marca, this is all my fault. I should have told her the truth a long time ago. Maybe if she'd known what could really happen she would have been more prepared to handle a guy like Ian."

"But you *did* prepare her—in a dozen different ways. I don't know what else you could have done, except maybe follow her around twenty-four hours a day."

Carly bit her lip, then let out a harsh sigh. "There must have been something else. Otherwise, why did this happen?"

"Carly, listen to yourself," Marca implored, shaking her gently. "Aren't you really saying that you think this is all Tracy's fault?"

Carly felt as though she'd just fallen through a hole in the floor. "God, Marca, what's wrong with me? You're right. I *am* blaming her—and myself—I even blamed Mitch." She raised a shaky hand to her temple. "I'm not thinking clearly."

"Oh, sweetie, of course you're not. Why should you be?"

Carly flattened her back against the wall and stared at the ceiling. "When I went into Mitch's bedroom to get Tracy, I saw this book upside down on the nightstand. He must have been reading it when Tracy showed up. It was the one written by my therapist to help other rape victims feel good about themselves again."

Marca winced. "I don't know what to say, Carly. This nightmare just keeps getting worse and worse."

"I feel so...helpless. I know that's just a result of shock, but—"

"Dr. Alderson?"

Carly whipped her head toward the man's voice, thinking it was another doctor. Instead, she found herself face-to-face with her daughter's rapist. She'd never quite internalized the term "killing rage," but suddenly, she knew exactly what it meant to want another person dead. "How dare you come here?" she demanded coldly.

Ian flinched. His face was a sickly gray, and his eyes pleaded with her to understand. "Look, you don't have to tell me what kind of scum you think I am. Coach Scanlon has already made that real plain."

Carly was too upset for tact. "What's Coach Scanlon got to do with this?"

"He and I had a kind of talk, and then he told me to come over here and be tested for HIV."

Carly went cold. "Oh my God, Ian! You're not—"

"No! Honestly, I'm not. I swear. I had a physical two months ago, and the test was negative. But Coach Scanlon, he said that I should have another test so Tracy wouldn't be worried. He said she had enough to deal with already." He hung his head and gnawed his lip. "I'm sorry, Dr. Alderson. I know that doesn't mean squat, but I am."

Carly didn't want to believe him, just as she hadn't wanted to believe Mitch. "The lab is downstairs, Ian. If the tech gives you any trouble, have her page Dr. Braddus."

He nodded, shifting from one foot to the other. "Uh, when you see Tracy, tell her I'm sorry. Okay?"

Carly simply nodded. She was too spent to do anything more.

Dr. Braddus kept Tracy in the hospital overnight, more to keep her sedated and calm than for any medical reason. In the meantime, the first of the two tests Ian needed to take had come back from the lab, and his blood showed no sign for HIV. It was encouraging news, but, as the doctor had quietly reminded her, both Ian and Tracy would need to be tested again in six months before they could be sure of the final result.

By noon the next day Carly was able to take Tracy home. Felicity and Tilly treated her like pampered royalty, plumping her pillow and plying her with magazines and herbal tea. But when Tracy began to look terribly tired, Carly shooed them out and closed the door.

"Nap time, I think," she said, fighting to keep her emotions level and her voice calm, but Tracy's face crumpled, and she began crying again.

Carly sat on the end of the bed and pulled her into her arms, smoothing her hair gently while murmuring the same words she'd used to soothe Tracy's little-girl hurts. Gradually the tears diminished to an occasional sob, then finally to sad little sniffs.

"Better now?" Carly asked, her voice thick with the tears she wished she, too, could shed.

Tracy's head bobbed against her breast, and Carly drew back and plucked a tissue from the box on the nightstand. "Here, blow," she murmured with her most encouraging smile.

Tracy did as she was told so meekly that Carly's heart tore. "Can you stand a little conversation?" she asked gently. "Nothing too deep, just some motherly words of wisdom?"

Tracy dropped her gaze to the tissue still wadded tightly in one hand. "You don't have to say it," she mumbled in a barely audible voice. "I know you hate me."

Carly closed her eyes and sent up a quick prayer for the right words. "I don't hate you. I've never hated you, and I never will. I love you dearly." She nudged Tracy's chin up and waited until her tear-streaked eyes met Carly's. "I love you," she repeated firmly. "Never, *ever* doubt that."

"That's what Mitch kept telling me you'd say."

Carly smiled. "It's true. Cross my heart."

Tracy smiled a little. "You warned me. I just didn't listen. Oh, Mommy, I feel so d-dirty."

Carly took her into her arms again and held her close. "Don't even think that, Tracy. You did nothing wrong. *Nothing!* You just trusted the wrong man, that's all. It's happened to other women, some of them a lot more experienced than you are. You've been hurt, and you'll never forget what happened to you, but you can learn to deal with it and then put it behind you."

Tracy shook her head, the picture of misery.

"Yes, Tracy, you will. And I'll help. Grandmother and Tilly, too. And Aunt Marca. We'll all be here for you. I promise." She took a deep breath. "But there's something we have to talk about now that's pretty unpleasant. Can you be strong for just a little longer?"

Tracy looked frightened, but she nodded timidly.

"I think we should call the police and have Ian arrested."

"No! Please don't do that, Mother," she begged, clawing at Carly's arm. "Everyone would know. I'd have to testify. I saw a show about that on TV. In court...the things they asked her. I couldn't stand it if they asked me the same things." She shuddered. "Please, Mom, can't we just pretend it didn't happen?"

Carly knew that was impossible, and so, eventually, would Tracy. But for the moment she simply held her daughter in her arms.

Chapter 14

The rain that had been coming down steadily all afternoon finally slacked off around three. Carly had left her office at noon, determined to take the afternoon off. Too much work and not enough rest over the past three months had her snapping at Sandy for inconsequential reasons and making stupid mistakes whenever she found herself forced to make anything but the simplest decision.

She'd taken a long, soothing swim, then slipped on her robe and hauled out her gardening tools. It was too soggy outside to prune the bushes that desperately needed attention, so she'd attacked the roses in the pots dotting the terrace. It helped to lose herself in the physical task. It helped more to concentrate on the flowers rather than her own misery. Heaven knows she'd tried everything else, including chocolate. Especially chocolate.

She'd put on five pounds since September, and every horrible ounce followed her around wherever she went. Scowling, she clipped another dead blossom from Felicity's favorite tree rose and stepped back to judge the effect. It was the week before Thanksgiving, a bit early to be doing a drastic pruning. But she'd needed the diversion.

The Timber Wolves were playing their last game in two days. And even though they were only seven and four and a very long shot to win the conference championship, they still had a mathematical chance. If they won this last game and the number one team lost *its* last game, they would end up in a tie.

She was still daydreaming about miracles and the man who was doing his best to make one happen when Tracy entered the pool enclosure through the outer door. She was wearing baggy jeans and an old Brown sweatshirt of Carly's. Raindrops still glistened on her hair from her dash from the garage to the house.

She'd moved back into the house shortly after that night-marish night, and Carly was secretly glad. She needed the diversion of worrying about Tracy to keep her from dwelling on her own anguish.

"Hi, hon. How was your session with Dr. Stein?"

"Pretty good. How come you're home so early?"

"It was in the nature of an ultimatum. Either I got myself and my 'impossible' mood out of the office for a few hours, or Sandy was going to pitch me out the window. Needless to say, I 'got.'"

"Good choice, Mom."

"I thought so."

Tracy wandered around, inspecting the newly shorn roses. Carly watched her surreptitiously, thinking that her little girl had come a long way in only a few months. She was still seeing a therapist in Medford once a week, but she no longer had nightmares, and she was talking about dating again.

"How about a snack? I think Tilly's been baking."

"She has. Gingerbread. I figured she needed an official taster to make sure it was a good batch, so before I left for my session with Dr. Stein I snatched a piece to eat on the way."

Carly nodded solemnly. "Every now and then one has to sacrifice for the common good."

Tracy giggled, and Carly's heart soared. For weeks after the rape Tracy had been morose and withdrawn. But time and intensive counseling had gradually helped her deal with her feelings.

Following the therapist's advice, Carly had told Tracy the details surrounding her conception and her own long, slow climb back from depression and guilt. She had not, however, told Tracy that the man she'd come to think of as a close and trusted friend was in reality her father.

"I hope you saved your poor hardworking mother some of that gingerbread," Carly teased, pulling off her gloves.

"Yeah, but only because Tilly insisted."

"You're all heart, kiddo."

"Hey, you're the one who's always talking about losing ten pounds."

"Fifteen, and I'm beginning to think that falls in the fat-chance category."

Tracy groaned. "Mother, is that a pun?"

"'Fraid so. Pretty dismal, huh?"

"Pathetic."

"I'll try to do better, I promise." Carly threw her gloves and shears into the tool caddy at her feet before slowly arching her aching back. Above their heads, rain pounded on the glass enclosure with renewed fury, and she grimaced. "If this storm doesn't blow over soon, the field is going to be mud soup by Saturday."

Tracy watched the rain sheeting the window in silence for a moment, then squared her shoulders and said softly, "I think I'll come with you to the game."

Carly felt a stab of worry. With Ian still at quarterback up until now, Tracy had gotten hysterical at the mere mention of football. On the advice of her therapist, she'd quit the cheerleading squad, using a "recently discovered medical problem" as an excuse, and even avoided driving past the stadium whenever she went in for classes.

"Are you sure you're ready for that?" Carly asked casually.

"Dr. Stein suggested it. She thinks I should start getting back into my old routine again, maybe even try out for the cheerleading squad next spring."

"How do you feel about that?" It wasn't necessary to point out that Ian would have graduated by then.

Tracy managed a tentative smile. "Okay, I think." She hesitated, then kicked at a crack in one of the flagstones with the toe of her sneaker. "I found out today that Ian is one of Dr. Stein's patients, too. He's in this group she started for rapists and abusers." She pulled a crumpled envelope from the back pocket of her jeans. "Dr. Stein gave me this during our last session. She's been holding it for me until she thought I was ready to read it. It's from Ian."

"What!"

Tracy grinned. "I told her you would react like that," she declared, nodding a bit smugly.

"Oh you did, did you? And what did Dr. Stein say to that?"

"She said you have stuff of your own you're dealing with, which is why you might be upset, but your stuff isn't my stuff, and I needed to read this letter."

Carly reminded herself that Silvia Stein was an outstanding therapist and swallowed her anger. "And did you?"

Tracy nodded. "Ian claims he's sorry and says he's working hard to change some things in himself that needed to be changed. He also said that none of it was my fault."

Carly took a deep breath. "He's right. I hope you believe him."

"I do." She smoothed her fingers over the envelope, a wistful look stealing over her face. "When I'm ready, Dr. Stein wants me to write an answer, telling him how I feel about what he did and about him. She also wants us to say the same things to each other face-to-face when we're both ready."

"Could you handle that?"

"I'll have to, if I want to get on with my life, because she said it's part of the healing process for both of us."

Carly smoothed Tracy's tumbled hair, her hand slightly unsteady. "I'm very proud of you, sweetheart. I know these past months have been hard, but you're doing wonderfully well."

Tracy drew a suddenly shaky breath. "Things will never be the same, though, will they?"

"No, but that doesn't mean the rest of your life can't be just as wonderful as it might have been if this hadn't happened. Perhaps, in some ways, even better, because you're so much stronger now."

Tracy carefully folded the envelope and tucked it into her back pocket again. Carly wondered if she would keep it or throw it in the trash. If it was her... but no, she thought. She didn't really know what she would have done if Mitch had written her such a letter.

They'd spoken briefly by phone after Tracy's release from the hospital, and she'd seen him at the games. He'd phoned once a week since to speak with Tracy, who always seemed more buoyant after their conversations.

Carly didn't know what Tracy and her father discussed, nor did she ask. Coach had come by several times, his extreme gentleness with Tracy touching Carly deeply. He and Felicity were seeing each other on a regular basis now, though Felicity still maintained that theirs was simply a friendly relationship. A friendly relationship that had her mother smiling more often than she frowned these days, in spite of her genuine concern for her granddaughter.

For his part, Gianfracco seemed younger to Carly every time she saw him. His pride in his coaching protégé seemed boundless, as was his pride in the Wolves. Even if they lost the last game and missed out on a bowl bid, the team had done what Bradenton had needed it to do. The TV money from the Jacks game and the revenue from the concession stands, combined with the money raised from the ticket sales and Marca's other promotions, had given them enough leverage to convince the bank to refinance the note.

The media had taken to calling Mitch a coaching phenomenon, using phrases like "a natural," "a born leader" and "master strategist." Carly was almost used to the sight of dozens of cameramen and women bunched around him during the games. Because of the publicity, enrollment applications had already increased by one-third, and the Trustees were falling all over one another to take the credit. Carly knew that she should be ecstatic. Instead, she was finding it harder and harder to find reasons to smile.

"So, is it okay if I sit with you and Aunt Marca on Saturday?" Tracy asked, nervously pushing back her hair.

"You bet it's okay. In fact, it's terrific. Aunt Marca and I have been yelling our heads off for eleven games now. It's about time we had some help." She picked up her tools and gestured toward the house. "How about we see if we can filch some more of that gingerbread before dinner?"

Tracy's dimples flashed. "Okay, but if we get caught, I'm going to tell Tilly it was your idea."

"Brat," Carly said, swatting her lightly.

"Ouch!" Tracy cried, feigning injury, and they both laughed as they walked side by side toward the house.

"Ohmigosh, Marca! Did you see that footwork?" Carly jumped to her feet, her presidential dignity forgotten. She and Tracy were sitting with Marca in the end zone, surrounded by students waving pennants and screaming nonstop.

Like nearly everyone else, Carly was wearing a bright orange Bradenton sweatshirt and slacks. Marca was wearing her old cheerleading sweater and jeans. Tracy looked far more formal in a wool shirt and hand-knit fisherman's sweater.

The storm had passed, and, as was usually the case with Oregon storms, the sun had come out and the temperature had risen a good ten degrees to the high sixties, with just enough wind to keep the flags at the top of the stadium fluttering against a deep blue sky. It was perfect football weather.

"Hey, that's my back you're pounding!" Marca exclaimed, cringing away.

"Stop complaining. Do you believe it? The bad news Wolves have finally had a winning season."

On the field, time out had been called, and the teams were huddling on the sidelines. "I'm going to get a soda and a hot dog," Tracy leaned over to announce. "Do either of you want anything?"

"Diet soda," Marca said immediately.

"Nothing for me, thanks," Carly told her, reaching for her purse.

"I'll get it, Mom." Tracy shouldered her outsize bag and slipped past the two students to her right into the aisle.

"She's almost like her old self," Marca said.

"I was afraid she'd be upset, seeing Ian again, even from a distance, but so far she's handling it just fine."

The referee blew the whistle, and the action began again. It was a pass play, and Carly could feel tension sweep through the crowd as Ian took the ball from the center and fell back, looking left.

Suddenly he uncorked a long pass to the right, catching the defenders going the other way. Ecstatic, Carly shot to her feet along with just about everyone else in the stands.

"All right!" she shouted as the ball settled into the running back's hands for a thirty-four-yard gain. The Wolves' bench emptied, and the crowd whistled and stomped and did all the things a college football crowd was supposed to do when their team was winning. Carly tried to find Mitch in the crowd of orange-and-blue jerseys, but he was too far away.

"Maybe you should follow Tracy's example," Marca suggested as they settled back into their seats.

"What's that supposed to mean?"

Marca shot her an impatient look. "When was the last time you had a good night's sleep? Or really laughed, instead of faking it the way you've been doing today?"

"I'm sleeping fine, and I can't help it if you don't like the way I laugh."

"Mitch and I had lunch the other day."

"Bully for you," she said, before she could stop herself. The sudden glint in Marca's eyes had her cursing her tired brain.

"Don't be mad at me," Marca said. "I tried to hate him, really worked hard at it, but I just can't hate a man who hates himself the way he does."

Carly stared down at the field, her stomach slowly twisting itself into a knot. "That's not what I wanted, Marca."

"He's had offers from a couple of NFL teams for next year. Of course, his contract with Bradenton has another year to run, but, as I told him, a sharp lawyer could probably find a loophole."

Carly slowly turned to look at her. "What did he say?"

Marca shrugged. "He laughed and said that he just happened to know the best lawyer in California, and maybe he'd better find out if that same lawyer was licensed to practice in Oregon."

The building housing the athletic department was quiet. The last class had been over for more than an hour, and the maintenance staff was already swabbing down the floor outside Mitch's office.

Holding the phone to his ear, he leaned back in his chair and closed his eyes. "Hey, I really feel sorry for you, old buddy," he growled into the phone when Dante paused to take a breath. "I sure would hate to find out my wife was carrying twin girls instead of just one. Hell, who wants three daughters, anyway?"

Dante bit off an obscenity, and Mitch laughed. "C'mon, Jess. Tell the truth. You're damn near busting your buttons, you're so proud of yourself."

"I'm also scared." His tone was dead serious, and Mitch frowned.

"Is Hazel okay?"

"So far, but she's also forty-four-years old. Having Tyler was hard on her. Now twins." Dante's sigh was ragged. "I can't lose her, Mitch."

"You won't, Jess. She's strong, and she's taking good care of herself. If I know you, you're damn near smothering her in attention."

"When she lets me, which isn't as often as I'd like," Dante groused.

Mitch winced as a cramp knotted his left thigh. Clamping the phone against his shoulder, he used both hands to massage it away. "Tell her I said to humor you. She's crazy about me, you know."

Dante's laugh was tinged with warning. "Like a brother."

"Sure, that's what I said."

There was a pause, and then Dante asked soberly, "Have you seen your lady?"

Just as it was starting to back off, the cramp seized hold again, worse this time, and he had to suck in hard to keep from groaning.

"Only from a distance. She came to all the games." And looked adorably huggable in her bright orange sweatshirt—and also totally out of reach. His reach, anyway. He dug his fingers more forcefully into the knotted muscle and winced.

"Are you still planning to spend the next few weeks in Sacramento?" Dante asked, changing the subject.

"Yeah. I should be able to get away from here by the end of the week. How's Jeannie doing?" Instead of hiring an outsider, Mitch had followed his gut and promoted Jeannie to manager. After a shaky start, she had taken to running things like the champ he knew she was.

"She was doing great, last time I checked. Has the place running like a Swiss watch."

"Maybe I should give her a raise." The cramp finally eased off, and he slumped against the chair. He needed to drag his tired bones home so he could get out of his braces and into a hot bath. And then he was going to sleep for a week.

"Hey, don't give away all the profits, partner."

"Don't worry, Pop. You'll still have enough to keep those twin cuties in diapers."

Dante chuckled. "Speaking of which, I hope you're prepared to be godfather to two instead of one."

Mitch felt a rush of emotions too complex to name. "Is that an official invitation?"

"Sure is. Any objections?"

Mitch swallowed hard. "Can't think of a one."

"Better not. You know Hazel when she's got her mind set on something."

Mitch heard the shimmer of love in Dante's rough voice and tried not to envy his old friend too much. "Give her a kiss for me and tell her I'm honored."

"I'll give her a kiss from *me* and tell her you'll see her next week. And, Mitch? Hang in there. It gets better."

"Sure it does," he said, before saying goodbye and hanging up.

An hour later Mitch was locking his desk drawer when he heard footsteps approaching. Glancing up, he saw Carly standing in the doorway, looking pale and determined and so lovely it stopped his heart. One smile, even a hint of longing in those green eyes instead of that maddening calm, and he would beg. Instead, he managed a decent enough smile and gestured her to the seat next to his desk.

She came toward him, bringing the scent of late fall with her. She'd put on weight, and it suited her. "I just came by to thank you in person for all you've done. And to bring you this."

When he didn't reach out to take it, she put the manila envelope she'd been carrying on the desk in front of him. "What's that?"

"The contract you signed, and a notarized affidavit releasing you from any and all future obligations to the college without penalty."

He'd taken a hit once that had cracked his ribs. He hadn't felt the pain at first, only a stunned jolt. "You're firing me?"

She frowned. "No, we're declining to hold you to your contract."

"You didn't like the job I did?"

She looked annoyed. "Of course we did! The entire campus is like a different place now. Everyone's talking about the Wolves."

"So you're canning me because we didn't make it into post-season play?"

"Scanlon, we are trying to do you a favor here. Why are you making it so difficult?"

He lifted his eyebrows. "I must be pretty damn dense, Carly, because I can't for the life of me figure out how losing my job comes out to be a favor."

"Marca told me that you'd received some offers from the pros, so naturally. . ." She shrugged.

"So naturally you assumed I would try to break my contract with you." His voice was silky.

"With Bradenton, you mean."

"Same thing." Mitch held back the anger that threatened to spill out in spite of his good intentions.

"All right, *I'm* releasing you from your contract. With my very deepest gratitude for all you've done."

He hooked a finger under the flap and extracted the contract. The attached cover letter on top was short and to the point and in essence said exactly what she'd just told him. With one addition—a buyout bonus. It felt like the crudest kind of insult, as though she thought he'd sweated bullets for six months simply for money.

Carly watched his face as he read. Other than a single muscle pulling at the side of his jaw, he seemed completely at ease. Apparently finished with the letter she'd agonized over for two solid days, he tossed the contract aside. Still relaxed, he angled a glance at her and smiled only a little.

"Does that mean you want me to go?" His gaze was locked on hers. His thoughts, however, were hidden.

"I want you to have what's most important to you. If returning to the NFL is what you want, then, yes, I want you to go."

Then she turned and fled before she compromised her pride and asked him to stay.

It was black as ink outside, with no moon and no stars. The overcast had come in around six and thickened steadily. Fog was rising from the ground, swirling around the security lights like the last heart-wrenching scene in *Casablanca*.

It wasn't quite midnight. Carly had gone home after she'd left Mitch's office. She'd even gone to bed. She just hadn't been able to close her eyes for more than a few seconds at a time. Whenever she did, the dry burn of grief seared the insides of her lids.

So she'd pulled on a pair of jeans and an old shirt and driven to the office. Bessie had finally given up, and the Otis people were in the process of replacing the old elevator with a shiny new one. Seeing Bessie so broken and sad had torn the remaining pieces of her heart into confetti.

Housekeeping was in the building somewhere. Every so often she could hear the whir of a floor polisher or the hum of a vacuum, but in every way that counted she was totally alone.

She'd worked steadily until the top of her desk was bare and her Out basket was piled high. She'd dusted then—the desk, her books, every knickknack and lamp. Finished with that, she'd decided to tackle her filing cabinet. Working from the bottom up, she'd gotten halfway through the top drawer when the campanile rang midnight.

"And all's well because Bradenton is solvent again. Right, guys?" she muttered, glancing at her paternal lineage framed for posterity on the wall before jerking another folder from the drawer. Inside she found three copies of a speech she'd given almost two years earlier and wondered what had possessed her to save three identical copies of the same speech. Because you're compulsive, she raged, throwing all three copies into the trash. And rigid and unforgiving and stupid, she added, pulling out another bulging folder. Snapping it open, she stared at the contents and realized she couldn't read a word. Everything was blurred. When a tear plopped onto the top document, she stared in disbelief.

She scrounged in her purse for a tissue. When it was sodden, she searched for another. The tears just kept coming, running steadily down her cheeks and dripping from her chin. She used the last tissue, but she couldn't seem to stop the tears. Sniffing and sobbing, she hurried out of her office and headed down the hall to the rest room—and stopped short.

Mitch was leaning against the wall at the top of the stairs, his face beet red and his shirt damp with sweat. His eyes were closed, and he was breathing in audible gasps.

"Mitch?"

At the sound of his name, he opened his eyes and glared at her. "You might as well make me a bed right here," he said between gasps, "because there's no way in hell I'm going to make it down three flights of stairs tonight."

Her heart was in her throat as she walked toward him. "What I want to know is why you climbed them in the first place."

He straightened, wincing visibly. He pulled free of one crutch and propped it next to him, then pulled the folded contract from his back pocket. "I came to give you this."

"Thank you." She took it without looking at it.

"I was on the way to the mansion, but, when I was driving by, I saw the light on in your ivory tower. Just my luck the elevator has gone belly-up." He looked angry and frustrated and endearingly mussed.

"Why didn't you just messenger the signed copies over to me tomorrow?"

"Because I'm not signing the damned thing, that's why."

She blinked, and the tears she'd forgotten splashed her cheeks. "You're not?"

He'd never seen her cry before. Seeing those tear-stained cheeks had his throat raw and his belly filled with acid.

"I'll admit there are a lot of things about myself that I have to change," he told her with total conviction, "but I'm not a quitter, and I'm not leaving here until you can find it in your heart to forgive me."

"You're not?" There was an odd little catch in her voice.

"Damn straight I'm not. Even it takes a lifetime, I'm hanging in here until you know in your heart that I'm sorry. And then we'll work on arranging a second chance so I can show you how much I love you."

She stared at him, certain she had somehow made up this entire scenario. If she blinked hard enough, the very determined, very disheveled man with tortured eyes would simply disappear.

"Aw, hell. You want me to crawl, right?" His mouth twisted. "To turn myself inside out telling you how I'd die before I'd ever hurt you again." He ran his hand through his hair, his eyes narrowing. "Okay, I'm so sorry, I'm sick with it," he all but shouted at her. "I go to bed at night and wake up after a couple hours in a cold sweat because I keep seeing your face looking up at me, those big eyes pleading with me." His voice choked, and he dropped his head. "Carly, I swear if you asked me to stop, it didn't get through. . . ." He shook his head, then lifted his gaze to hers. "But that's not an excuse. What happened was my fault, all my fault. I'm supposed to tell you all this in a letter, but—"

She stiffened. "A letter? What kind of letter?"

He felt his face getting hot. "It's in the nature of an assignment for this sort of class I'm taking." He saw a strange look come into her eyes, but he was too whipped to even attempt to define it. As it was, he was lucky he hadn't already keeled over at her feet.

"The same 'class' Ian is taking?" she asked in a quiet voice that had him backing down hard on the sliver of hope he'd nurtured while he'd dragged himself up three endless flights.

"Yeah." He dropped his gaze. "He's a good kid, Carly. I know that's hard for you to believe."

"I don't want to talk about Ian. I want to talk about you."

He brought his gaze up slowly, and she saw him quickly brace his shoulders. And then he waited, his eyes steady and dark with shadows. "Whatever you want."

"First, I want a handkerchief, if you have one."

He drew his eyebrows together, but he reached into his pocket and pulled out a folded handkerchief.

"Thanks," she murmured before using it to wipe her cheeks and blow her nose. "I never cry, you know," she said. "It's so self-indulgent."

He looked puzzled, and then a little gleam came into his eyes. "Why do I think that's a quote from your mother?"

"Because it is." She moved closer, and her scent enveloped him, leaving him raw and needy. "Can we go back to the first part of this conversation?" she asked solemnly, her hand toying with the middle button of his shirt.

"Uh, which part?"

"When you were talking about the contract."

He scowled. "I'm not signing, period."

She had one button undone and started on the one above it. "After that part."

Mitch was having trouble getting past the distraction of her fingers brushing his chest. "I think I said something about getting you to forgive me."

"And after that?"

A shudder ran through him, splintering his control. He grabbed her wrist and worked to level the sudden spiking of his temper. Part of him knew he was using anger as a substitute for the agony of not being able to hold her, but the man who'd always had a notoriously low boiling point didn't want to think about that.

"What the *hell* do you think you're doing?" he demanded in a rough tone.

Her eyes flashed, and she jerked her hand free. "I'm trying to get you to tell me you love me again, you stubborn jackass."

He felt something give way inside him, but he wasn't ready to believe in miracles just yet. "That comes after the forgiving and second chance parts," he said, his voice suddenly thick. "You're in charge of those."

She nodded slowly, her heart full. "I'll need to write you a letter, too," she murmured. "And I'll need to say things that might hurt you more than you deserve to be hurt. But once we can get that out of the way, we can pretty much consider the rest a done deal."

"Maybe you'd better explain that," he said warily.

"The forgiving and second chance part. I'd already decided to do both. I was just waiting for you to ask."

Mitch figured he was going crazy. Just in case, though, he decided to check it out before he headed for the nearest locked ward.

"Does that mean you might stop hating me some day?"

"I don't hate you. I think I might even like you a little." She grinned. "More than a little."

He let out the breath he wasn't aware he'd been holding. "Okay, we'll start there."

Her eyebrows swooped together as she stared up at him. "Start what?" she asked carefully.

A long climb back, he thought. "Whatever you want. Maybe dinner sometime? Just to talk. Nothing heavy."

"All right." She managed a teasing smile. "I'll put it on my calendar."

It wasn't much in the way of encouragement, but he grabbed for it like a drowning man grabs for a shadow on the sea. He cleared his throat. "Remember when I told you I didn't want your charity?"

She opened his mouth to blast him, but the lopsided smile on his face stopped her. "What about it?" she asked instead.

"I've changed my mind. I want anything you're willing to give me."

"Anything?"

"Or nothing." He cleared his throat. "To tell you the truth, I'm not crazy about that option, though." That won him a tiny smile, and his hopes soared.

"You aren't the only one who's sweated through therapy, Mitch. I did the same thing years ago. And one thing I learned to do was ask for what I wanted. I've decided I want something from you."

"Whatever you want, it's yours."

She drew in courage along with a breath. "I want you to forgive yourself. Right now, this minute. No more beating up on yourself."

He felt a jagged hole open in his gut. "I can't give you that."

"You promised me anything. At this moment, that's what I want most."

Mitch hung his head. "I don't know how."

"Will you try? Please, Mitch. I can't stand to see you in so much pain."

He brought his head up slowly. "I'll give it a shot. I can't promise I'll succeed. Good enough?"

"For now." She drew a shaky breath. "Well?"

He drew his eyebrows together. "Well what?"

Cocking her head, she planted a fist on her hip and threw him what she hoped was a challenging look. "Why is it that when I wasn't sure I wanted you to kiss me, you were dead set on kissing me every chance you got. Now, when I *do* want you to kiss me, you're just standing there."

His jaw tightened. "Because, damn it, I'm afraid to touch you."

"I won't break."

"No, but you have to be remembering—"

"No," she said very firmly. "I'm not. What I do remember is how good you can make me feel with just a touch or a smile or one of those growling noises you make when you're frustrated and out of sorts and determined not to show it."

"Oh, God, bright eyes." He reached for her awkwardly, and she went into his arms, arms that closed around her so tightly she could scarcely draw breath.

She felt his chest heave as one sob after another shook him, deep, soul-baring sobs that came from deep inside. His body shuddered with each one until she was afraid he would break apart.

Murmuring his name over and over, she rubbed his back and nuzzled his hair until, finally, he regained control. When he lifted his head to look at her again, his eyes were filled with so much tenderness that she went weak inside.

"I thought the odds were a million to one that you'd forgive me. I still can't believe—" He couldn't go on. He dropped his forehead to hers and squeezed his eyes shut. "Let me into your life, Carly. I promise I'll spend the rest of mine trying to make you forget the pain I caused you."

Carly drew back so that he could see what was in her eyes. "You already have, Mitch." She framed his worn face with hands that were surprisingly steady. "I love you, too," she murmured, "and if you don't kiss me pretty soon, I'm going to knock you down and have my way with you."

His mouth was fierce as he took what she offered. Liquid fire ran through her, warming all the lonely places she'd ignored for so long. But just as she was luxuriating in the stir of pleasure, he groaned and pulled back.

"I'm sorry as hell to have to say this, bright eyes, but if I don't sit down pretty soon, I'm going to be laid up for a week."

Her smile was only slightly shaky as she stepped out of his arms and handed him his crutch. "C'mon, Coach. Let's go find you a chair, and then we can continue this discussion where we left off. I can't wait to find out what comes after the 'I love you' part."

Epilogue

Spring had come to Bradenton two weeks earlier than usual. Wildflowers bloomed in the fields surrounding the campus, and the air was perfumed with their fragrance. Carly slid down the window of the Jaguar and inhaled the glorious scents. Today was her first wedding anniversary and she was taking her hardworking husband to lunch.

Turning her head she glanced at his strong profile. Sensing her gaze, he glanced her way and smiled. "Have I told you how great you look today?" he asked in that shivery voice that always sent a thrill down her spine.

"Not often enough," she murmured.

"Give me a kiss, and I might be persuaded to tell you again."

Because he had to use both hands to operate the manual controls, she released her seat belt, then leaned over to steal a quick kiss.

"Not only do you look terrific, but you smell great too," he declared firmly. "Very sexy."

Carly pouted as she belted herself in again. "You used to say I smelled classy."

"That was before you started wearing me out in bed on a regular basis."

Smiling smugly, she rested her head against the seat and watched him through half-closed eyes. The first few months after she'd accepted his proposal had been rocky for both of them. With Silvia Stein's help, they'd managed to say all the things to each other that had to be said, the good as well as the painful. Mitch, especially, had gone through some black times, trying to convince himself that she wasn't cringing inside whenever she felt his hands on her.

The worst time had come when he'd tried to make love to her and couldn't. He'd been in a black mood for days—until she'd surprised him at his house by showing up with champagne and candles and a black lace nightie that had had him eating his pillow.

After much agonizing and consultation with the therapist, they'd agreed never to tell Tracy that Mitch was her real father. Instead, he'd adopted her through the courts, and she'd accepted him without hesitation, even calling him Dad at least as often as she called him Mitch.

She was blooming now, a junior on the Dean's List and a cheerleader with a boyfriend who adored her and a ton of plans for the future. But there were still times when Carly caught Mitch looking at her with a quiet sadness in his eyes, and she knew that he regretted not ever being able to acknowledge his paternity.

Still, in the months since they'd married, the good days had far outnumbered the bad, and she was happier every day. Only one small shadow hovered over them, and that was Mitch's infertility.

The doctors had been cautiously optimistic, but Carly had watched him become more and more discouraged. Hazel and Jess Dante had been wonderfully supportive, especially Hazel, who was in blooming good health after the birth of the twins, Amanda and Amelia.

Two months before, when they'd attended the girls' christening, Carly had been deeply touched to see tears in Mitch's eyes. Since then, he'd been a proud godfather, showing the team picture after picture of the girls and bragging about their brilliance and incomparable beauty. Only at night, when they were alone in bed, did he ruefully admit how much he envied Jess for the ease with which he'd given Hazel the children she'd always wanted.

"Pull over here," Carly instructed, pointing toward the shoulder of the road.

Mitch stopped the Jag where she'd indicated, then turned to look at her expectantly. "Okay, bright eyes. Now what?"

"See that tree with the giant leaves?"

He turned his head to look where she pointed. "The Alderson elephant ear magnolia," he intoned with one hand over his heart. "Amen."

Carly swatted his hard shoulder. "Be serious. I'm trying to give you your anniversary present."

"Okay, I'm serious." He released his seat belt and leaned over to nuzzle her neck.

"See the tree next to it, the one with the pink blossoms?"

"Yeah, I see it." He kissed the spot under her ear that always made her crazy, and she shivered.

"Ah, stop distracting me," she murmured, then squeaked when he pulled her across his lap.

"Who's distracting whom?" he drawled, the extent of his 'distraction' prodding her belly.

She inhaled slowly, relishing the power she had over him. Sometimes she had only to look at him in a certain way, and he was aroused. She snuggled close, loving him so much.

"Where was I?" she murmured, breathing in the clean soapy scent of his skin. Beneath her thighs, she felt the hard edges of his braces, and smiled to herself. It was difficult to believe now that they used to make love in the dark because he'd been shy about revealing his body to her. Nowadays he was anything but shy. And half the time, she was the one who took off his braces because she couldn't wait for him to get around to it.

She nuzzled his shoulder, then drew back. His eyes glittered as he whispered a very explicit, very arousing suggestion in her ear.

"Behave yourself," she murmured, but she couldn't keep from smiling. "We're talking trees here."

He tried for little-boy earnestness, but only succeeded in looking impatient. "Okay, make it fast."

Carly fought down a grin. "I brought you out here so we could plant another tree next to the plum."

Curiosity crowded some of the heat from his eyes. "Any particular reason, or do you just want to see me get red in the face and breathe hard climbing up that hill?"

"That piddling little hill?"

"That Alp, you mean."

Carly laughed. "Anyone who can climb three flights of stairs can climb a little hill."

"Yeah, but I had an incentive to climb those stairs. Planting a tree is not what I'd call a high priority."

She took his left hand and ran her finger over his wedding ring. "I planted that plum on the day I decided to keep our first baby. Now I want you to help me plant the one to celebrate our second."

He went still. "You had a call?"

She nodded. "From Dr. Matsuka himself. The last insemination worked. I'm pregnant."

For an instant Mitch couldn't speak. "I'd pretty much given up hope," he admitted gruffly. It had been humiliating as hell submitting himself to Matsuka's probes and syringes—not to mention painful more often than not. But he'd done it because Matsuka had pulled off some pretty amazing results with other paraplegics, and because Carly wanted another child—and so did he.

"I'm sure it's another girl," she murmured. "I feel exactly the same way I felt when I was pregnant with Tracy."

He laced his hand with hers and kissed her fingertips one by one. "I love you," he said thickly. "I'll die loving you, and if I find out I can come back in another lifetime to love you again, I'll fight the first damn angel that tries to stop me."

Carly laughed, her heart full to bursting. "And I'll be right in there with you." She kissed him hard, then drew back. "So, will you help me plant that tree or what?"

His smile was crooked. "Give me enough time, and I'll plant an entire forest." Humbly, gratefully, he lowered his head to kiss her again. His love. His life.

* * * * *

OFFICIAL RULES
PRIZE SURPRISE SWEEPSTAKES 3448
NO PURCHASE OR OBLIGATION NECESSARY

Three Harlequin Reader Service 1995 shipments will contain respectively, coupons for entry into three different prize drawings, one for a Panasonic 31" wide-screen TV, another for a 5-piece Wedgwood china service for eight and the third for a Sharp ViewCam camcorder. To enter any drawing using an Entry Coupon, simply complete and mail according to directions.

There is no obligation to continue using the Reader Service to enter and be eligible for any prize drawing. You may also enter any drawing by hand printing the words "Prize Surprise," your name and address on a 3"x5" card and the name of the prize you wish that entry to be considered for (i.e., Panasonic wide-screen TV, Wedgwood china or Sharp ViewCam). Send your 3"x5" entries via first-class mail (limit: one per envelope) to: Prize Surprise Sweepstakes 3448, c/o the prize you wish that entry to be considered for, P.O. Box 1315, Buffalo, NY 14269-1315, USA or P.O. Box 610, Fort Erie, Ontario L2A 5X3, Canada.

To be eligible for the Panasonic wide-screen TV, entries must be received by 6/30/95; for the Wedgwood china, 8/30/95; and for the Sharp ViewCam, 10/30/95.

Winners will be determined in random drawings conducted under the supervision of D.L. Blair, Inc., an independent judging organization whose decisions are final, from among all eligible entries received for that drawing. Approximate prize values are as follows: Panasonic wide-screen TV ($1,800); Wedgwood china ($840) and Sharp ViewCam ($2,000). Sweepstakes open to residents of the U.S. (except Puerto Rico) and Canada, 18 years of age or older. Employees and immediate family members of Harlequin Enterprises, Ltd., D.L. Blair, Inc., their affiliates, subsidiaries and all other agencies, entities and persons connected with the use, marketing or conduct of this sweepstakes are not eligible. Odds of winning a prize are dependent upon the number of eligible entries received for that drawing. Prize drawing and winner notification for each drawing will occur no later than 15 days after deadline for entry eligibility for that drawing. Limit: one prize to an individual, family or organization. All applicable laws and regulations apply. Sweepstakes offer void wherever prohibited by law. Any litigation within the province of Quebec respecting the conduct and awarding of the prizes in this sweepstakes must be submitted to the Regies des loteries et Courses du Quebec. In order to win a prize, residents of Canada will be required to correctly answer a time-limited arithmetical skill-testing question. Value of prizes are in U.S. currency.

Winners will be obligated to sign and return an Affidavit of Eligibility within 30 days of notification. In the event of noncompliance within this time period, prize may not be awarded. If any prize or prize notification is returned as undeliverable, that prize will not be awarded. By acceptance of a prize, winner consents to use of his/her name, photograph or other likeness for purposes of advertising, trade and promotion on behalf of Harlequin Enterprises, Ltd., without further compensation, unless prohibited by law.

For the names of prizewinners (available after 12/31/95), send a self-addressed, stamped envelope to: Prize Surprise Sweepstakes 3448 Winners, P.O. Box 4200, Blair, NE 68009.

RPZ KAL